Dra

Rebecca took a jar of honey and very slowly and deliberately poured the liquid between the crevice of Esther's thighs. Esther could feel the sticky substance trickling over her sex. The honey slid between her buttocks and formed a small pool on the sheet beneath her. It felt both bizarre and blissful as Christopher and Rebecca began to lap at the honey.

Dramatic Affairs

FREDRICA ALLEYN

BLACK
lace

Black Lace novels are sexual fantasies.
In real life, make sure you practise safe sex.

First published in 1998 by
Black Lace
Thames Wharf Studios,
Rainville Road, London W6 9HT

Typeset by SetSystems Ltd, Saffron Walden, Essex
Printed and bound by Mackays of Chatham PLC

ISBN 0 352 33289 1

Chapter One

*E*sther had first learnt she'd been dumped by
Marcus on the Monday. It was now Sunday,
and she was sitting at the kitchen table, staring at
the front of the tabloid newspapers spread out
before her. Each of them carried a similar picture
of Marcus and his new love on the front page. Only
the headlines varied, but by very little. Probably
the most hurtful one was the quote from Marcus
where he said: 'At long last I've found my true
soulmate'. Esther could hardly believe that one. She
could remember Marcus saying the same thing to
her at least three years earlier. She thought that
perhaps when she was feeling stronger she might
fax this information to Claudine, the new love of
his life, but she knew in her heart that she
wouldn't. It simply wasn't in her nature, and anyway she wouldn't want to inflict the kind of hurt
that she was feeling on to another woman, however
deserving.

With a sigh she got up from the table and

glanced out the window. Reporters and photographers were still gathered outside the tiny North London home that she and Marcus had shared for the past three years since leaving drama school. At first it had been a genuine ordeal to face them at all. It wasn't as though the breakup had been amicable or even expected. Marcus hadn't informed her that their relationship was even over. He had gone to America six months previously and had become an overnight star. He was now lined up for a major movie, and they had intended for Esther to join him as soon as she had finished filming her latest TV play.

The first she had known about his new girlfriend was when she had received a telephone call from a friend in America warning her that Marcus had been seen around a great deal with Claudine. That had been exactly twenty-four hours before the news had broken in England. Even now, Marcus had not had the decency to pick up the phone and tell Esther in person.

She knew that she had to go shopping this morning and that, once again, she would be pursued by the paparazzi, all clamouring and shouting at her, prompting quotes, and asking her how she was and what she was feeling. She wondered if they genuinely expected her to tell them the truth or if they were simply hoping to goad her into bursting into tears or breaking down in a heap, slumping on to the pavement to give them some of the wonderful pictures their editors were no doubt longing for. Being an actress, she had an advantage over other women in a similar situation; there was always a small part of her that stood back from what she was doing and watched her own performance. It was a trait she'd found rather disconcerting at first but now it was proving to be extremely useful. She knew that her performance as heartbroken but brave was becoming Oscar worthy, and she wondered how she was going to differentiate between truth and reality in the future. How would she know, she wondered, when the true grief had worn off and she was merely putting on a mask to show the rest of the world how hurt she was? You're disgusting, Esther, utterly disgusting, she told herself fiercely, but she couldn't help it. She supposed it went with the profession.

The trip to the shop, which normally took her about five minutes, took twenty-five, and when she arrived back clutching her carrierbag of low-fat milk, low-fat spread, low-fat yoghurt and low-fat everything, she felt utterly exhausted as she slammed the door on the baying horde outside. It wasn't that the pictures of the pencil-thin Claudine had made her particularly weight conscious, but all the same she decided it was time to be a little careful. She liked her curves – there had been a time when Marcus couldn't keep his hands off them – but if she wanted to extend her range it would possibly be better if she were slightly less voluptuous. She suspected this display of virtue wouldn't last very long but it gave her a small glow of satisfaction at the moment.

She ate a piece of toast and Marmite and a low-fat yoghurt while gazing at the pictures and re-reading the articles. Finally, however, even she had had enough of reading about herself and Marcus. She gathered them all up, scrunched them into a pile and threw them into a corner. Just as she was wondering whether or not she could set light to them the telephone rang and she waited for the answerphone to click in so that she could work out whether or not she wanted to speak to the caller. She'd been screening her calls ever since the news broke. Journalists had been calling, and her mother hadn't helped matters by saying that Marcus had always dominated her and had been holding her back in her career. Fellow actors and actresses had all expressed their sympathy, but Esther was sure they were gloating at the downfall of one half of the country's young golden couple. There had been calls from genuine friends, though, and this proved to be just such a call. She was delighted to hear Lydia's voice coming through the speaker. Quickly, she grabbed at the receiver.

'Lydia, how lovely to hear from you. I'm sorry about the answerphone but I'm still being plagued by "Oh I'm so sorry" calls or "How are you feeling, Esther?" calls.'

'That's OK,' laughed Lydia. 'I wasn't expecting you to pick the phone up yourself. I can imagine what it must be like at the moment. Actually I rang because I've heard some really exciting news and I think you might be interested.'

Esther couldn't think of anything that would excite her at the moment, unless it was hearing that Marcus's film contract had fallen through and Claudine had run off with a hunk of American beefcake. However, she was too polite to say this to Lydia who had been a friend to her for as long as she and Marcus had been together. 'Do tell then,' she said, mustering as much enthusiasm as possible into her voice.

'It's about Christopher Wheldon,' Lydia said excitedly. 'Apparently he's decided to leave the

4

RSC and set up his own theatre company. He wants to gather a few like-minded people around him and then tour the country putting on popular classics in the traditional style. He's going to take them on the road to country homes and small theatres, as well as better-known venues. He says he's going to bring the theatre back to the people.'

'What does he mean by that?' she queried.

'You know perfectly well what he means,' said Lydia, sounding a trifle annoyed. 'It's just the kind of thing that Marcus would have been interested in once, before he got carried away by all the Hollywood hype. Besides, I seem to remember that at drama school you were always saying that theatre was the only true form of acting.'

'Did I really say that?' asked Esther. She thought for a moment. 'Yes, I believe I did. Well, everything changes and the truth of the matter is . . .'

'The truth of the matter is,' Lydia said firmly, 'that Marcus has ruined your career. I hate to say this to you, Esther, but I think you're really lucky he's dumped you. I mean, I know it hurts and everything but you gave up all the things you wanted for him just so you could be at his side and then, the moment you're not, what happens? He runs off with someone else, some French breadstick.'

Esther giggled. 'You shouldn't say that about her. She's very attractive.'

'She's all right if you like them immaculately groomed, perfectly made-up and with a face like a blank canvas,' said Lydia. 'Personally I think he's a fool. You're worth ten of her but at least you're free now. You can stop doing all those crap TV parts playing blonde bimbo girlfriends and show people that you can really act. It's different for someone like me, I'm never going to get anywhere until I'm older. I'm far too plain to be anything but a character actress and to be a character actress you have to be forty. I shall spend most of my life waiting at tables until I'm old enough to be a character.'

Esther laughed again. Lydia was the only person who'd been able to make her laugh in the past week. 'I don't think that Marcus held me back at all,' she said. 'Everything that I did I chose to do. I must admit Christopher's idea is rather intriguing, though. It would be nice not to have modern directors of the kind who make you play Ophelia in a mini skirt while all the men wear Armani suits.'

'Exactly,' Lydia said triumphantly. 'And he's going to do all the classics. He's going to do Coward and Priestley, Shakespeare and Marlowe.'

'How big's this company going to be?' asked Esther in astonishment.

'Oh not that big; apparently they're all going to be potted versions.'

'If you ask me he's a bit weird,' said Esther. 'Marcus never did like him.'

'Marcus never liked anyone he thought might outshine him,' Lydia pointed out.

'But Christopher isn't such a good actor as Marcus,' protested Esther. 'He thinks he is but he isn't; just like he says he's six feet tall and he isn't. I don't think he's more than five ten.'

'You should hear yourself,' said Lydia. 'You sound just like Marcus.'

Esther drew in her breath sharply. It was true that the opinions she was voicing were Marcus's opinions and not her own. She wasn't particularly keen on Christopher Wheldon but, on the other hand, she didn't know him that well and she'd thought that his *Henry V* had been one of the best ever. 'I suppose I could ring my agent and find out what's needed in order to get an audition,' she said slowly.

'Just think how sick Marcus will be if he hears that you're doing classical acting,' crowed Lydia.

'That isn't why I'll do it, if I do do it,' Esther said crossly. 'It's just that I need something different to take my mind off Marcus and, by the sound of it, this would be different and keep me busy. Have you any idea how long his season will last?'

'None at all,' said Lydia. 'I'm not the sort of person who's going to be involved. I only heard this on the grapevine but you can get all the details from your agent. Go for it, Esther, please, for my sake if no one else's. This could open up a whole new world for you.'

'I doubt if he'll take me,' Esther said. 'I haven't had much stage experience.'

'Exactly, and that's because of Marcus. Now do you accept my point?' asked Lydia.

'Not that it's because of Marcus,' said Esther, 'but I agree that I have neglected the stage. Mind you, offers haven't exactly poured in. It's hard enough to get TV work. Anyway, I'll ring my agent, find out all that I can, and let you know how I get on.'

'That's great,' enthused Lydia. 'I look forward to hearing from you, and remember, Marcus is the loser – not you.'

'You'll never guess what that was about,' remarked Christopher Wheldon, replacing the telephone and

7

looking across the bedroom to where Rebecca was lolling on the large four-poster bed.

'Do tell,' said Rebecca.

'That was Esther Reid's agent. Apparently Miss Reid would like to audition for my new company. What do you think about that?'

Rebecca shrugged, tossing her long shoulder-length dark hair back off her face and staring at him with slanted hazel eyes. 'I didn't know she could do stage work,' she remarked. 'I saw her in an absolutely dire TV play the other night.'

'Never mind the play, what was *she* like?' asked Christopher with interest.

'Didn't really think about it. She's sort of curvy, blonde, pretty and vacant-looking.'

'Meow!' laughed Christopher, walking towards the bed. 'Well I've said that she can come along and have a chat with me. I thought that sounded more polite than asking her to audition. After what Marcus has just done to her she's probably anxious to get away from the public eye for a bit.'

'She's hardly going to get away from the public eye by joining a touring theatre company,' Rebecca pointed out dryly.

'I meant escape from the house, not be on TV so much, carve out a new career for herself,' remarked Christopher.

Rebecca gazed up at him. He really was incredibly attractive. He had fair highlighted hair that flopped forward over his forehead, a handsome face, grey eyes and was very well built. He prided himself on keeping fit and it was one of the things she liked most about him. That and his enthusiasm for sex; an enthusiasm that was equally matched by her. She'd been a bit player at the RSC when

8

they'd met two months earlier but, for some reason, Christopher had homed in on her and, like the rest of the company, she could hardly believe her good luck. However, having now got hold of him she had no intention of letting go.

She was, and she knew it, a very fine actress, but she was already aware that it would be unwise to make this clear too early to Christopher. She was more than willing to subjugate her performances when playing opposite him until he was thoroughly in her thrall; only then would she allow him to see how talented she really was. For a man like Christopher Wheldon there was only room for one star – and that star had to be him.

Rebecca also knew how furious he was at Marcus's success in America. Christopher had been certain that after his successes at the RSC he would be snapped up by Hollywood scouts and whisked off following in the footsteps of Kenneth Branagh and Ralph Fiennes. Unfortunately, Marcus had beaten him to it and now Christopher, by creating his own company, was making it clear that fame and fortune were not everything. In other words he was hiding his own disappointment and at the same time telling the great theatre-going public in Britain, 'Look at me. I'm loyal, I'm true and I'm not lured away by money.' Rebecca assumed that Christopher must imagine the public wouldn't know that he had never been offered any money. In fact, Hollywood had shown no interest in him at all.

'Are you going to get Esther Reid to audition for you once she arrives,' she asked. 'If so, what are you going to make her do?'

Christopher sighed. 'I hadn't really thought about it,' he murmured.

Rebecca found this hard to believe. Christopher never did anything without thinking about it and she was very surprised that he was even considering allowing Esther to join their company. She couldn't imagine what his reason was but she had no doubt that he had one.

She hadn't yet dressed, although it was past midday, and she noticed that Christopher's eyes were lingering on the amount of bosom that was revealed by the plunging neckline of her crimson satin nightdress. She looked up at him trying to gauge his mood. Christopher liked two kinds of sex, and it was important that she caught his mood correctly.

Sometimes, he liked to dominate her. She sensed that some of her attraction for him lay in her slender bones and long neck. He got a huge sexual thrill from wrapping his large fingers around her wrists and sometimes clasping his hands tightly round her neck as though about to strangle her. But there were other times, usually late at night after a few drinks, when the real Christopher began to show through, then things would change entirely and Christopher would want Rebecca to take charge.

These were the times Rebecca enjoyed the most. The surge of power she felt when she had Christopher at her mercy, those blissful moments when he would be moaning and begging or grovelling at her feet, provided the most exciting sex she'd had so far. One thing she understood very clearly was that this private side of Christopher – this need to be dominated – was a side that she must never discuss with anyone or she would be cast out, not only from Christopher's life but possibly from the whole world of acting. Christopher Wheldon held a great deal of power. He could open doors for people and he could also slam them shut in their face. Rebecca had no intention of having any doors slammed in her face.

'You're not jealous of Esther are you?' asked Christopher, sitting on the bed and running a finger lightly down the inside of Rebecca's right arm.

'Why on earth should I be jealous of Esther?' asked Rebecca in astonishment. 'After all, what's she ever done except TV work and go out with Marcus Martin?'

Christopher's hand wandered higher up Rebecca's arm, lingering on the fine-boned shoulders and then stroking the flesh across her collarbone. 'Come to that, what have you ever done except go out with me?' he queried.

'Well, she simply isn't the kind of person that arouses any feeling in me except contempt,' Rebecca said sharply.

Christopher laughed. 'I think you're lying to me,' he said softly. 'I don't think you want Esther to join our company. I think you're afraid I might fall for her.'

Rebecca wanted to laugh but she realised that Christopher was serious. He genuinely wanted Rebecca to start feeling jealous about Esther, and from this she reasoned he must be intending to let Esther join the company. Well, she wasn't jealous of Esther, and she couldn't imagine for one moment that Esther would provide the kind of sexual thrills that Christopher wanted. Nevertheless, if this was

11

what he wanted then she was willing to play the game.

'Perhaps I'm just a tiny bit jealous,' she admitted in a soft voice.

Christopher slid his hands up her throat, caressing beneath the base of her chin with his thumbs and at the same time drawing her upright so their faces were close together. 'I knew it,' he said triumphantly. 'Well, don't worry, Rebecca. At the moment I'm perfectly satisfied with you.'

He leant towards her. Rebecca closed her eyes and felt his mouth start to plunder hers. His tongue probed fiercely between her lips, and one of his hands strayed down inside her nightdress to tweak sharply on her nipple. Rebecca's breath caught in her throat and her body instinctively drew away from him a fraction but he pulled her back tightly and his fingers closed around her breast. Her desire was mounting rapidly now and her breathing grew quicker. She sometimes wished that she could resist him just a little longer, make him work harder, but his sheer physical magnetism and the knowledge that she was with the great Christopher Wheldon always proved too much for her self-control.

With a soft moan she wrapped her arms around him and pulled him down on top of her. Christopher tugged sharply at the hem of her nightdress until it rose up above her thighs. She heard the sound of him unzipping his trousers and then he was lying on top of her. She could feel him hard against her, the tip of his penis rubbing against her outer sex lips. Rebecca began to move her hips, arching them upwards, trying to spread her legs further apart despite the restrictions of the nightdress. Christopher pushed her back down on to the bed.

'Don't be in such a hurry. You're always greedy aren't you, Rebecca?' he teased, his tongue flicking in and out of her ear.

'I can't help it,' moaned Rebecca, wriggling frantically as she felt his erection sliding slowly into her. 'Please, please hurry.'

Sometimes Christopher liked to make her wait, but this was not one of those times because he was in a hurry too. Within a few seconds he was thrusting forcefully into her and, as he moved, the hand that was gripping her breast squeezed and released in matching time with the movements of his hips. Rebecca felt her orgasm starting to build but she needed something else, something extra, if she was to climax as fast as she knew Christopher was going to.

Suddenly, Christopher stopped moving, wrenched the nightdress higher so that it was bunched round Rebecca's waist, and slipped a hand beneath her bottom. With a grateful sigh Rebecca allowed her feelings to take over as Christopher carefully inserted his forefinger between the cheeks of her bottom. He moved it lightly around the rim of her second opening and then, as he felt all her muscles tense in their pre-orgasmic explosion, he gave two extra powerful thrusts with his hips and at the same time pressed firmly against the wall of her rectum. With a scream of delight Rebecca climaxed and, at the same time, Christopher uttered a shout of pleasure before collapsing on top of her.

For a few minutes he lay there, his head resting in her neck, her long dark hair covering his

13

shoulders. But, as usual, once he'd finished he'd finished, and was ready to move on to other things.

Sometimes Rebecca wished that he would lie longer with her, but that only ever happened after the other kind of sex – the kind where she took control. This particular day was no exception, and within ten minutes Christopher was walking out of the bedroom and leaving her, presumably to make arrangements for his meeting with Esther.

Three days later Esther arrived at the small community hall in Clapham where her agent had arranged for her to meet with Christopher Wheldon. She felt very nervous, and realised that part of the apprehension was fear of how Christopher would behave towards her. Marcus had never made any secret of his feelings for Christopher, and had given several interviews in which he had referred to his rival in somewhat scathing terms. While Esther herself had never spoken about Christopher, she realised it was probable he would assume she shared Marcus's views.

She'd quite expected to find several other people waiting in the hall but there was only Christopher. He was standing at the opposite end of the room and, when he heard the door opening, turned so that he was caught in a ray of sunlight shining through a window high above him. Esther realised at once that Christopher had arranged this deliberately. It certainly showed him to full advantage. She hadn't appreciated quite how boyishly good-looking he was and, when he smiled at her, she realised that he did indeed have a great deal of charm, even if it wasn't necessarily genuine.

'Esther, how lovely to see you!' he exclaimed.

14

'It's very nice of you to see me,' responded Esther. 'As my agent told you, I haven't done stage work for a long time and I'm afraid I might be a bit rusty.'

'I shouldn't worry about that,' laughed Christopher, walking towards her with his hand outstretched. 'By the time we've all rehearsed and got used to one another I'm sure that any rough edges will have disappeared. Besides, you've been doing a lot of television work and I admire that. It's a very demanding discipline.'

Esther was surprised to hear this. As far as she knew, Christopher regarded television drama in any form as little better than appearing in a commercial. Nevertheless, she appreciated his kindness and the effort he was making to help her feel at ease. 'My agent didn't tell me whether I should prepare a piece for you to hear,' she explained awkwardly.

'I really only wanted us to have a little chat,' said Christopher. 'I tell you what, though, perhaps it would be a good idea if you and I read something through. That way we'll get an idea of how we work together and, let's face it, in a company the size of the one I'm hoping to have it's important that everyone gets along with everyone else. Really and truly this is going to be ensemble acting.'

Esther's heart sank. She loathed the term ensemble acting and knew perfectly well that Christopher didn't mean what he was saying. No one with an ego like his would have any intention of merging into the background. He didn't expect to be part of a team; he expected to be the star, and everyone else in his company was presumably expected to help him shine brightly. She didn't mind this, though, and indeed she had fully accepted that this was how it would be. What she did object to was Christopher trying to pretend it would be otherwise.

'Well?' queried Christopher. 'What do you say?'

Esther gave him a shy smile. 'Did you have anything special in mind?' she asked.

'As a matter of fact, yes I did,' said Christopher briskly as his boyish charm dropped away from him, leaving behind the intense actor that she had been expecting to meet in the first place. 'I thought we'd try a piece from *Hamlet*, Act III scene 1. You can be Ophelia opposite my Hamlet of course!'

Esther was horrified. Like most actresses she had always thought Ophelia a thankless task. She seemed to go from slight depression to total madness at incredible speed, and it was almost impossible to make her believable.

'Do you have a problem with that?' asked Christopher.

'No, of course not,' Esther said hastily. 'Do you have a copy here? I'm afraid it isn't a part I know very well. I mean, I've never played it or anything.'

'I don't suppose you've played any of the parts that I have in mind for you if you do join the company,' said Christopher. 'All this really is is a test to see how you and I rub along together. You see, I'm actually very anxious to have you on board and, as long as the reading goes reasonably well, then I think you can safely assume that you'll be part of my company.'

Esther was amazed. This wasn't the way auditions went in the normal course of affairs, and it certainly wasn't the way she'd expected this one to go. It seemed that provided she didn't actually trip

16

over her tongue and make a complete fool of herself then Christopher was going to make her part of his company, despite the fact that in the theatre-going public's minds she and Marcus were probably still inextricably linked.

Christopher handed a copy of *Hamlet* to Esther. 'I've marked the place,' he said encouragingly. 'We'll start from where I finish my speech "the fair Ophelia. Nymph in thy orisons be all of my sins remember'd".'

Esther glanced at the book, her eyes running swiftly down the page. It was absolutely ghastly. She couldn't think what she was going to do with it, and was horribly aware that Ophelia was going to sound an utter drip. Remembering all her drama school training she slowed down her breathing, relaxed her muscles, and mentally prepared for the reading.

'Good my lord, how does your honour for this many a day?' Once she'd begun she found it easier than she'd expected. For one thing, Christopher was giving a very good reading of Hamlet. He wasn't simply reading the lines, feeding her cues in order that she could do her speeches. He was acting the part and this made it much easier for her to respond. By the time she came to her last lines, 'Oh! Woe is me, to have seen what I have seen, see what I see!', she knew she'd done a far better job than she would have imagined possible half an hour earlier.

Closing the book, she looked at Christopher and he smiled broadly at her. 'There,' he said with pleasure. 'That was pretty good, wasn't it? I think you'd make a very good Ophelia. Well, is there anything you'd like to ask me?'

Esther wondered if this meant that she was definitely in. She assumed that it did and there were a lot of questions that she wanted to ask him, but some of them she felt it better to save until he had definitely confirmed the fact she would be on board. 'I was wondering how many people were going to be in your company?' she asked.

'Twelve of us in all,' explained Christopher. 'Six men and six women. Most of us will be young. I only need a couple of character actors, one male and one female; the other ten will all be young and, to be honest with you, they've got to be quite good-looking, especially the girls. There aren't many parts for unattractive women in any of the plays that I intend to put on. Also I want them to be ambitious; you need that hunger in order to get good performances.'

Esther agreed, but she also realised that Christopher's desire to be surrounded by six attractive young women was probably based more on personal need than on the needs of the playwrights. It was quite easy with the aid of make-up to make fairly ordinary girls appear highly attractive. However, she wasn't going to argue with him. It didn't matter to her what the girls looked like as long as she was given parts that would really show off her capabilities as an actress.

'Were there any particular plays you had in mind or haven't you decided that yet?' she asked.

'Well, I've settled on what's going to be the mainstay,' explained Christopher, 'and that's going to be Priestley's *Time and the Conways*. What do you think of Priestley's time plays?' he added.

'I rather like them,' admitted Esther. 'I suppose

my favourite is *An Inspector Calls* but I do like *Time and the Conways*.'

'What role do you think you'd be best suited for?' queried Christopher, smiling at her encouragingly.

'Perhaps Hazel,' suggested Esther. 'It's quite challenging because she has to change so much. I mean at the beginning she's young and pretty and has the world at her feet but by the end it's all gone wrong for her, hasn't it?'

'Well yes,' agreed Christopher. 'And I suppose you could play it, but actually I'm considering you for Kay.'

Esther was amazed. Kay was a larger part and had some long monologues. She'd always pictured Kay as being tall, elegant and somehow less curvy than she was. Also, by the end of the play Kay has a kind of melancholy about her that wasn't something Esther associated with herself. She supposed it was rather flattering she was being considered for the part, but then realised that he might well be saying this to all the girls.

'How would you feel about playing Kay?' persisted Christopher.

'Well, of course I'd love it,' said Esther. 'Any actress would jump at the chance to play Kay. I'm a little taken aback, that's all.'

'Well that's fine,' said Christopher. 'Anyway, there's a lot to be settled before we start casting plays and, to carry on with answering your question, I'm also hoping to do some Coward, probably *Private Lives*. The problem with that is there's only four people of any importance in it, but I thought we'd probably vary the cast from venue to venue. Then there'll be some potted Shakespeare, you

19

know, like potted operas – they're all the fashion these days. To be perfectly honest, if we're touring some of the smaller towns, people won't want the uncut *Hamlet* or the entire *Henry V*. They'll probably want all of *Macbeth*, though. I find that no matter where you go the public enjoy plenty of blood and gore. Also, thank God, there isn't much comedy to deal with in that. That's a real killer when it comes to modern audiences.'

'It all sounds very exciting,' said Esther. 'Are there any big venues planned or haven't you decided on them yet?'

For the first time Christopher looked a little vague. 'That's rather up in the air at the moment,' he admitted. 'The thing is though, once I've got my full company together and decided for certain on the plays which – apart from *Time and the Conways* – are still fairly flexible, then I can't approach managers of theatres anywhere because I can't tell them exactly what we'll be doing. I don't imagine it's going to be a problem though. I don't wish to sound immodest, but I do feel that my name counts for something in this country.'

After all her years with Marcus, Esther knew her cues very well when it came to this kind of conversation. 'I don't think you're being immodest, Christopher,' she said with a smile. 'It would be very silly of you to pretend that you weren't a famous name.'

'The problem is,' Christopher said slowly, 'that I'm not a TV name. These days I regret to say that it's the stars of TV who put bums on seats. It's a terrible state of affairs but something we've got to face up to.'

20

'Does that mean you're hoping to have some TV stars in the company?' asked Esther.

'Absolutely not,' said Christopher. 'I'm just explaining that we may not always play to full houses in some of the smaller towns.'

'That's not a problem for me,' said Esther. 'Unlike you I'm not used to playing to full houses in theatres. After the RSC, though, this is going to be something of a challenge for you, isn't it?'

'It's going to be a challenge in more ways than one,' said Christopher with a wry smile. At that moment his eyes locked on to Esther's and what she saw there astonished her. Christopher was most definitely showing that he found her attractive and his words indicated that she, like the whole venture, was part of the challenge he had just mentioned.

'Well, perhaps you'd let me know when you've decided for sure,' she said hastily, getting up from her chair and throwing the strap of her canvas bag over her shoulder.

'I obviously haven't made myself clear,' said Christopher in surprise. 'I've already made up my mind about you, Esther. I want you to join my company. The only question is, are you interested in me?'

Esther tried not to look too excited. Inside she was bubbling with delight, but she knew better than to show it. 'It all sounds very interesting and, as soon as I've spoken to my agent, one of us will be in touch with you,' she said with her most dazzling smile.

'Fair enough,' Christopher agreed amicably and then, as she was about to leave, he put his hands on her shoulders and kissed her lightly on both cheeks. This in itself was nothing unusual but, when he'd finished, he allowed his hands to slide down the sides of her arms before he released her. This apparently insignificant gesture caused tiny flickers of excitement deep within her.

As Esther walked out of the hall, her cheeks flushed a becoming shade of pink, Christopher Wheldon smiled to himself with satisfaction. He'd been going to take Esther into his company anyway, no matter how bad her reading. In fact, to his surprise, she'd been unexpectedly good. That was a bonus. The real reason for her inclusion was that he was determined to make Marcus realise that in giving up Esther and going out with Claudine he had made the wrong decision. If everything went as Christopher planned then by the end of this tour the Hollywood scouts would be clamouring at his front door, and when he finally flew off to America he would have Esther by his side. It would be the ultimate revenge.

It was seven o'clock that evening before Christopher returned to the house that he and Rebecca shared in London. She was already waiting, fully dressed, ready to go out to dinner that evening. It was only then that Christopher remembered the party they were meant to be attending.

'God, I'm sorry, Becky, everything's been complete chaos today,' he called as he dashed upstairs for a quick shower. He saw with relief that Rebecca had laid out his dinner jacket, shirt and tie on the bed so that all he had to do was literally wash and go. She followed him up the stairs. Her ankle-length embroidered silk dress – sleeveless and with

22

a square neckline – clung to her like a second skin. Round her neck she had a tiny black and crystal necklace, an antique that he had bought her to celebrate two months together. She was wearing very high-heeled strappy shoes and, by the time he had showered and was dressing, Rebecca was pulling on a pair of elbow-length black gloves. Christopher gave a sigh of pleasure. This was exactly how he liked Rebecca to look in preparation for one of their special evenings together.

'Can't wait for the party to end,' he remarked casually.

'That sounds promising,' said Rebecca, a half-smile playing around her lips. She had planned this in advance, well aware that Christopher would have spent the entire day interviewing countless beautiful young women for his company. It was important that tonight she reaffirmed her status as his lover.

They returned home at one in the morning. Christopher had been quiet in the taxi and, once they were inside the house, he turned to Rebecca. 'I hope you're going to be nice to me tonight,' he said softly.

'I don't think I will be,' Rebecca said. 'You didn't behave very well tonight.'

Christopher looked suitably chastened, and Rebecca's pulse began to quicken. This was going to be an exciting evening. 'What did I do wrong?' he asked.

'You spent far too much time talking to the other girls and ignoring me,' Rebecca said angrily. 'I think you're going to have to be punished.'

Turning on her heel she walked swiftly up the

stairs, well aware of the provocative sight that she would be presenting from where Christopher was standing in the hallway. Walking into the bedroom she began peeling off her long gloves and, as she did so, Christopher joined her in the room.

'You're right,' he said in a little-boy voice. 'I did behave badly, and I think you should punish me.'

'Right then,' said Rebecca. 'Take your clothes off and hang them up tidily.' Christopher obeyed with alacrity. Within a couple of minutes he was entirely naked, standing in front of her with his erection already fully formed. Apart from removing her gloves Rebecca was still fully clothed. She glanced down at the glistening purple glans and her upper lip curled scornfully.

'I don't think we want to see that, thank you,' she remarked.

Christopher hastily covered himself with both hands. Rebecca stepped forward and slapped his hands away.

'I didn't mean for you to hide it. I meant I wanted it to go away,' she said coldly. 'I shall have to see what I can do about it, won't I?'

'I'm very sorry,' murmured Christopher, brushing his hair back off his forehead in an awkward gesture.

'You certainly will be,' promised Rebecca. At her words, Christopher's excitement grew even more visible and Rebecca had to turn away to hide her satisfaction. 'Lie face down on the bed,' she ordered him. Without a protest Christopher did as she asked. 'Now spread yourself out in the shape of an X,' continued Rebecca and, once Christopher's wrists and arms were in the right position, she fastened them to the four corners of the bedposts with long silk scarves.

Christopher turned his head and looked up at her. 'What are you going to do?' he asked, sounding rather too eager for Rebecca's liking. Leaning over him, she drew one long fingernail down the centre of his spine, leaving a thin red line in its wake. Christopher's whole body shivered with delight.

'I'm going to do something very special,' Rebecca said at last. 'Something that I only do when I'm very, very cross with you.'

Christopher gave a soft sigh and then uttered a tiny yelp as Rebecca tugged on his long fair hair, lifting his face off the pillow so that she could stare into those magnetic grey eyes. 'Right,' she said with frightening gentleness. 'Now I think we can get down to business.'

Chapter Two

Rebecca moved to the head of the bed so Christopher could watch as she slowly removed her long black dress, allowing it to fall into a silky heap at her feet. Beneath it she was entirely naked, apart from shiny black hold-up stockings and a tiny black G-string. She saw Christopher swallow hard and his tongue flick out to moisten his dry lips. Turning her back on him and walking with a provocative sway of her hips, Rebecca crossed the room. Making sure that she remained in his line of vision she picked up a silver-backed hair brush that she kept on their dressing table. Many times she would get Christopher to brush her long dark hair, but this time both he and she knew that it was intended for a very different use.

When she returned to the side of the bed, Rebecca eased her thumbs into the sides of the G-string and slowly tugged it down her legs until all she had on were the stockings. She then collected together the other items that she would need for their session, deliberately taking her time so that Christopher, watching her every move, would grow even more excited.

Finally she climbed on to the bed then straddled herself across the middle of his back while facing his feet. Then, very carefully, she tapped lightly against the cheeks of his bottom with the bristles of the hair brush. At first Christopher remained completely still but, after a few moments, his hips began to move as he tried to press himself against the mattress beneath him. Immediately Rebecca lifted the brush into the air.

'If you don't keep still I shall leave you tied up like this and go and sleep in the spare room,' she said shortly.

'I'm sorry,' mumbled Christopher, and Rebecca smiled to herself. She knew very well how difficult this must be for him and how excited he was growing. Her own excitement was growing too, but there was a long way to go before the session was over.

Once Christopher was still again, she resumed her use of the brush. This time she flicked it far harder against his tightly muscled buttocks and, slowly, a red flush began to appear on the surface of the skin. Once both his buttocks were glowing she moved lower, using the brush against the tops of the backs of his thighs and only stopping when she reached the soft flesh of the backs of the knees. She then straightened up again so that she was sitting upright. She then placed the brush to one side.

Slowly she climbed off her lover's back and then, standing beside the bed, slid a long-fingered slender hand beneath his helpless naked body. She

27

could feel, by the size of his erection, that he was already perilously close to climaxing. This was something that had proved a problem early on when they had first begun to play these games. Now, however, Rebecca was an expert at preventing him from coming too soon. Carefully she squeezed his penis firmly, her thumb on the underside, with her fingers on the top of the penis just below the glans. As she gripped firmly she heard Christopher give a tiny groan of disappointment but, as usual, the technique worked well and after a few minutes she knew that his urge to come had gone.

'You're being rather quick tonight,' she said in her most bossy voice. 'It looks as though you're going to keep me very busy.'

Christopher didn't answer; he simply buried his face deeper in the pillow uttering tiny sounds of mixed pleasure and despair. This was what they both loved the most and Rebecca began to tremble from the excitement of it all. She couldn't help wondering what his fans would think if they could see him now, spreadeagled and tied on the bed, entirely at her mercy and loving every minute of it.

Next, Rebecca resumed her earlier position sitting astride him, only this time she held a bottle of massage oil. Carefully she began to apply it liberally to his back. Using long strokes she moved her hands up and down and then round and round in small circular movements. She moved her hands ahead of herself, slowly sliding them down his body until she reached the faintly pink buttocks. Ignoring those for the moment she poured a little of the oil into the palm of one hand and carefully anointed the tips of her own breasts. Then she crouched on all fours, leaning forward so that she

28

could anoint the backs of his thighs with oil using her breasts instead of her hands. This drove both of them wild with delight, and Rebecca's internal muscles tightened as she felt the pressure of Christopher's legs against her rapidly hardening nipples. The pleasure for her was so great that she almost forgot Christopher, and it was only when he uttered a muffled groan that she realised that once more he was dangerously near to reaching a climax.

Swiftly twisting round so that she was facing his head, she again reached beneath him and applied the squeeze technique until his burgeoning erection had lessened. It was always at around this point that Christopher started to become irritated. Although he enjoyed being dominated, there came a moment when he wanted to be allowed to climax and was torn between his desire to be dominated and his desire for gratification. Rebecca had decided long ago that it was best if she remained in control. Although he might make a fuss at the time, afterwards he was always incredibly grateful and the end result was wonderful for both of them.

After allowing him a short break she resumed her original position, and then slowly tipped the bottle of oil so that drops of it fell on to the base of his spine and began to seep down into the crack between his buttocks. Then, using her fingers, she began to knead them slowly and sensuously while all of Christopher's muscles began to tighten and his hips started to move restlessly once more.

Rebecca continued this for so long that she knew it was almost beyond the kind of cruelty that Christopher really wanted, but she couldn't help it – she was enjoying herself and her power so much.

Her breasts felt large and tight, and deep within her stomach she could feel tiny flutterings while between her thighs she was already damp and more than ready for him. Eventually, she replaced the stopper in the bottle of oil and picked up the final implement for the evening's entertainment. Christopher twisted his head round to try to see what was going to happen but she sharply ordered him to look away again. Then, very carefully, she lifted up the small but flexible rod that held a number of Thai beads.

This was one of Christopher's favourite forms of stimulation. Rebecca prised his buttocks apart with her hands and then spread some of the oil that had seeped between them carefully around the opening to his rectum. It was only when she began to slide the tiny rod into the puckered mouth of the rectum that Christopher realised exactly what delights she had planned for him and he gave a tiny cry of delight. Rebecca inserted the rod very slowly, twisting and turning it as it slid in, the small beads rubbing against the incredibly sensitive sides of the opening. Once the rod was inserted as fully as possible, Rebecca had a choice. She could either continue twisting it or she could flick the protruding end, allowing the beads that were inside Christopher to vibrate even harder against him. After pausing for a moment to decide which would be best, Rebecca flicked at the rod and immediately Christopher's body started to rise up from the bed.

'If I have to tell you to keep still again,' said Rebecca, 'then I'm going to stop the game and leave. This is your last warning, do you understand?'

'Yes,' groaned Christopher. His voice was thick,

barely recognisable, and beneath the mounting excitement there was also resentment at her total power over him. Rebecca continued to flick remorselessly at the rod until Christopher was groaning aloud with his ever-increasing need to climax as the stimulation intensified.

Finally, Rebecca decided that the time had come for her to gain more pleasure as well. While still flicking occasionally at the protruding end of the Thai beads, she began to slide herself up and down Christopher's oiled back, widening her legs so that her clitoris was stimulated by the hardness of his well-muscled body.

She moved slowly at first but then with increasing speed as the wonderful hot liquid sensation at the pit of her belly intensified. As she moved herself, Rebecca also massaged her already-oiled nipple with her own fingers, and after a few moments the combined sensation meant that her entire body shivered and shook as she found a moment's release in her first orgasm.

Beneath her, Christopher, who was not yet allowed to come, bucked furiously as he tried to throw Rebecca off him. It was double torture for him when Rebecca gained satisfaction during his torment of frustration and domination, but this only added to Rebecca's excitement.

Suddenly, she was seized by the desire for yet another orgasm before she allowed him any kind of release. She reversed her position, which meant that she was now facing the back of Christopher's head, then spread her entire body over his so the front of her body covered the back of his. Placing her hands on the tops of his shoulders, she used these to pull herself up and down over his oiled flesh. She knew that, quite apart from the sensations he would be feeling from her breasts and belly, he would also be driven half mad by the feel of the stockings against his legs. He loved to feel silk against his skin and, as she moved faster and faster, allowing her own excitement to mount and the flickering flame to burst into an orgasm, she heard him muttering curses into the pillow.

After her second orgasm, Rebecca carefully removed the rod from Christopher's rectum. She did it very slowly and deliberately, allowing one bead to pop out at a time and, as each bead slowly appeared through the opening, Christopher's body jolted. Only when it was finally removed did Rebecca climb off the bed and start to unfasten the silken scarves that tied him there.

Even though he was now free, Christopher knew better than to try to do anything on his own initiative. He remained lying face down until Rebecca gave him permission to turn on to his back. Once he was positioned there, she proceeded to re-tie him and, in addition, covered his eyes with a piece of black cloth. This meant that Christopher had no idea of how he was going to be allowed to achieve his long-awaited orgasm but, as she looked at his naked body, Rebecca could see that every well-defined muscle was taut and quivering with anticipation. His erection was huge, the glans purple with tiny clear drops of pre-come slowly oozing from the slit.

Rebecca decided that she would give Christopher a running commentary on what she was doing. This was an entirely new idea, but she felt that it would probably be almost more than he could stand. Tonight, that gave her a strange kind of satisfaction, since she was still well aware that he had spent the afternoon interviewing attractive actresses. In a way, quite apart from giving them both intense pleasure, this session was a kind of sensual revenge.

'I'm lifting myself up now,' she murmured to him seductively. As she did so she squatted over his penis and then rubbed it against her clitoris.

'Now I'm going to move my hips around and you must keep perfectly still,' she told him calmly. Christopher's mouth was tightly closed in a desperate effort to control himself but, despite this, a small groan escaped him. Rebecca was so carried away that she really didn't care if Christopher was enjoying himself or not. His reward would come at the end; she was getting hers all the time. As she allowed his penis to stimulate her clitoris a hot throbbing pulse began deep within her, somewhere behind the clitoris itself, and she knew that very soon she was going to have her final orgasm. She wanted to postpone it for as long as possible in order to make it more intense. Reaching down, she grasped the root of Christopher's penis in her hand and then descended swiftly on to it so that penetration was incredibly deep.

'Now I'm going to move up and down on top of you,' she whispered to Christopher.

'I don't think I can wait much longer,' he gasped.

Rebecca didn't care, but she remembered to pretend that she did. 'You'd better, Christopher,' she said with a tone of menace to her voice. She could feel his hardness within her increase, and smiled at the realisation of what even a simple command given in the right tone could do to him. She sensed that, despite the fact he was so close to the edge,

Christopher would strain to carry out her orders, and this additional excitement only increased her own build-up to orgasm.

Now, with a keen edge of cruelty, she moved her hips around and around, sank slowly back on him, then lifted her hips in the air until only the tip of him was inside her, before plunging her body back down on to his. All the time she kept up a running commentary on what she was doing and how she was feeling.

She described how her muscles were tightening, how she felt hot and liquid in her belly, and how her breasts were feeling tight and swollen while her nipples tingled remorselessly. All at once she felt the warm glow begin to spread throughout her entire belly and up through her breasts, while between her thighs the tension increased and a deep ache started. She knew that she was only seconds away from a huge orgasm and, leaning forward with her hands on either side of his head, she dangled her breasts in front of Christopher's face.

Although he couldn't see them, Christopher could feel them only too well. His mouth opened and he lifted his head, searching blindly so that he could draw one of her nipples into his mouth. Taking pity on him, Rebecca carefully allowed one of the throbbing hard tips to enter his mouth. Christopher licked and sucked on it greedily, his tongue swirling around the tissue that surrounded the tip of the nipple, and Rebecca quickened the pace of her hips as she moved up and down on him.

Suddenly, Christopher drew his head back, releasing Rebecca's nipple with startling speed as he shouted out in agonised ecstasy. Rebecca knew he could no longer control himself. Immediately she sat back so that her arms were free at her sides and, as she continued to move up and down, stimulating his desperately straining penis, she allowed the fingers of her right hand to rub slowly against her clitoris.

Rebecca had judged the moment to perfection. As Christopher gave a giant shout of satisfaction while his hips pumped furiously, Rebecca too was flooded with one of the most intense climaxes she had yet experienced with her lover. It felt as though her whole body had suffered an electrical charge, and when her muscles were finally still and the sensations slowly began to ebb away, she slumped down on top of him with her head resting on his chest.

Beneath her she could hear his racing heartbeat and, as he murmured words of gratitude and affection, she knew that this time she had managed to surpass herself. It didn't matter how pretty the girls were he had seen that afternoon, she was well aware that, if she were able to continue satisfying him in this way, then Christopher would not look anywhere else for a permanent girlfriend.

After she had released him and they were both getting ready to sleep, Christopher held her tightly against him. 'That was really incredible, Becky,' he said slowly. 'I've never met a woman who was so versatile. You always seem to know what it is that I need and the best thing of all is it's what you need too.'

'We make a very good pair,' agreed Rebecca softly. Then, snuggling up against him, she fell happily asleep.

* * *

Exactly two weeks after her audition, Esther returned to the hall in Clapham in order to meet the other members of Christopher's new company. He'd already announced to the press that the company would be known as 'The People's Theatre'. This had amused both Esther and Lydia, since they were well aware that this was Christopher's theatre and the people were merely expected to come and adore him.

Christopher was standing at the door in order to greet everyone as they arrived. This would have been a more heartwarming gesture if it hadn't been for the fact that on the opposite side of the road several press photographers were busy snapping away as he warmly welcomed each arrival. Esther was greeted with hugs and kisses and she heard the frantic clicking of the cameras. She smiled to herself. It would be wonderful if a photo of this were to appear in one of the American papers for Marcus to see, but she doubted if that were likely to happen. Nevertheless, it showed her that she had been right in deciding to take this job. There would clearly be plenty of publicity and, by the end of the tour, she should be more firmly established as a theatrical actress. As far as she knew, Claudine was nothing but a model, although she called herself a model and actress. This was a term that had previously caused both Esther and Marcus considerable amusement and was generally looked down upon by fully trained professional actors and actresses.

Once everyone was inside the hall, Esther looked about her with interest. She very much hoped that the other members of the company would be people she could get along with easily. It made such a difference, especially when touring was involved.

A circle of chairs had been arranged in the middle of the room and within about ten minutes Christopher had organised it so they were all sitting down. He then proceeded to introduce them to each other and Esther, with a horrible sinking sensation, realised that once the introductions had been made they were probably going to be expected to play some bonding games.

She'd had more than her fill of those at drama school and one of the big advantages of working in television was that you were not required to carry out this kind of exercise. There simply wasn't the time. You learnt your lines, turned up on set and acted. In the theatre, as she knew from Marcus, it was all very different and these bonding games were, for some reason, considered a vital part of company work. Personally, she thought they were utterly ridiculous.

'Right then,' said Christopher, getting to his feet and proceeding to walk round the backs of the chairs. 'First of all I'll introduce the girls. This is Rebecca Leslie. Rebecca and I met at the RSC, and so I do know a little about her work. She's as enthusiastic about this project as I am, and indeed as I hope you all are. Rebecca, is there anything you'd like to say to everyone?'

Esther wondered if they were all going to be asked to say something about themselves to the company. Her mind went utterly blank as she tried desperately to think of something intelligent or helpful that she would be able to say. While she was thinking about it, Rebecca, who Esther thought had a beautiful face with extremely dramatic features, gave a small smile. 'I really just want to say how very grateful I am that Christopher has allowed me to be part of his wonderful idea,' she said softly. 'I only hope that I don't let him down. I just know this is going to be a huge success and I'm sure we're all going to be great, great friends.'

Looking round the circle, Esther's eyes met those of a tall dark-haired man sitting opposite her. His face was totally impassive, and he showed none of the forced enthusiasm that was reflected in the faces of the other company members. Indeed, he looked as though the only thing he was likely to do was vomit. Esther bent her head in order to hide a grin.

Christopher moved on round the circle. 'This is Rosie Meyer. Rosie, as you may know, has had a small part in *Brookside*. She's also done quite a bit of pub theatre and is extremely enthusiastic, aren't you, Rosie?'

Rosie smiled and nodded her head. She had brown curly hair and was a rather buxom girl with high colouring. She seemed more natural than Rebecca and, glancing round the circle said, 'Hi everyone. Like Rebecca I'm just absolutely thrilled to be here.'

Christopher gave a smile of acknowledgement – clearly he expected everyone to say how thrilled they were to be a part of his company – and then he moved on to a red-haired girl. 'This is Theresa Wilson,' he continued. 'Theresa did a wonderful audition for me. It was a most unusual reading of Lady Macbeth. I think she's going to prove really innovative, and that's something I hope we'll all strive for. I believe that plays can be traditional and yet innovative at the same time.'

'How interesting,' murmured the dark-haired man softly.

Christopher's eyes flickered in the direction of the speaker and he opened his mouth as though to reply but then seemed to think better of it and closed it again. 'Is there anything you'd like to say, Theresa?' he asked.

'Not really,' she replied. Her voice was quiet, and Esther wasn't surprised that her Lady Macbeth had been innovative. It was probably the most subdued reading that anyone had ever heard. However, Theresa looked the kind of girl who might have hidden depths. 'I'm very pleased that you liked my audition piece,' continued Theresa, 'and like the others I'm just so excited. I can't wait for us to get going.'

There were only two more girls for Christopher to introduce. The first, Ellie Ford, was baby-faced in appearance but there was something slightly predatory about her, and Esther noticed that Ellie spent most of her time looking at the male members of the cast. When asked if she had anything to say, she simply shook her head and murmured her appreciation of the fact that she had been accepted into Christopher's company. Mary Fuller, the character actress, looked to be in her late fifties. She had silver-grey hair, was slightly above average height, and had remained slim. Esther knew that she had once been a well-known ingenue but that she had kept her career going by turning in some very fine character performances. Esther had also heard rumours about Mary's sexual preferences, but she couldn't quite remember what they were. It was either for young men or young women and Esther would have to wait to see which was right.

When Esther herself was introduced she cringed as Christopher burst into a paean of praise, stressing the brilliance of her reading of Ophelia, and saying how lucky they were that she had been free to join them for the project. It was obvious to Esther that everyone else in the circle was as stunned as she was. After all, she had done very little except appear in some television plays and be seen on Marcus's arm. As for her Ophelia, while it had been better than she'd expected, it certainly wouldn't have won her best actress of the year. Obviously Christopher had his own agenda for making such a fuss of her, but she wished that he hadn't done it. It had put her at an immediate disadvantage. Now everyone would be watching her, waiting for her to make a mistake. If you were the director's favourite then no one else in the company was likely to be very fond of you.

When Christopher introduced the men he was far quicker about it and, while his hand had lingered on the shoulders of the actresses, he never touched any of the men. The dark-haired man, who was almost too good-looking but was saved by an edge of danger in his features, was called Damon Dowden. Esther remembered that a couple of months earlier he had turned in a brilliant Iago at the National. Apart from that she knew very little about him, but it seemed to her that Christopher was far more fortunate to have Damon in his company than he was to have Esther. Damon refused to make any comment about himself at all; he simply nodded curtly at the company and then looked at the floor.

Another of the men, Nicholas Maxwell, had been on television quite a lot. He informed them with

40

great pride that he had once owned a street market stall and this had paid his way through drama school. Esther sensed that he disliked most actors and actresses of Christopher's kind, but understood that he needed them if he were to make his mark. She wondered exactly what parts Christopher had in mind for him, but then realised that because of his TV appearances he was possibly to be used as a draw for the general public in some of the smaller towns.

Two of the other male actors were almost indistinguishable from each other. Noel Daniels and Michael Lester were both average in appearance with fairly long mid-brown hair, light-brown eyes, average height and, Esther suspected, of average acting skills. They seemed cheerful and energetic and were the type of actors who helped to make life easier on the road. It was obvious they knew each other well. In fact, Michael said that he had first met Noel at LAMDA and they had remained friends ever since, only ever falling out now and again over a girl. This brought the first laugh of the morning.

Finally there was George Hickey. George had to be at least sixty, thought Esther. He had grey hair, light-blue eyes and, while he looked as if he had once been slim, he was now suffering from late middle-age spread. When Christopher asked him if there was anything he wanted to say he actually got to his feet and issued what was plainly a prepared speech in which he praised Christopher, the work that Christopher had already done, and the work he was planning to do. Esther thought that, if he felt it would have helped, George would have got down on his hands and knees and grovelled round Christopher's feet. The one thing that was obvious was he had a beautiful speaking voice and excellent diction. This was more than could be said for Nicholas Maxwell, whose market stall origins did not seem to have been ironed out by his drama school education.

When the introductions were finally over, Esther's worst fears were realised. Christopher took his seat again and looked round at everyone with a broad smile. 'Right then,' he said cheerfully. 'Now, I believe it's essential that if we're to work well together we learn to lose our inhibitions and trust each other. I'm sure all of you here will agree with me, and so I thought it would be a good idea if, before we started discussing or reading any of the plays, we spent a little time in getting to know each other. Let's start with a game of zip zap boing.'

Damon Dowden uttered an audible sigh, but Noel and Michael looked extremely enthusiastic. 'Hey, that's a great idea,' agreed Michael. 'Noel and I are really good at that.'

'Really,' said Rebecca, sounding incredibly bored. 'Are you any good at anything else?'

Michael grinned at her. 'That's for me to know and you to find out,' he retorted.

'Thanks, but I don't think I'll bother,' replied Rebecca.

'I don't think I've ever played it,' said Ellie. She looked helplessly around the circle. 'Perhaps someone could tell me about it?'

'Don't look at me,' said Damon, his voice surly. 'It's Christopher's idea. I'm sure he can tell you what it's all about.'

Christopher seemed surprised that Ellie didn't know the game. 'Is there anyone else apart from

42

Ellie who doesn't know how to play it?' he asked. His tone was such that Esther doubted if anyone would confess to not knowing, even if that was the case. No one else did say anything, so Christopher explained patiently for Ellie's benefit.

'It's a game where you pass round the clap,' he said earnestly.

Both Damon and Theresa Wilson sniggered. Ellie giggled nervously while Mary Fuller watched her with interest. No one else said anything. Christopher's ready smile deserted him. 'I hope you're not all going to be childish about this,' he said shortly. 'What I mean, Ellie, is that one of us – say Damon over there – claps, and as he claps he turns to his right and Mary, who's sitting on his right, catches the clap and passes it on by clapping –'

'There's something I never knew,' commented Damon.

'I'd appreciate it, Damon, if you didn't keep interrupting me,' Christopher said irritably. 'Now, Ellie, everyone carries on like this turning slightly to their right and clapping, catching the clap and passing it on saying zip. Then if they say boing as they take the clap it starts going round the other way in a clockwise direction. This carries on until someone says boing again, then the clap goes back anti-clockwise. If someone says zap they're throwing the clap across the circle to the person opposite them. You'll soon get the hang of it; it's fast, it's fun and it breaks down inhibitions.'

'I see,' said Ellie, sounding unsure.

'It's really quite easy,' Esther assured her. 'We used to play it loads at drama school.'

'So did we,' confirmed Rosie. 'Mind you, none of

43

us got on very well so I don't think it really worked.'

'Well I think it's useful,' said Christopher firmly. 'Can we start now please?'

They played zip zap boing for at least ten minutes and Esther was amused to notice that Damon never once made any attempt to alter the direction of the way the game was going. He simply clapped and turned to his right or clapped and turned to his left as though it was a matter of supreme indifference to him whether the game was played properly at all. However, some of them, particularly Noel and Michael, began to get noisier and noisier and the speed of the game picked up. By the end of the ten minutes there was a lot of giggling and laughter going on and Esther wondered if she was the only one feeling prematurely old and out of it. She tried hard to disguise it but had the feeling that Rebecca – who for some reason had been watching her closely right from the start – was aware of this.

'OK,' called Christopher at last, just when Esther thought that she couldn't stand any more of it. 'Now then, George, could you and Damon move that table from the end of the room and bring it just a fraction further forward. We're going to play the falling game.'

'If you think I'm falling off that table and letting this lot catch me you've got another thing coming,' Damon said irritably. 'I've joined this company to act, not play stupid games.'

Rebecca stood up, shaking her long dark hair back from her face and moving sensuously towards Damon. 'Don't be like that,' she murmured, 'it's really important, Damon. I know you're very

44

experienced, but not everyone here is. It's really up to people like you and Christopher to help the rest of us. I'm quite happy to go first. I know I can trust you to catch me.'

'Don't rely on it,' said Damon as he and George started to move the table.

'Who is he?' whispered Rosie Meyer to Esther as the pair of them stood together while the table was being moved.

'Damon Dowden,' explained Esther. 'He's been at the National and before that I think he was at the Royal Court. He's had some brilliant reviews for the past year or so.'

'He's a bit frightening, isn't he?' said Rosie. 'I don't think we're going to get a lot of laughs out of him.'

'He isn't really that kind of an actor,' said Esther. 'Noel and Michael look good fun though.'

'Yes,' agreed Rosie. 'You know,' she confessed, 'I didn't expect to be picked for this company. I thought Christopher would want people with far more experience. It was only when I read what he said to the press, about trying to give young people a chance now that rep had nearly died out, that I realised why he'd taken me on.'

Esther thought that Rosie's buxom figure and natural enthusiasm had probably played as great a part as anything in her acceptance, but she nodded and smiled. She had decided before arriving today that she was going to be very careful what she said. She had always, in the past, found it best not to get too involved with anyone but simply to get on with her work. As far as she was concerned this was her chance to show she could act. She wasn't going to become involved in any personality clashes. In any case, she had some sympathy for Damon, who must have thought he was long past the time of having to play these kinds of games.

The falling game was always tricky. Esther had never found it easy to stand on a table, close her eyes and then simply launch herself into space relying on everyone else's outstretched arms to safely catch her. Even at drama school it had taken all her courage and now, after such a long gap, it was even worse. She knew that she actually took far too long to launch herself off the table and heard the edge of irritation in Christopher's voice as he urged her to jump. Of course she was safely caught, and as she opened her eyes and was set down on her feet again, she caught Damon watching her with a strange expression in his very dark-brown eyes. However, the moment he realised that she'd seen him looking, he looked away again.

Esther remembered that in the reviews of his performance of Iago, there had been tremendous enthusiasm about his extraordinary charisma on stage. She couldn't help but think that this abundance of stage personality appeared to drain him of any charisma off it. It was also clear that he was not a good 'group' person.

By the end of the day they all knew each other a little better. It seemed to Esther that alliances were already being formed, although this had not been the idea of the exercises. It was impossible, though, to prevent this from happening. You could never expect twelve people, each with their own huge ego, to get on. The best you could hope for was that some of them would get on very well and that all of them would be able to tolerate each other's foibles.

'Tomorrow,' said Christopher, 'I'm going to get you to start the first read-throughs of *Time and the Conways*. I'm going to play around with the roles quite a bit, which means that, although you may read one role tomorrow morning, you'll probably read a different one in the afternoon. I certainly haven't made up my mind about casting yet.'

'Not even yourself?' asked Damon.

There was a sudden silence. Christopher turned and looked at Damon. 'No, not even about myself,' he said with an attempt at lightness.

'Well you do surprise me,' murmured Damon. He picked up his jacket and then walked out of the hall and off into the London streets.

'God, he's going to be a pain,' said Rebecca. 'Do you think it's really worth having him with us, Christopher?'

'Rebecca, I don't want to hear any more remarks like that,' said Christopher. 'Damon's a marvellous actor, as you know very well. Maybe he isn't the easiest of people, but that's not the point. I think I'm more than capable of dealing with him.'

Rebecca looked suitably chastened. 'Sorry,' she said.

'Well, I think it's been a terrific day,' Noel said enthusiastically. 'I can't wait for the reading tomorrow. What part do you want me to read first, Christopher?'

'I thought probably Gerald Thornton,' said Christopher.

'The solicitor chappy? Oh great, I'd like that.'

'Yes, well that's not to say you'll be playing Gerald, it's just the part I'd like to hear you read in the morning,' Christopher reminded him. 'OK, everyone, well I think we'll call it a day for now.

By the way, if anyone from the press asks you any questions about the company, I'd really prefer it if you passed them on to me. I think it's best to have just one spokesperson for the group otherwise things can get very complicated.'

'So much for the people's theatre company,' George Hickey murmured in a low voice to Mary Fuller.

Mary smiled at him. 'Did you really expect anything different, George?' she asked. 'I certainly didn't. I'm just grateful to have the chance to do this.'

'Oh I agree,' George replied hastily. 'Perhaps we should go for a drink, Mary. It must be all of six years since we last met, and if my memory serves me correctly you and I could probably be quite useful to each other during this tour.'

Mary nodded in agreement and the two older actors disappeared out of the door. Eventually everyone except for Christopher, Rebecca, Esther and Nicholas had gone. Esther had been expecting to leave with Rebecca, but Nicholas drew her to one side and explained that Rebecca and Christopher were an item. 'I thought you knew,' he said. 'I should think everyone else here does.'

'I'm afraid I don't know very much about Christopher at all,' confessed Esther. 'I know about his acting, of course, but not his private life.'

'I suppose you've been pretty caught up in your own over the past few weeks,' Nicholas replied tactlessly.

Esther had the feeling that she wasn't going to like Nicholas Maxwell very much but, nevertheless, she smiled sweetly at him. 'It's all been pretty traumatic,' she confessed. 'The important thing

48

now is to put it behind me and get on with my career. That's why this is such a great opportunity.'

'I'm hoping it'll give me some street cred with all those arty directors who are stuck up their own arses,' said Nicholas. 'They seem to think that unless you talk in an old-style BBC voice, and come from a good background – whatever that may be – you can't be a classical actor. They only have to look at me and they start talking *EastEnders*. It's not fair. Why can't I be just as good as Christopher?'

'No reason at all,' said Esther.

Nicholas accompanied her as far as the tube station and there they parted. As she travelled back to her house, Esther allowed herself a small smile. Somehow, she didn't think that Nicholas Maxwell's Henry V would have quite the same impact as Christopher Wheldon's, not unless he made some attempt to improve his vowels and his voice projection.

Despite that, she felt that the day had gone well and at last she was doing what she'd trained to do – being a proper actress. For the first time in months she was looking forward to going to work the next day. Also, she realised that the entire time she'd been with the company she had only thought about Marcus once. That was such a huge improvement it was barely believable. It's cheaper than therapy, she thought to herself as she got off at her stop.

Once she got home she prepared a light meal, had a shower, went to bed and was asleep within fifteen minutes.

Chapter Three

*I*t was during the following morning, just after
Esther had read the role of Carol in the first act,
when she suddenly decided she was going to seduce Christopher Wheldon. Originally, it had
seemed to her that simply by joining his company
and becoming well known as an actress she would
be getting her revenge on Marcus. However, after
watching Christopher and the way all the girls in
the cast were clearly fascinated by him, she decided
it would be even more of a triumph for her if she
were able to supplant Rebecca in his affections.

The problem was, it was Damon Dowden who
really attracted her. There was something fascinating about him, something dark and forbidding,
that made her want to learn what he was like in
bed as well as an actor. Despite this, she decided it
was Christopher she would pursue. In any case,
Damon didn't seem in the least bit interested in
Esther. On the whole he wasn't interested in anyone, but as the day wore on she did notice him

exchanging a few comments and even laughing once with Ellie Ford.

To Esther's way of thinking this was not a point in Damon's favour. Ellie, although baby-faced in appearance, was clearly a very ambitious and sexually voracious young lady. Her light-brown urchin haircut and her wide round-eyed expression were effective with men but, whenever she was talking to any of the other girls, her face would change and it was then that the other side of her would show through.

Time and the Conways was a good play, but Esther thought it would be a difficult one to pull off successfully. Set in 1919, shortly after the end of the First World War, the middle-class Conway family epitomise everything that was solid about their kind at that time. In both Acts I and III the scene is consistent but, in the middle act, Kay, one of the Conway daughters, seems to have a vision about the future of her very English family. It is this vision that makes the play so special. If Kay's apparent dream is indeed to become true then nothing the audience sees in the first and last acts is of any true and lasting importance. Values will change, and the young people's lives will be blighted by tragedy and disastrous love affairs or marriages. The problem in Esther's mind was whether or not a modern-day audience would accept the concept of this vision.

When she voiced this fear to Christopher he brushed it to one side. 'A well-written play, acted proficiently, can't fail,' he assured her with one of his most attractive smiles. 'I think that audiences today want the reassurance that this play can give them. They want to be reminded of a time when

51

there were standards and morals because, despite our so-called liberal age, most people are looking for boundaries, you know. It makes them feel safe.'

Esther certainly wasn't going to argue with him; she just hoped that he was right. Although most of the cast read several of the roles, Damon Dowden read only one. That was the role of the outsider, Ernest Beevers. In the first and third acts Ernest is an insignificant outsider not even considered worthy of the hand of the pretty and popular Hazel Conway. However, in the middle act, during the vision, when he is married to Hazel, his character changes entirely.

In the morning Damon read Ernest as portrayed in Acts I and III. In the afternoon he read the very different Ernest as portrayed in Act II, and Esther sensed that the entire company was startled by the powerful display he gave. Now she wished fervently that she'd been to see his Iago. She also understood exactly why Christopher Wheldon wanted Damon in the company. He would provide a marvellous contrast for Christopher, who was clearly – despite his protestation of uncertainty – going to play the rakish Robin. The contrast between the fair-haired, lively, anything-for-fun Robin and the dour, mercenary Ernest Beevers, portrayed by the dark and sinister Damon, would be wonderful.

It was a tiring day because, quite apart from reading for various roles in this play, all of the company performed small pieces from some of Shakespeare's most popular plays. Esther was somewhat amused to see that Nicholas was given a role in *Macbeth* – but only as Banquo. She could tell that he was annoyed by this, but if he had seriously thought that Christopher was going to let anyone but himself play the title role then he had to be quite mad. She only hoped that Nicholas managed to keep his resentment under control during the forthcoming tour, especially since she couldn't quite make out what part, if any, he was going to be given in *Time and the Conways*. It seemed most likely to her that he would finish up as an understudy and that Banquo was simply a consolation prize – and not a very good one at that.

During the lunch break, they all went their separate ways. Esther found herself with Rosie, Noel and Michael at a nearby pub. Rosie was good fun to be with; she had an excellent sense of humour and so far had been unfailingly cheerful. Noel and Michael made it obvious they were both attracted to her and, while Rosie clearly relished their attention, this did not stop her from including Esther in their conversation.

'How are you coping with all the publicity you've been getting lately?' Noel asked Esther when Michael was at the bar ordering a round of drinks.

'It was pretty ghastly at first,' confessed Esther. 'Actually, I think some of the attention's beginning to drift away now and I feel much better in myself simply because I'm involved in this project. There's nothing like work to take your mind off your personal troubles.'

'It must be difficult, though,' sympathised Noel. 'I make a point of never getting heavily involved with anyone. Michael and I are agreed on that. We don't think that it's possible to have a settled relationship with anyone in this profession. Let's be honest, there are far too many temptations along the way. Isn't that right, Rosie?' As he spoke he squeezed Rosie's right knee and she giggled.

When Michael returned from the bar he sat down between the two girls. One of his arms rested along the back of Rosie's chair and she smiled happily, turning her head from one man to the other.

'We share a flat near here,' said Michael to Esther. 'If you ever want to come back for a coffee one evening we'd be delighted, wouldn't we, Noel?'

'We certainly would,' Noel agreed enthusiastically.

'We like to share everything,' continued Michael. As he spoke he glanced at Rosie and then his eyes met his friend's over the top of her head. It was then that Esther realised exactly what he meant, and she wondered if Rosie realised too. If she did it clearly didn't bother her. By the time they returned to the rehearsal room, Rosie was walking with her arms linked with both men.

Esther was secretly fascinated by the thought of two men sharing one woman. She wondered what it would be like to have two men attending to her, doing all the things she liked best at the same time. Somehow, she couldn't imagine being able to take part in such a scenario but the idea was fascinating. She wondered if Rosie would tell her about it if she were to make up a threesome with them.

While Esther and her group had been at the pub, Christopher and Rebecca had taken Theresa out to a nearby café. Christopher had mentioned to Rebecca the previous evening that he found Theresa 'rather fascinating'. Her mass of red curly hair, and the pencil-slim figure combined with exceptionally large breasts, had attracted his attention from the moment she had first auditioned. Occasionally, he and Rebecca had been joined by a second girl during one of their sex sessions and it had always proved very successful. Rebecca had quickly picked up on his hint and was now going out of her way to be friendly with Theresa.

Theresa, who desperately wanted to play the part of Madge – the one Conway girl who was not in any way a sex symbol – was flattered by the attention of the great Christopher Wheldon. She knew that he and Rebecca were an item and thought that Rebecca's interest in her must be based on the fact that Christopher was impressed by her acting.

'You know, Theresa,' said Christopher as they ate toasted sandwiches and drank cappuccino, 'there's a great deal more to you than meets the eye.'

Theresa smiled shyly at him. 'That's very kind of you,' she said. 'I feel that I've been rather typecast in the past few months. If you're built like I am then I suppose it's only natural, which is why I'd really like to play Madge. I mean, no one can say Madge is glamorous; she doesn't even get a man, does she? But the thing is, would the audience believe in me playing a part like that?'

'Well,' said Christopher slowly, 'I think they might, but you'd have to put in a lot of hard work. The point is really, exactly how dedicated are you, Theresa?'

'I'm a hundred per cent dedicated,' Theresa said indignantly. 'I'd do absolutely anything to get the part of Madge.'

'Would you now?' murmured Rebecca. She

glanced across the table at Christopher and he nodded slightly.

'You know,' he said to Theresa, 'I think that if you had some extra tuition, say from me, then I could almost certainly promise you the part of Madge.'

'Extra tuition?' asked Theresa in surprise. She was no fool, and knew perfectly well what that usually meant in the theatre, but this time she couldn't believe she was hearing right. After all, Christopher lived with Rebecca and Rebecca was sitting there with them while he talked about extra tuition.

'That's right,' said Rebecca. Reaching out, Rebecca caught hold of a strand of Theresa's hair and she idly played with it. 'You've got really beautiful hair,' she said. 'Christopher's got a thing about red hair, haven't you, Chris?'

'I don't know if it's the hair,' confessed Christopher. 'Perhaps it's the character of people with red hair that really fascinates me.'

Theresa felt her face going hot. There was no doubt that the pair of them were toying with her, and there was a definite feeling of sexual tension in the air. At first she felt slightly uncomfortable as Rebecca touched her hair, but when she released it she felt a momentary pang of loss.

'If you did have extra rehearsals,' said Rebecca at last, 'then I'd be there too. I'd be putting the woman's point of view, as it were.'

Then, Theresa understood what was being suggested. Like all the girls in the company, she was besotted with Christopher. She'd have given almost anything to have slept with him just once. What she hadn't bargained on was sharing him with

Rebecca. Now that the idea had been put forward, though, she couldn't help but feel excited. She realised that the pair of them were waiting for an answer, and as she hesitated she felt Christopher's leg rub against hers beneath the table. He was watching her intently and she shivered slightly with a mixture of desire and apprehension.

'I think it sounds a super idea,' she said at last.

With a sigh Christopher leant back in his chair, a smile of contentment on his face. Rebecca looked equally pleased. She looked like someone who knew she had played her part well.

Rebecca glanced at her watch and the three of them suddenly realised that it was time they were back at the rehearsal room. 'Come on, Chris, we're going to be late,' Rebecca said.

'You go on ahead,' Christopher said lightly.

After Rebecca had left the café, Chris helped Theresa into her coat and then, putting an arm round her waist, squeezed her lightly. 'I think you're going to be an excellent Madge,' he said reassuringly. 'As for the extra tuition, well, that's going to be a total delight.'

It was nearly seven in the evening before they were all finally told what parts they were to play in *Time and the Conways*. Everyone sat around the room trying hard to look casual but inside Esther knew that each of them would – like her – be feeling strung-up and anxious. If you'd set your heart on a part – and after her reading she had set her heart on playing Hazel – then it was horrible if you failed to get it. Normally this failure was never witnessed by anyone else but, in this case, the entire company would know full well whether or not each person was happy with the role they'd been given. Of course there would be false commiserations, or even false congratulations, but it wasn't a comfortable situation to be in.

It did cross Esther's mind that perhaps Christopher should have taken them to one side individually as he told them what parts he'd chosen for them, but clearly this was another part of his ensemble attitude. No one was to be kept in the dark; there were to be no secrets. Not that that were entirely true; there would be plenty of secrets and Esther thought that most of them would centre around personal relationships within the company. However, the façade of openness was to continue.

'Here we go then,' Christopher said cheerfully. 'Quite a few of these parts have been cast against type. I think that this makes for a far more exciting production. Naturally, I haven't gone to ridiculous extremes. I'm sure none of you will be surprised to hear that Mary is playing Mrs Conway. It would be rather difficult for any of you girls to play her, particularly since she's in her late fifties in the middle act. There will be some other surprises, though, but I hope that none of you will be too disappointed and some of you should be very excited. I certainly am.'

'I wish he'd stop talking and just get on with it,' muttered Rosie, who was sitting next to Esther. Esther nodded in agreement.

'The part of Kay,' said Christopher, smiling round at them all, 'is going to be played by . . .' He paused for a moment and Rebecca sat upright, looking keen and eager. 'Esther,' he concluded.

Esther didn't dare look at Rebecca. She knew only too well how the other girl must be feeling and couldn't understand why she'd been given the role. Certainly it would stretch her to her limits, but she had the dreadful feeling that she might fail. She knew, as most actors and actresses do know, that the role of Hazel, the blonde beauty with the soft centre, had suited her down to the ground. Intelligent, sensible Kay, with her visions and her analytical approach to life, was simply not Esther.

'Hazel,' continued Christopher, apparently oblivious to the feelings of the people around him, 'will be played by Rebecca.' Again, Esther kept her eyes fixed firmly on the ground but she could hear some whispers among the group and knew that everyone was as puzzled as she was by his casting.

By this time Christopher was looking quite pleased with himself. He'd clearly intended to make an impact and had succeeded. He carried on casting the play and Esther was amused to find that Ellie was to play the impulsive, excitable sixteen-year-old, Carol. It was true that with her young appearance she was probably the best person for the part but her character was another matter. Rosie was to play Hazel's friend, Joan – a pretty but rather foolish girl. Again, this piece of casting was not illogical. However, when it came to Madge – a girl who was meant to have been to Girton College, was brisk, bookish, self-confident and not very pretty with the air of a schoolmistress about her – there was a collective intake of breath when Christopher announced that Theresa was to play the part.

'Well, I have to say,' said Damon in a low voice to Ellie who was sitting on the other side of Esther, 'she's not at all like any schoolmistress I've ever seen depicted in the early twentieth century. I wonder how he intends to flatten her bust.' Ellie snorted with laughter and quickly changed it into a cough when Christopher glanced her way.

When it came to the roles of the two brothers, the part of Alan – a lance-corporal, rather dull and introverted – went to Noel; Robin, a dashing good-looking RAF officer – charming and attractive – was, to no one's surprise, to be played by Christopher. As expected, the role of Ernest Beevers – the socially awkward lower-class but upwardly mobile outsider – went to Damon. As he hadn't read for any other role this was certainly not a surprise. Michael, the young man who shared a flat with Noel, was to play Gerald, the pleasant good-looking young solicitor, which meant that there was no part in the play for Nicholas Maxwell.

Glancing across the room at him, Esther could see that Nicholas wasn't pleased. He had read for the role of Ernest Beevers and also for Alan. Neither of the parts had suited him in the least, but this hadn't prevented him from making it clear he expected to be in the play. He was frowning now and Theresa, who was sitting on his left, was whispering what Esther assumed to be words of consolation in his ear. The only other member of the company without a part was George Hickey. This wasn't a surprise to anyone, least of all George. There was no role suitable for him in the play and in any case he'd been promised Lear when Christopher presented his mini version during the tour. Obviously for someone like George this was the chance of a lifetime and next to it *Time and the Conways* paled into insignificance.

'Right,' said Christopher briskly. 'I can tell some of you are rather surprised by the parts you've been given, but I can assure you I have every confidence you're all more than capable of doing excellently in them. I'm sorry there's nothing for Nicholas and George but later on in the season there will be times when none of us are acting.'

'I'll be astounded if Christopher's ever not acting,' murmured Damon.

'The point of a company like this,' continued Christopher, 'is that even if you're not on stage you're part of the production. Everyone is equally important. After all, where would we be without the prompt, the props man, the publicity? No, as far as I'm concerned this company has no stars and no passengers.'

'I wonder if he really believes that,' Esther said to Rosie. Rosie looked a little uncomfortable. 'It isn't really true, is it?' continued Esther. 'After all, Christopher Wheldon *is* a star; he can't change that.'

'Sssh,' hissed Rosie. 'You know what he means and I think it's very sweet of him.'

Esther supposed that was one way of looking at it, but remembering Marcus she couldn't help feeling that some of them were being patronised. This didn't mean she wasn't still eager to seduce Christopher. His ego didn't bother her; in fact it was probably his ego that attracted her the most. After Marcus, it would be almost impossible to be attracted to somebody who had no star quality. In any case, Christopher was extraordinarily attractive. Unlike Damon, who was so good-looking in a dark secretive way that one found it difficult to see beneath the handsome mask, Christopher's boyish charm brought out not only sexual desire but also

61

a streak of maternalism. The combination was irresistible.

'Well, that's about it then,' said Christopher. 'If any of you want to discuss your parts with me then I think tomorrow morning would be the best time. Right now I think we should all get off home. It's been a long day and you've all worked very hard. Thanks a lot and see you tomorrow, ten o'clock sharp.'

Damon immediately got up from his seat. Esther watched him stride to the far end of the room, pull on his long navy wool coat, throw a maroon scarf casually round his neck, and then, with Ellie close at his heels, he hurried out of the door. Nicholas Maxwell started to move towards Christopher but Christopher deliberately turned his back on him and became very busy talking to Theresa. Rebecca stepped forward and intercepted Nicholas so that within a few minutes the pair of them were talking in an animated fashion together.

Esther would rather have liked to have talked to Rebecca herself. She wanted to know how Rebecca felt about playing Hazel and whether or not her influence on Christopher would enable them to change roles. She supposed that was very unlikely. Christopher was not the kind of person who would want to be seen to be influenced by anyone. Besides, he clearly had very strong ideas of his own.

Noel and Michael got up and Noel turned to Esther. 'Do you want to come back and have a coffee at our place?' he asked. 'Rosie's coming, aren't you, Rosie?'

Rosie nodded. 'Do come, Esther, we can talk about everything. You must be very excited at getting the part of Kay.'

'Not really,' confessed Esther. 'I thought I was going to be Hazel.'

'Well, Rebecca thought she was going to be Kay so that makes the two of you equal,' laughed Michael. 'Are you sure you won't come back with us? It must be a bit lonely going back to that house you used to share with Marcus at the end of every day.'

'It's really nice of you but I honestly don't mind,' said Esther. 'I feel exhausted now. All I want to do is have a meal, a shower and go to bed. I'll take you up on your offer some other time, OK?'

'Sure,' Noel agreed easily. 'Come on, then, Rosie, let's get going.'

Esther followed Noel, Michael and Rosie out of the hall and they all called good night to Christopher as they left. He acknowledged with a warm smile but as Esther looked back one last time he gave her a wink and a wave. To her surprise, she was quite excited by this. It hinted at an intimacy that had so far been lacking and gave her hope that her plan for seduction might not be so difficult as she'd begun to fear.

Once she was home Esther picked up the phone and rang Lydia. She'd promised Lydia that as soon as she knew what part she was to play she'd let her know. 'Hi, Lydia,' she said briskly. 'Guess what role I've got?'

'Well, I think I can safely say that I'd put money on it being Hazel,' said Lydia with a laugh.

'I hope it's not too much money,' laughed Esther. 'I'm to play Kay.'

There was a long silence at the other end of the line. 'Kay?' queried Lydia. 'Surely that's not really you?'

'Well thank you very much,' said Esther. 'That's pretty insulting. Thankfully, Christopher has more faith in my acting ability than you do.'

'Hey, there's no need for that!' exclaimed Lydia. 'Only last night you were telling me you wanted to play Hazel. I know Christopher had mentioned Kay to you early on but once you'd read the play through you could see that you were made to play Hazel. Anyway, Hazel's pretty and blonde and Kay's not meant to be nearly as pretty. Who on earth's playing Hazel?'

'Rebecca Leslie.'

'Who the hell's Rebecca Leslie?' asked Lydia.

'She's Christopher's girlfriend. She's tall and very dramatic-looking with long dark hair.'

'Well she sounds as though she should be playing Kay then,' said Lydia. 'What on earth's Christopher Wheldon doing?'

'He said it's very exciting to cast against type,' said Esther, somewhat defensively. She was quite surprised to hear herself. If the truth were told she secretly agreed with Lydia but for some reason she wanted to defend Christopher's actions. Also, she felt that perhaps Christopher was paying her a compliment. If he thought she could play Kay then he had clearly seen more depth to her acting than Lydia imagined she possessed.

'Well, there's no point in arguing about it,' said Lydia. 'At least it's taken your mind off the ghastly Marcus. Tell me, who's Damon Dowden playing?'

'Ernest Beevers of course,' said Esther. 'The only problem is, in the play Ernest is described as a small thin man. Well, Damon's certainly not small

– he's about six foot two – and, although he's slim, he's big-boned. Not that it matters; his reading was terrific.'

'He's terrific in everything he does,' said Lydia. 'I think he's incredibly good-looking. I wish I was in the same company as him.'

'He's a bit strange,' said Esther. 'I'm not sure why he's joined us. He doesn't seem to think very much of Christopher and he spends most of his time making sarcastic remarks in a quiet voice, mainly to Ellie Ford.'

'Ellie Ford!' said Lydia. 'My God, I was once in some fringe with her. I think she slept with every male member of the cast and the play only lasted a week.'

'How many men were in it?' asked Esther with a laugh.

'About two dozen,' giggled Lydia. 'No, that's not true, but there must have been half a dozen. She looks such a girly type, you know all innocent, but apparently she's a real man-eater. He'll have his hands full there.'

'Well that's up to him,' said Esther. There was no way she was going to admit to Lydia that she too found Damon Dowden extremely attractive. There was no point. Firstly, he wasn't in the least interested in her and, secondly, she had her sights set on Christopher Wheldon.

'Anyway,' said Lydia after they'd chatted for a further twenty minutes or so, 'I must let you go. I expect you're shattered. I'm sorry if I sounded rather rude earlier; I just hadn't pictured you playing Kay but I bet you'll be terrific. Congratulations. Now, you go off and get a good night's sleep and make sure that you let me know when and where you open. I wouldn't miss this for the world.'

'I'm sure you won't need me to tell you,' said Esther. 'I imagine Christopher is going to make sure the whole itinerary is published in the national press. He isn't going to bring the classics to the people quietly. There wouldn't be any point, would there?'

'There certainly wouldn't,' agreed Lydia. 'Keep me informed how it goes, won't you?'

Esther promised that she would and replaced the telephone. Somehow she didn't think she'd be ringing Lydia quite so often in the future. Lydia reminded her of her times at drama school and days shared with Marcus. Now she was moving on. In any case, she had no intention of letting Lydia in on her secret itinerary. No, it would be better if she only rang her friend once a week during the rehearsal period and then, once they were on the road, she wouldn't need to have any further contact with her until the tour was over.

Unusually for her, despite her exhaustion, she took the play to bed with her and read the first act through before falling asleep. Deep down she knew, even though Christopher had denied it, that she was going to have her work cut out playing Kay.

Noel and Michael's flat was in total chaos. Rosie could hardly get in through the front door for discarded clothes, dirty plates, glasses with small amounts of liquid going mouldy in the bottom, and the almost inevitable overflowing ashtrays. She felt at home at once. This was a typical young actor's flat. The fact that two of them were sharing it had compounded the problem but Rosie didn't mind. Luckily, she wasn't a tidy person herself.

'Let's see if we can find somewhere to sit down,' said Noel. 'Michael will fix you a drink, won't you, Michael?'

'Sure,' Michael said agreeably. 'What do you fancy?'

'Have you any wine?' queried Rosie.

'Loads of red, but we're out of white.'

'Red's fine,' said Rosie, sitting down on the three-seater settee and nearly sinking to the floor. Either the springs had broken or it was a very soft settee.

'You'll be great as Joan,' remarked Noel as she began drinking. 'You're certainly pretty enough.'

'Well I hope I'm not as foolish as she's meant to be,' giggled Rosie.

'Of course not,' said Michael. 'We both think you're a very intelligent girl, isn't that right, Noel?'

'Anyone who likes us has to be intelligent,' confirmed Noel.

For a while they chatted about the company and their parts but very soon Rosie realised that each of the men had their arms along the back of the sofa and that Noel's hand was gently stroking the side of her neck. She snuggled up closer to him and, as she did so, Michael began to stroke her arm. She felt very warm and cosy between the two of them and, when Noel started to nibble her ear and blow gently into it, Rosie knew they were going to have a terrific evening. Within half an hour she was following them eagerly into a large bedroom. This was only slightly less untidy than the other room, and was nearly filled by the vast bed.

'Which of you sleeps here?' she asked with some amusement.

'We take it in turns,' explained Michael. 'It rather depends on which of us has someone staying over. It's also extremely useful for threesomes.'

There was a short silence as Noel and Michael looked intently at Rosie. Rosie knew this was the moment when she could choose. They were making their intentions perfectly plain and it was up to her to decide whether or not she wanted to enjoy them both. It really wasn't a difficult decision to make. Rosie thought that most women, given the chance, would be delighted to have two men making love to them at the same time, especially when they were both as good-looking as Noel and Michael. Without a word, she began to unlace the trainers she'd been wearing for rehearsals and then, as provocatively as she could, she removed the baggy tracksuit bottoms that were traditional rehearsal costume.

She sensed that both men were somewhat surprised by the fact that beneath the sensible clothes she was wearing black, high-cut, all-lace briefs. They too began to strip, but they watched her keenly as she removed the clothes from her upper body until she was down to her black lace underwired bra. Her pale full breasts spilt out of it and Noel gave a low whistle of appreciation. 'God, you've got a fantastic body,' he said, his voice thick with desire.

'You certainly have,' Michael agreed whole heartedly.

Rosie felt a surge of power at the expressions on their faces. She clambered on to the middle of the bed, spread her arms out on each side of her, and sat looking at them. 'Right then, who's first?' she asked with a grin.

'I don't know about first,' said Noel sliding naked on to the bed next to her. 'What we'd really like is to make love to you at the same time.'

'Providing that's all right with you of course?' added Michael.

Rosie sighed with contentment. 'It all sounds fabulous,' she said, taking her glass of wine from Noel's outstretched hand and draining it.

Within a few seconds the two men had stripped Rosie so that she was lying naked on the bed between them. Noel was behind her, his erection brushing against her buttocks, while Rosie's breasts were pressed against Michael's chest. For a few minutes they lay pressed tightly together, and then both the men moved away from her a little as Noel propped her up on her right-hand side. This lifted her body up, thus freeing her breasts for Michael. Michael cupped them between his hands and then buried his face between them for a few seconds before starting to lick at the underside of one breast while fingering the nipple of the other.

While he was busy, Noel was reaching round her and slowly gliding his hand along the smooth skin of her slightly rounded belly. He raised himself up off the bed and she then felt his hand going lower until it was playing softly with her pubic hair. He moved his hand in easy circular motions, tugging on the flesh beneath so that it pulled the skin between her thighs, moving it over her slowly swelling clitoris.

Just as she felt the first tingle of excitement in both her breasts and her vulva, Noel removed his hand and started to pat and stroke her buttocks. At the same time Michael, while still keeping hold of each of her breasts and gently massaging them, started to trail his tongue down the middle of her ribcage until he reached her bellybutton. Once there, he poured the few remaining dregs of red wine from her glass into the cleft and then, as her body jerked, he lapped it up and the whole of her belly quaked with excited anticipation.

After continuing this stimulation a little longer the two men, moving in rhythm, rolled over so that Michael was lying on his back. Noel then rolled Rosie over until her back was on Michael's chest. Her head was tucked into his neck, and she felt his arms go round her so that his hands could continue teasing and titillating her burgeoning breasts. Her nipples were already rigid and had nearly doubled in size. Michael's fingers kept pulling and stretching them, although occasionally he would massage her whole breasts.

Noel arranged Rosie so that her legs were lying directly on top of Michael's. He then fastened a hand round each of Rosie's ankles and, as he did so, Michael moved his legs apart. This meant that Rosie's legs were parted and the sensation that she was being manipulated by the two men in order to give her maximum pleasure was so exciting that she felt herself becoming very damp between her thighs.

Rosie started to lift her head to see what Noel was going to do but Michael pulled it back again so that she was once more lying with her head in the hollow of his neck. Suddenly, she felt Noel's tongue on the inside of her thighs, and she drew in her breath sharply. As she did so, Michael pushed her breasts closely together, rubbing them so that the inner sides stimulated each other. Tiny sparks of pleasure shot from her breasts down between her thighs where Noel was making tiny circular motions as he eased his way upwards.

Rosie's clitoris felt hot, and she could feel her sex lips were swelling. She gave a sigh of satisfaction when she felt Noel's hands gently parting them and then, very lightly, he started to trail his tongue around the highly sensitive flesh that surrounded the nub of nerve endings. However, he didn't allow his tongue to touch it and she started to strain her lower body upwards and move her hips to get some stimulation there, where she most craved it.

With a soft laugh, Noel pushed her back down so that she was again flat on Michael's body. 'Michael likes to feel skin against skin,' he said seductively. 'See if you can keep him happy, Rosie. If you keep your body against his he'll be perfectly happy, won't you, Michael?'

Michael gave a murmur of agreement, and Rosie realised they were playing a game with her. A game that would tease and torment her but which only increased her excitement.

Michael suddenly bent his legs, which meant that Rosie's legs were lifted into the air as well. But for Noel's helping hand her legs would have fallen off and back on to the bed but he managed to drape them over Michael's knees so that she was now wide open for him. It was at this moment that she fully expected, indeed longed, for his tongue to touch her aching clitoris but, instead, he used it to trace a slow path along her perineum. At the same time his fingers were teasing her buttocks and the rim of her anus. Then Michael suddenly tweaked hard on her right nipple and, as Rosie gasped at the searing flash of pleasure that coursed through her breasts, Noel popped his tongue into her vagina and used it as he would his penis. Suddenly, Rosie felt her belly start to contract and she heard Noel murmur, 'She's coming, Michael,' just a split second before she had her first orgasm.

Both men waited until her body was still again then, after allowing her a few seconds to recover, Noel moved his tongue so that it descended on her clitoris with a feather-light touch. She thought that she was going to climax again immediately, but Noel prevented this by switching to a gentle sucking motion with his lips. It was absolute bliss, and she felt as though the hot tightness that was again building in her lower belly and breasts would never end. Michael's hands were constantly busy with her breasts and, as her muscles grew tight with an impending second orgasm, Noel suddenly withdrew his head from between her thighs and instead inserted two fingers into her and started to slowly massage her G-spot.

Rosie felt like screaming. It was a glorious sensation, but it had spoilt the build-up to her second orgasm. She murmured her frustration, but Michael whispered reassuringly into her ear, promising her that it would be worth waiting and that they both knew what they were doing.

Noel repeated the exquisite torture several times, working on her with his tongue and his mouth and then, every time she reached the brink of orgasm, withdrawing his mouth and returning to her G-spot. It was only when both men seemed to sense that she could take no more that he finally used both tongue and lips on her clitoris at the same time. As her body began to buck, his fingers returned to her vagina so that as she came she felt as if her entire sex was being plundered.

Her moment of ultimate release was shattering, and she cried out with delight. When it was over, Noel carefully rolled her off Michael and they returned her to her original position, sandwiched between the two of them. 'There, wasn't that great?' asked Noel.

'Incredible,' murmured Rosie, still in a daze and with every nerve ending alive and tingling.

'Now I think it's time we had some fun as well,' said Michael. It was then that Rosie realised, with a surge of excitement, that the evening was far from over.

'We want to make sure you go on enjoying it as much as you have been,' said Noel quickly, 'so we'll get you thoroughly prepared first.' The way Rosie's body was feeling, she thought that she was probably already very well prepared. That, plus the additional excitement of knowing that she was going to satisfy both men at once, was driving her into a frenzy. Clearly the men had further delights in store for her before they finally gained satisfaction for themselves.

They both moved away from her slightly but each of them kept one hand reassuringly on her body so that she never lost complete physical contact. After a few moments, Noel straddled her upper abdomen and, while Michael licked gently around the nape and side of her neck and her ear, Noel – his hands well oiled – began to massage her breasts.

First of all he slid the flat of his right hand diagonally across her right breast, trailing it towards her left shoulder. Then he slid his left hand across her left breast in the same manner. The sensation was exquisite and he repeated this movement time and time again until she felt she could no longer stand it. As her breathing quickened, Noel smiled down at her. 'Time for a change I think,' he said seductively.

Next, using one well-oiled fingertip and the lightest possible touch, he drew a spiral on one of her breasts, beginning on the outer side and moving inwards until he reached the nipple. She had never been touched on her breasts so delicately before, and when he repeated the stroke on the other breast she gave a tiny cry of delight. 'Does it feel good?' he queried.

'It's absolutely fantastic,' whispered Rosie. 'Don't stop, whatever you do.'

'I've no intention of stopping,' he assured her. 'In fact, there's plenty more to come.'

Rosie shivered. This was proving to be the most exciting evening of her life. Next, Noel, his eyes narrowed slightly in concentration, carefully squeezed a little skin on each side of her right nipple then, very lightly, he slid his fingers outwards moving along the ridge of flesh that he had raised. Streaks of excitement and pleasure were coursing through Rosie's breasts and she could feel her nipples hardening once again. After endless repetitions of this, Noel, noticing her rigidly erect nipples, carefully squeezed the right one between his oiled forefinger and thumb and slid his fingers up and off the nipple. Rosie's breathing was now audible in the otherwise silent room and, just when she thought the sensation couldn't possibly be bettered, Noel began to use both hands alternately on the same nipple, sliding each hand up and off.

The searing pleasure was no longer confined to her breasts alone but was shooting down between her ribs, through her abdomen and into her vulva. It was only after Noel had repeated the movement on her left nipple so that both breasts had been equally stimulated that she was finally allowed a moment's breathing space. Her senses had never been so heightened and, when Michael rolled her on to her left side and gently pushed her knees up towards her chest, she gazed into Noel's face, her eyes shining with excitement and sexual desire. 'What's he going to do?' she asked.

'Wait and see,' said Noel. 'I know you'll love it.' As he spoke, he started to massage her breasts again and instantly every nerve ending leapt beneath his skilled touch.

When Rosie felt Michael start to part her buttocks she tensed slightly, wondering what was about to happen. 'It's all right,' Michael assured her, 'we'd never do anything to hurt you. This is just to make it easier for all of us to climax together.'

For some reason, Rosie trusted them completely. She felt the rim of her rectum being touched with a well-lubricated finger and then the finger was inserted very gently just inside the opening, spreading some gel inside her. After that, she heard Michael get off the bed and move around the room but, when she tried to turn her head to see what he was doing, Noel clasped her face between his hands and bent down to kiss her. His tongue licked and teased the corners of her mouth, and his lips were firm and demanding against hers. She responded instantly, forgetting about Michael, and it was only when she felt the weight of his body on the bed again that she remembered he was there.

'I'm going to use this to open you up a little bit

more,' Michael explained quietly. 'It should feel really good; if it doesn't, let me know.'

For a moment Rosie felt anxious but Noel reassured her at once. 'It'll be great,' he promised her. 'Honestly, it'll drive you out of your mind with pleasure.'

His words alone were almost enough to do that; she had never before been to bed with someone as skilled, as creative, as these men.

In the meantime, Michael fitted a thin ribbed latex wand on to the end of a vibrator and then, with the greatest of care, began to ease it into the already lubricated opening between Rosie's buttocks. Once it was in past two of the ridged marks he turned the vibrator on to a low setting. As it began to move, Rosie felt the most incredible sensation as the fragile, nerve-filled walls were stimulated and shafts of pleasure shot through her. At the same time, the nerve endings behind her clitoris began to tingle so that suddenly she was desperate for stimulation between her thighs. Noel seemed to understand how she was feeling.

'Touch yourself there,' he suggested. 'We don't mind; in fact we'd love to see you masturbate.'

Rosie wondered briefly where all her inhibitions had gone, but she was so carried away by the sheer sensual delights of the evening and the incredibly relaxed atmosphere that there no longer seemed to be any limits to what was acceptable. Quickly she lowered her hand between her thighs and began to move her fingers in slow circles over her outer sex lips so that the clitoris was indirectly stimulated.

Noel could see the muscles of her abdomen tightening and rippling. 'You can come if you like,' he assured her. His words, together with the magic of his hands and the fantastic sensations between her buttocks, were enough to tip her over the edge and her whole body shivered and shook as once again she reached the pinnacle of pleasure.

When her orgasm was over, Michael turned off the vibrator and very carefully removed the plastic extension from her rectum. As he did this, Noel stopped massaging her breasts and kissing her and gently sat her upright on the bed. A somewhat dazed Rosie watched as Noel positioned himself on the side of the bed with his feet on the floor. He then lay back flat. His erection was very impressive. 'Time for you to do some work now, Rosie,' he said with a grin.

'What would you like me to do?' she asked with a smile.

'Just sit on it and then lean forward with your arms each side of my shoulders,' said Noel.

Rosie needed no second bidding. She positioned herself above his swollen penis and then lowered herself slowly down on to him until she was fully impaled. Then, remembering his instructions, she leant forward and her breasts, well oiled from his earlier massage, were within easy reach of his mouth. She tipped herself lower still, desperate for him to take one of her aching nipples into his mouth, which he obligingly did.

It was then that she heard the sound of a condom being unwrapped and, glancing over her shoulder, she saw Michael preparing to enter her from behind. Rosie had never tried sex this way before, but she felt certain that it was going to be terrific. Noel's lips were clamped tightly round her left breast and he moved his head up and down so that he was stretching her nipple to its fullest extent and then releasing it, just as his fingers had done earlier.

By now Rosie was trembling, tense with rising desire and in keen anticipation of what was about to happen. She felt Michael part the cheeks of her bottom and then, very, very slowly he was easing himself into her. The incredible sensation of full-ness in both her vagina and her rectum was as exciting as Noel had promised. Once Michael was fully inside her, he stopped moving.

'It's up to you now,' Noel said gently. 'We can't move; you have to. If you thrust your hips back-wards and forwards you'll be bringing us both off at the same time.'

She began to move, slowly at first but then, as she heard both men's gasps and groans of mount-ing excitement, she quickened her pace. She could tell by the expression on Noel's face when he was about to come and, just seconds before he reached release, she froze in mid-movement. Noel's eyes widened in astonishment and he stared up at her. 'Don't stop now, please,' he groaned in mock despair.

'I thought you'd like to wait a few more seconds,' laughed Rosie. 'After all, you only get the one chance, unlike me.'

Behind her Michael too was groaning with exquisite frustration. They both knew that Rosie was playing with them as they had played with her but knew also that she wouldn't keep them waiting very long. She couldn't because her own climax was building so rapidly that she would be prolonging the agony for herself as well as for them.

To encourage her, Noel managed to reach down

and his oiled finger located the centre of her pleasure. He tapped very lightly on her clitoris and then slid his finger up and down the side of the small shaft. Almost immediately Rosie felt everything inside her start to bunch up in a pre-orgasmic spasm and, in order to stimulate herself beyond the point of no return, she started to move her hips frantically faster and faster with complete disregard to the men.

Within seconds the wonderful hot melting feeling was beginning and the dreadful tightness suddenly exploded into flooding release that surged through every part of her. At the same time both the men uttered huge groans and gasps as they too reached shattering orgasms.

When the last tingling sensations died away, Rosie felt utterly exhausted. She had never been so sated, and was grateful when the men withdrew from her and she was able to collapse into a heap on the bed. She was vaguely aware that both of them were climbing on to the bed with her, then one of them drew a duvet around them all and they fell into a deep and satisfying sleep.

Chapter Four

It was at the beginning of the second week of the four-week rehearsal period when Esther realised that she was definitely in trouble. As she'd suspected from the beginning, the role of Kay didn't really suit her. For a start, she knew that her looks were against her. Kay wasn't meant to be as pretty as Hazel, and she was meant to be far more intelligent and sensible. Although Rebecca was tackling the part of Hazel with gusto, and giving a more than creditable performance, there was still no disguising the fact that she looked far more like Priestley had intended Kay to look, and her delivery of lines was far more like Esther imagined Kay's would have been.

At the beginning she'd hoped that it was simply her imagination and lack of confidence, and that the rest of the company wouldn't be aware that she was struggling. However, when she confided to Rosie that she wasn't sure she was getting it right Rosie pulled a sympathetic face. 'I can't think why he cast you as Kay,' she said. 'We can all see it was stupid. I don't know why he doesn't change you and Rebecca round even now. It isn't too late, and we all think you'd both be more comfortable that way.' After that, Esther realised that she was right. She'd been miscast.

On the Tuesday of the second week, shortly after lunch, they resumed rehearsals at the point where they had finished in the morning. Esther particularly hated the end of Act II. It was at this point in the play that she had to discuss with her brother Alan – played very well by Noel – her thoughts on the terrible changes that had taken place in the time-warp section. She had to look back to the girl she'd been at nineteen, and reflect on the hideous passage of time. She had a line in which she had to say: 'There's a great devil in the universe, and we call it Time.'

She knew perfectly well that her delivery of this was quite appalling. She sounded either over-melodramatic or, when she attempted to tone it down, totally disinterested. It was with considerable trepidation that she resumed the scene and, although Noel did his best to help carry her through, when they came to the end – and Esther was left supposedly looking out of the window in reflective mood – there was absolute silence in the rehearsal hall.

'Right then,' said Christopher just when it had seemed to Esther that the silence was never going to end, 'I think this calls for a bit of discussion. Let's all sit round and have a bit of a chat about what Priestley intended here, shall we?'

'I'd really rather not,' said Damon audibly to Ellie. 'In my opinion if we don't know what he intended by now then we shouldn't be in the play at all.'

Esther flushed. She knew perfectly well that the remark was aimed at her, because everyone else seemed to be coping with their roles far better than she was.

'We can do without that kind of destructive remark, Damon,' said Christopher. 'Gather round, everyone.'

Esther could tell that no one was in the least enthusiastic about this, apart from Rosie, who was pretty enthusiastic about everything including – if Esther understood her correctly – Noel and Michael. She wished she had some kind of sexual distraction at the moment. Although at first she'd been too upset to miss the constant supply of sex that Marcus had given her, she was beginning to feel somewhat irritable. Her libido was high and, because she was struggling so hard with the play, she certainly wasn't making any inroads into Christopher's affections. If anything, it seemed that Theresa was the one most likely to supplant Rebecca in his affections.

'Now,' Christopher said seriously. 'We can all see that you've worked very hard on this, Esther. How do you feel that you're doing?'

It was a stupid question and Esther wished that he hadn't asked it. 'I feel reasonably comfortable in the first and last acts,' she explained, 'but I find the middle act really difficult.'

'You don't seem any different in the middle act,' said Ellie Ford.

'I wouldn't say that,' interrupted Rebecca. 'You do seem different, Esther, but you don't seem like Kay.'

'I don't feel like Kay,' confessed Esther. 'Quite frankly, Christopher, I'm not sure I'm right for this part.'

'Of course you are,' said Christopher with a note of irritation in his voice. 'You don't think I'd have chosen you if I hadn't known you were perfectly capable of doing it, do you?' Esther shook her head. 'Right, then I suggest we do some hot-seating,' said Christopher.

Esther wanted to groan aloud. She absolutely loathed hot-seating and didn't feel that it served any useful purpose at all. However, she knew it was extremely popular with a lot of directors and many actors, and by the looks on the faces of those around her she sensed that she was in the minority. Only Damon looked as horrified as she felt, which was no surprise because it was clear that Damon was one of those people who thought that acting was something you simply got on with.

'OK, Esther, you sit in the middle of the circle and we'll ask you questions,' said Christopher. 'Remember now, you answer them all as though you're Kay. Who wants to start?'

'I will,' Noel said enthusiastically. 'What's your favourite food?'

Esther's mind went totally blank. She couldn't even think what her own favourite food was, never mind what Kay's might have been. In fact, she wasn't certain what sort of food Kay would have eaten back in 1919. 'Italian!' she blurted out.

There was a collective burst of laughter and Christopher frowned. 'Don't be silly, Esther,' he said. 'I hardly think Kay was likely to be eating Italian food, do you?'

83

'I'm really sorry,' apologised Esther. 'I wasn't thinking like Kay, was I?'

'Exactly,' said Christopher, far more cheerfully. 'And that's at the root of the whole problem. Now then, answer the question again, but as Kay.'

'I can't think of anything,' confessed Esther. 'I mean, what sort of food did they eat in 1919?'

'Roast beef?' Rosie suggested.

'Probably,' said Damon. 'I don't suppose they'd heard of mad cow disease in those days.' Again everyone giggled, with the exception of Christopher.

'I can't say roast beef, can I?' Esther remarked crossly. 'Even if that was Kay's favourite food it isn't my idea, it's Rosie's.'

'She was only trying to be helpful,' drawled Damon, giving her a tight-lipped smile.

Esther wished that she wasn't so attracted to him. He was horribly sarcastic and plainly thought her acting diabolical, but there was still something about him that fascinated her.

'For goodness sake, Esther,' continued Christopher. 'Let's try you on another question and do concentrate. Think Kay. Think *Time and the Conways*. Think anything but bloody Esther for God's sake!'

There was a sense of awkwardness in the room now. For the first time a slight wave of sympathy engulfed Esther. No actor or actress ever liked being bawled out in front of other people and it was considered rather bad form on Christopher's part. He seemed to realise this because he quickly softened his tone. 'Sorry, it's just that I don't think you're really trying.'

'I am,' Esther assured him, 'but I'll try harder.'

'What's your favourite colour?' asked Rosie helpfully.

'Pale blue,' Esther said at once. She could imagine Kay wearing long elegant pale-blue dresses, or a pale-blue twinset and a tight-fitting pencil skirt in the middle act.

'What's your favourite animal?' asked Nicholas.

'A cat,' replied Esther. Somehow she knew for certain that Kay would like cats; cats were aloof and independent. It would be Hazel who liked dogs. For at least twenty minutes the question and answer session continued and, by the end of it, Esther realised that she could have told an audience almost anything they wanted to ask her about Kay except how she should be acted. She didn't feel that this was really the point of the exercise.

'OK, let's run through that scene again,' said Christopher. 'Hopefully the hot-seating will have helped considerably.'

'I'm really sorry about this, Noel,' muttered Esther as the pair of them took up their places again.

'Don't worry,' Noel said reassuringly. 'I love being the centre of attention; it's every actor's dream.'

'Well I could do without it at the moment,' confessed Esther. 'It's only nice if you know you're doing well.'

'You'll get it in the end,' he promised her. 'I'm sure Christopher's telling the truth. After all, why would he have cast you in a role that he didn't think you could do?'

'To make him look better,' Esther suggested in a quiet voice.

'No, I don't think he'd do that,' Noel replied.

'Kay's such a pivotal character that it would ruin the whole play no matter how good Christopher was himself. Come on, really go for it this time.'

Esther did really go for it and she thought that she'd done better but when it was over there was still silence in the hall. When it became apparent that Christopher wasn't going to make any comment the group all started talking to each other, breaking up into the sub-sections that were beginning to divide them. It was only then that Christopher came across to Esther.

'That was better, darling,' he murmured. 'On the surface you were certainly more like Kay, but I didn't feel that you *were* Kay, if you get my drift.'

Esther did get his drift. He meant that she was using tricks and gestures to convey the character and not feeling the part. The problem was, he was right. 'I think it's coming,' she answered.

Christopher put a hand on her arm and stared intently into her eyes. 'I'm sure you're going to be really great,' he said in a low voice. 'Why don't we go into the kitchen at the back there and I'll help you run through some of the lines. Noel's fine, no question about it, but I think that perhaps if I read Alan I could get a better response from you. After all, I got a very good response from you when you were playing Ophelia opposite my Hamlet, didn't I?'

'You certainly did,' agreed Esther, wondering why the touch of his fingers on her arm seemed to be sending a glow of heat through her clothing.

'I think you'd respond very well to me in any situation,' Christopher added meaningfully.

Again Esther began to believe that she might be successful in her desire to seduce him. There was no mistaking his interest now, and as he led her through into the tiny kitchen she sensed that both Rebecca and Theresa were watching the pair of them very carefully.

Once in the kitchen Christopher made them both a cup of coffee and then, as they stood in the corner of the tiny room, he slid an arm round her waist. She felt his hand gently slide up beneath her long jersey until he was able to lightly stroke the bare skin around the side of her waist. 'You're beautiful you know,' he said. 'I can't imagine what Marcus was thinking of. He must be mad to prefer Claudine. I can tell you this, if you were my girlfriend I'd make sure I'd keep you.'

With a smile Esther moved away from him, pulling her jumper down over her leggings. 'As I'm not your girlfriend it doesn't really matter, does it?' she queried lightly.

'Not at the moment,' agreed Christopher. 'I can't believe that you don't feel there's something special between us though.'

Esther widened her eyes in mock innocence. 'Professionally?' she asked.

'Professionally and personally,' he said quietly.

'I think we ought to concentrate on the professional side at the moment, don't you?' Esther retorted briskly. Some instinct told her that this was the right way to keep his interest. By the expression on his face after she'd spoken she knew she was right. If anything, he looked even more interested now than he had a few moments earlier.

'As you like,' he agreed. 'We'll deal with the professional side first and see what develops on the other side later, agreed?'

Esther gave him the benefit of her most seductive smile. 'Agreed,' she said warmly.

After that Christopher got down to the business of the play and for the next half-hour the pair of them worked tirelessly. By the time they'd finished Esther had to admit that she'd improved. Christopher was good, there was no question about it, and somehow his truthfulness as Alan improved her performance immeasurably. It was rather like playing tennis or dancing, she thought – it was always easier to be good if your partner was good too.

When they returned to the hall the rest of the company were working on their potted Shakespeare scenes. 'Glad to see you've all kept busy,' Christopher said. 'Who organised this?'

'I did,' said George. 'I knew you wouldn't want us to waste time, but on the other hand I didn't think I should take over directing *Time and the Conways.*'

'No, no that's excellent,' said Christopher. Esther watched as Rebecca walked over to her boyfriend and whispered something in his ear. He glanced back at Esther and then across the room to where Theresa was standing. Theresa's expression was hard to fathom. She looked fascinated by Christopher and yet slightly awkward and nervous, as though she wasn't quite certain herself what her feelings were.

Shortly after that, the company adjourned for the day and Esther found herself swept along with Christopher, Rebecca and Theresa to the nearby pub. Christopher chatted easily to them all but once he was at the bar and the three girls were sitting together Esther felt an uneasiness in the air. Surprisingly, it didn't come from Rebecca but from

Theresa, who looked less than happy at Esther's presence.

'Here we are then, girls,' said Christopher, putting down their drinks. 'Now, we can talk about anything but work, agreed?'

'Agreed,' said Rebecca with obvious relief. She looked at Esther. 'I suppose you had this problem when you were with Marcus. Presumably he liked to talk about work morning, noon and night?'

'Well, not at night,' said Esther.

Rebecca laughed. 'Oh, I see. Well, I didn't mean it literally. Naturally Christopher has better things to think about at night than the play. I make sure of that, don't I, Chris?'

'Don't call me Chris,' he said shortly. 'You know I hate it.'

'How's Marcus getting on in America?' asked Theresa.

Esther looked at her in astonishment. She couldn't believe that Theresa really thought she'd want to discuss Marcus and America. 'I've no idea,' she said curtly. 'He and I haven't been in contact since he left England.'

'It must have been an awful shock for you,' continued Theresa, smoothing her tight top down over her extraordinarily large breasts and thereby drawing all eyes in the pub to them.

'I'd like to suggest that there are two things we don't talk about,' said Esther. 'That's the play and Marcus.'

'Sounds a good idea to me,' agreed Christopher. 'I must say Marcus was never my favourite topic of conversation.'

'I don't suppose you were his either,' Rebecca remarked idly.

Esther hoped they weren't going to ask her for confirmation of this and to her great relief they didn't.

The four of them continued to gossip for a while, the usual showbusiness gossip about who was going out with whom, performances that had hit the headlines recently or – more interestingly – scandals known only within the profession itself. Esther was enjoying herself immensely; she'd missed this kind of conversation since Marcus had left and realised that she was probably spending far too much time alone. However, Rebecca suddenly glanced at her watch and then tapped Christopher lightly on the arm.

'I think we'd better be going,' she said. 'You did promise Theresa some extra tuition, remember?'

Christopher looked slightly taken aback and his eyes caught Esther's for a fleeting moment before he turned to face the now silent Theresa. 'Of course,' he said charmingly, 'I hadn't forgotten, Theresa. I suppose this is one of the problems of both acting and directing. As an actor I always enjoy the winding-down period when rehearsals end, but there's no rest for the director – or the wicked!'

'You should certainly know about that,' murmured Rebecca, and Esther felt a strange tension creep into the air. It was plain that Christopher no longer wanted to linger in the pub and within a few minutes the girls were collecting their coats. While they were gone he leant towards Esther.

'I meant what I said earlier, back in the rehearsal room,' he said earnestly. 'I really do think there's a very special rapport between us, and I'm sure you know it too. If there's ever anything I can do for you, you've only to let me know. I'm sure I don't need to spell out what I mean, do I?'

Esther shook her head. Her mouth felt slightly dry because although she knew that Christopher was now pursuing her, which was what she'd wanted all along, she also felt that there was something strange going on between him, Rebecca and Theresa. She didn't believe that Theresa was his lover; she was far too unsure of herself in his presence for that to be true, but there was certainly something brewing and it crossed her mind that perhaps Rebecca was bisexual. If so, then possibly Christopher watched them, although somehow she didn't believe that he was the sexually passive type.

'We're ready,' Rebecca said sharply, standing just behind Christopher's chair and putting her hands on his shoulders as though to affirm that he was her possession. Esther would have expected Christopher to object to this but instead he glanced up and she saw a look of pure sexual excitement pass between the pair of them. All at once she couldn't wait for them to be gone.

When she was finally alone she decided that after she'd finished her drink she'd go back to the flat and carry on working on the play. She knew that it was silly – Lydia would always be happy to see her, but somehow *Time and the Conways*, Christopher, and the whole company were becoming more important to her than anything else. Before she could leave she was suddenly joined at her table by Damon Dowden.

'Drinking alone?' he remarked. 'One of the signs of alcoholism, I believe.'

'I wasn't alone,' Esther said acidly. 'The others have just left.'

91

'And who were they, or shouldn't I ask?' enquired Damon.

'Christopher, Rebecca and Theresa,' Esther told him. 'Why on earth should I want to keep that secret?'

'You tell me,' said Damon.

Esther felt that she should say something more agreeable, something to improve the relationship between them. Not that she'd ever done anything to be difficult, but she sensed that Damon didn't like her, and quite apart from the fact that she fancied him like mad she felt it would be better for the whole company if the pair of them were on good terms.

'I really liked your reading of Ernest Beevers,' she said. 'It's not the kind of part I'd have expected you to be so good at.'

'Really?' Damon raised his eyebrows. 'What sort of roles did you have in mind for me then?'

Esther felt slightly uncomfortable. 'Well, stronger roles I suppose, although it's true that Ernest Beevers becomes very strong in the middle act. It's just that after your Iago and –'

'Did you see it?' Damon enquired.

'No,' confessed Esther, 'but I read all the reviews.'

'Don't tell me that after all your experiences with Marcus you believe what you read in the papers!' Damon laughed. 'Have you seen me in anything at all?'

Esther was beginning to feel more and more awkward. 'No,' she admitted. 'Mind you, there's lots of good actors I haven't seen but that doesn't mean that I don't know they're good.'

'Name me one,' demanded Damon.

92

'Alex Jennings,' Esther said firmly. 'Somehow, probably because of Marcus's commitments, I've never got round to seeing him but I'm sure even you wouldn't deny he's one of the best stage actors around at the moment.'

'Agreed,' conceded Damon. 'I hadn't realised how busy you were,' he continued. 'I've managed to get to see Alex in quite a few things but obviously you've been busier than me. Tell me, what's your favourite stage role so far?'

'I've mostly done TV,' confessed Esther. She was beginning to feel angry now. It was plain that Damon was deliberately needling her and she wondered why she'd bothered to try to be pleasant. The problem was, despite his attitude she was still incredibly attracted to him. Like the other members of the company Damon dressed casually, but somehow on him even casual clothes looked smart. This evening he was wearing a pair of khaki chinos, a burnt-orange shirt, open-necked to reveal a white T-shirt beneath, and casual brown loafers. With his thick dark hair swept back off his high forehead and his dark eyes looking intently at her from beneath even darker brows, he was heart-stoppingly handsome and he had cheekbones that would be the envy of any male model.

'I bet you photograph well,' said Esther without thinking.

Damon softened. 'What on earth makes you say that?'

'Only the fact that you've got such good bones.'

'I inherited them from my mother, so it's luck not a skill,' he confessed. He was still smiling and for the first time Esther felt that he was really looking at her. She wished that she was wearing

93

something slightly more figure hugging than the long, ice-cream pink, polo-necked jersey over her usual rehearsal garb of black leggings.

'You ought to get your hair cut,' he said.

Marcus had loved her long fair hair flicked up at the shoulders; the thought of cutting it still seemed like sacrilege. 'That's a very personal remark,' she said.

'No more personal than telling me I've got good bones,' he retorted.

'That was a compliment. I wasn't telling you to go out and have plastic surgery.'

Again Damon laughed. 'Sorry, that's one of my problems. I always say what I mean and in our profession that's both dangerous and unusual.'

Esther drained the last of her drink and started to get up but Damon put out a hand to restrain her. 'Let me get you another. This is the first time I've really enjoyed myself all day. What are you drinking?'

'White wine spritzer.'

Damon went off and returned with drinks for both of them. 'All I really meant was,' he said slowly, 'it would make you look different if you had a more modern hair cut. Something short and sharp. Let's face it, generally you're pretty typecast, aren't you? Something like a change of hairstyle can dramatically alter the way agents look at you.'

'Taken another way,' pointed out Esther, 'it can also ruin your chances of getting any work at all. When we were at drama school we were told that if we had a hit playing a certain kind of role and with a certain kind of look the last thing we should do was go out and change it.'

'Oh I agree,' said Damon. 'Do tell me, what was your big hit?'

Esther flushed with annoyance. 'I'm not saying I've had a big hit; I'm just pointing out that there are advantages to a certain look, particularly for a woman of my age.'

'I think we'd better drop the subject,' Damon suggested. 'I was sorry to hear about you and Marcus,' he added, his voice off-hand but his eyes surprisingly kind.

'Why?' asked Esther rudely. 'You didn't know either of us.'

'No, but I know what utter shits people like Marcus Martin and Christopher Wheldon can be, which is why I'm rather surprised that you're quite as friendly with Christopher as you are. I'd have thought one nasty experience with a massive ego might have warned you off at least for a little while.'

'I'm not particularly friendly with Christopher,' Esther said defensively.

'No? Then how come you've been given the part of Kay?'

'I've no idea,' said Esther. 'I wanted to play Hazel.'

'Well you'd certainly have played her better than you're playing Kay,' said Damon. 'Are you trying to tell me that you didn't know you had a chance of playing Kay? That you didn't have an opportunity to tell Christopher you didn't want to do it?'

'When I auditioned he did discuss the possibility of it with me,' Esther confessed reluctantly. 'I seem to remember saying something about of course I wouldn't turn it down because any actress would love to have a chance of playing the role, but I was only being polite.'

'Not polite,' Damon pointed out, 'you were just making sure you didn't slam the door on a chance of joining his company. You wanted to show you were an adventurous spirit, isn't that true?'

'I've no idea why I said it,' Esther replied. 'Whatever the reason I'm being paid back in spades now.'

Damon stretched his arms above his head and she felt his long legs brush against hers as he spread them out beneath the table. 'I imagine there's some consolation in all the private tuition you're getting,' he said with deceptive charm.

'If you mean those few minutes we spent in the kitchen,' said Esther, 'then they were helpful, yes.'

'I'm sure he'll find somewhere more private for your next lot of lessons,' said Damon. 'Don't play the naive ingenue with me, Esther. I've been around far too long to fall for that one. You've made it pretty plain that you like him, so don't pretend you haven't.'

'I admire him as an actor,' was all Esther could think of to say.

Damon gave a bitter laugh. 'It's amazing what that expression can mean to girls,' he said at last. 'Well, don't blame me if you get your heart broken again. And this time, I certainly won't feel sorry for you. Once bitten twice shy I'd have thought.'

'Why do you have to be so deliberately offensive?' demanded Esther.

'I enjoy it,' drawled Damon. 'Anyway, it makes a change from the fawning charm of our actor-director.'

Esther's eyes were now sparkling, and she could

see that Damon too was enjoying their repartee even though some of his comments had hurt her more than she cared to admit. Before either of them could speak again there was the sound of the pub door opening and then Ellie Ford was standing next to them at the table.

'There you are,' she said to Damon with relief, not even bothering to glance at Esther. 'I went back to the flat and you weren't there. I thought you were coming round for something to eat tonight.'

'I fancied a drink first,' said Damon. 'There's no law against it, is there?'

Obviously taken aback by the sharpness of his tone, Ellie backed off hastily. 'No, of course not, it's just that . . .'

'What?' Damon demanded.

'Nothing,' said Ellie deciding to sit down next to him. She looked across the table at Esther. 'Are you trying to get some help from Damon, too?' she asked.

'Help about what?' Esther asked.

'Playing Kay of course. I should imagine that's the thing uppermost in your mind at the moment. It must be horrible to be struggling so badly at this stage.' The forced sympathy in her voice was even more irritating than Damon's outright condemnation of some of her acting and Esther felt her temper rising.

'Well,' she said sharply, 'I don't suppose you'll have any problems playing Carol. I mean, it's easy for you to assume the mentality of a sixteen-year-old, isn't it? Admittedly you're not as naive as she was, but if you used a little less make-up then no doubt even that problem could be overcome.'

'I think I'll take that as a compliment,' said Ellie.

'It's quite useful to be able to play a sixteen-year-old when you're twenty-four; it opens up a lot more roles for you. You're younger than me, aren't you?'

'Just,' conceded Esther.

'Well I don't suppose you've ever been offered any roles of sixteen- or even seventeen-year-olds, have you?' queried Ellie.

'No,' Esther replied. 'I think casting directors find me rather more mature than that.'

Damon laughed with delight and Ellie seemed to decide that she would be better off keeping quiet. Within a few moments Damon had finished his drink and got to his feet. Ellie linked arms with him and once again Esther was left feeling an outsider.

'See you tomorrow, then, ten o'clock sharp as our esteemed director keeps telling us,' said Damon.

'See you,' Ellie said vacantly, and the pair of them drifted out into the night.

Esther was surprised to realise how much she disliked Ellie. Normally she could rub along with most people but there was something about the baby-faced young actress that she found cold and calculating. Unlike most other actresses, she didn't even pretend to be interested in anyone but herself and men. It seemed extraordinary to Esther that a man like Damon Dowden would be at all attracted to someone like Ellie, although she wasn't certain that it was a sexual relationship. It was always possible that he enjoyed Ellie's barbed comments, which were in tune with his own.

Unusually for her, once Esther got home she realised that she was feeling quite sorry for herself.

For a start she was finding her role difficult. In the past acting had come relatively easily to her and she realised that this was because she hadn't been stretched. The only other time she'd ever had a problem Marcus had been on hand to help her and, to give him his due, he'd been generous with his time. Of course, that part hadn't in any way been related to his work; if it had been then it might have been a different story. Marcus, like Christopher, couldn't bear competition.

Quite apart from her professional difficulties, Esther was seriously concerned that it wasn't going to be possible for her to actually get into bed with Christopher. Rebecca was always on hand and now there appeared to be an even more complex situation involving Theresa as well. Esther wondered if this had something to do with the strange casting of Theresa as Madge. Admittedly Theresa was coping rather better than Esther would have expected, but she was still a mile away from what Esther thought J B Priestley had intended.

She wished that she wasn't so drawn to Damon; it complicated things too much. By joining the company she had set her mind on a two-fold revenge plan. The first, to shine as an actress, and the second to bed Christopher and hopefully have this news leak across the Atlantic to Marcus. Even if he didn't want her any more, she knew that it would infuriate him. Now, although it was admittedly early days, it seemed that she was going to have trouble on both counts.

There was always Lydia to talk things over with but she still didn't want to involve her friend. The whole business was too complicated and she didn't feel that she could really admit to her true purpose in joining Christopher's company. Lydia would have understood, but Esther felt that it showed her in a bad light. If she hadn't fancied Christopher at all then she wouldn't have considered the second part of her plan, but the truth was that she did fancy him. If it wasn't for the unsettling presence of Damon then she would probably be even keener on Christopher, but even the brief time she had just spent with Damon in the pub had set her pulse racing. She could picture him naked in bed, his long-fingered hands demanding and yet knowing.

It was more difficult for her to imagine what sex would be like with Christopher. If Marcus was a guide then it would probably involve mirrors. Even during their most intimate moments Marcus had enjoyed being able to watch himself. Usually when mirrors were involved in sex Esther gathered that it was to enable the men to watch the women but in their case she was quite sure that Marcus had had eyes only for himself.

Although she'd intended to go over the play, Esther's body felt tingling and tight. She wished that she had a casual lover, someone that she could just enjoy a robust session of sex with in order to relieve the tension that had been building up in her throughout the day. Because she and Marcus had been going out together for so long sex had never been a problem for her. Now she realised that she was feeling more and more frustrated and she hoped it wouldn't be too long before she achieved her aim of getting Christopher into bed with her.

Accepting for the moment there was no chance of that, she went to take a leisurely shower. After she had lathered herself well, she stood beneath the warm spray and allowed it to play on her breasts and upper torso. This had the effect of heightening her sexual desire and she decided to soak her breasts again, but more slowly and luxuriously, taking special care with the nipples, which she gently caressed between her fingertips.

After a few moments she unhooked the shower-head and, holding it in her right hand, allowed it to play between her thighs. Then she raised it a little and let the water drip down over her lower stomach and pubic hair. As the tension began to gather in her vagina she allowed her thoughts to wander. She'd intended to fantasise about Christopher but instead it was Damon's dark face that appeared in her mind. Slowly and sensuously she began to lather the soft golden fleece over her pubic mound and, as she did so, she allowed herself to imagine that it was Damon's fingers caressing her so tenderly. After a few moments she stood with her legs clenched tightly together. Then she crossed her legs and started to contract and release her genital and thigh muscles until slowly she felt the wonderful build-up of warmth that told her an orgasm was on the way.

She loved this particular moment, the moment when she knew that she would soon be flooded by the hot bliss of sexual release. When she couldn't stand it any longer she stood with her feet planted firmly on each side of the shower cabinet, thrust her hips forward slightly and, using her fingers, slowly started to stimulate herself with two fingers. She refused to allow herself to touch the incredibly sensitive clitoris, concentrating instead on the area around it so that the build-up was slower but more intense.

All at once she felt a heavy ache deep inside her

vagina. This was something that frequently happened to her as her orgasm approached and what she really liked best was to have Marcus slide inside her just after the ache began. It would ease as she was filled by his wonderful hardness. This time, that wasn't possible, and the ache was almost a source of pain to her – but a delicious kind of pain because she knew that it was a sign of impending pleasure. Finally, when she heard herself uttering tiny gasps of need, she let her fingers lightly move over the slippery swollen bud. Instantly her orgasm broke, with waves of muscular contractions spreading through her lower body. As she climaxed, Esther kept her hand pressed firmly against the whole of her vaginal area. She needed the pressure and the contact in order to gain maximum satisfaction.

When it was over she gave a soft sigh of contentment and then carefully sprayed herself down once more before climbing out of the shower and wrapping herself in a warm fluffy towel. Suddenly she felt relaxed and sleepy. She only wished she'd been with Christopher tonight instead of on her own.

It would have surprised Esther to learn that Christopher was thinking the selfsame thing at exactly the same moment. He'd just showered and was sitting in the bedroom of Theresa's flat wearing only a silk dressing gown while he waited for Rebecca and Theresa to get ready for him. He was already excited at the prospect of what lay ahead of him, especially since he thought that Theresa was going to be slightly shocked by the events. He enjoyed it when girls were shocked; it added an extra frisson of pleasure to watch their innocence dissolve under his and Rebecca's skilful ministra-tions and urgings. He had no doubt at all that Theresa would be a very quick learner and that she would gain maximum enjoyment from their session but, all the same, he wished it was Esther who was with them.

Originally he had intended to bed Esther simply to show Marcus how stupid he'd been to reject her, but now it was more personal. She was an exciting mixture of strength and vulnerability and he found her hourglass figure and soft, blonde beauty an intriguing contrast to Rebecca's dark, detached, haughty sensuality. Not that he intended to share Esther with Rebecca, at least certainly not to begin with; he wanted to have her entirely to himself, to feel those round breasts pressed against him and to watch her trembling with ecstasy as he brought her again and again to the pinnacle of pleasure.

He was so excited by his thoughts that, when the door finally opened and Rebecca and Theresa entered, he was already fully aroused. At least, he thought that he was, but when he saw what Ther-esa was wearing his erection grew so hard that it was painful.

Naked, Theresa was even more attractive than he'd expected. Her cascading red hair fell nearly to her waist while her body was amazingly slim apart from her very large breasts. Tonight, these breasts were accentuated by the harness that she was wear-ing. The whole outfit was designed to drive him to a frenzy of desire.

She was wearing a leather mask with rivets round the eye holes, and a black-leather studded collar with buckles and a leather ring. Straps ran from beneath her thighs, up each side of her lower body, round her breasts, across her shoulders and down her back again. In her hand she was carrying a long latex domination strap and, although it was clear by her hesitant movements that this was an entirely new experience for her, he could tell by the redness of her erect nipples, and the faintest of pink rashes on her upper chest, that she too was already aroused.

'We thought it would be a good idea if we started some tuition now,' said Rebecca.

'Who's the teacher and who's the pupil?' asked Christopher.

'I thought we'd take it in turns,' Rebecca drawled, and, as Theresa glanced from Christopher and back to Rebecca, Christopher knew that for once he would enjoy being the teacher just as much as being the pupil.

Chapter Five

*I*t took Christopher and Rebecca some time to teach Theresa how to enjoy being dominant. It was clear that this was not what she'd expected when she first joined them, and Christopher was very pleased that they were using the rooms Theresa was renting. In general he always preferred to play away from home unless he was with his steady girlfriend of the moment. That was one drawback to courting the press as assiduously as he did: he never knew when they were about. Since his home was so well known, there would frequently be a freelance photographer somewhere within range of his front door.

Christopher wouldn't have been quite so pleased had he known that George Hickey and Mary Fuller were in the room adjoining Theresa's bedroom. He didn't know, because Theresa hadn't seen any reason to tell him, that George had managed to rent the adjoining flat to hers. Both were very convenient for the rehearsal room and had been available for short-term renting prior to the company moving on.

As soon as George had moved in, he'd drilled a small hole in the wall in order to be able to watch Theresa dressing and undressing morning and night. It was a bonus that was as unexpected to him as it was unknown to Theresa. However, tonight was a bonus not only for George but also for Mary Fuller. George had originally invited her round for a drink and some company simply because, as they were so much older than the other members of the group, they had become reasonably friendly.

The fact that both of them were turned on by the sight of attractive young girls, although Mary preferred to watch hers with young men, proved a common talking point and they each had favourites in the company. All that was forgotten for the moment, though, as they took it in turns to watch through the tiny spy hole. Another advantage to the flat was the fact that sound carried easily and so even when they weren't actually able to see what was happening they could hear almost every word that was said.

Most of the tutoring of Theresa had fallen to Rebecca. To her surprise she didn't find this quite as exciting as she'd expected. She realised that, while dominating Christopher was thrilling, having to teach another girl how to do it was less of a turn-on. For the first time she hoped that Christopher's desire for being dominated wasn't going to take over their sex life entirely and was quite grateful for the fact that she knew that by the end of the night he would assume the dominant role again. He would have to because Rebecca knew he certainly wouldn't want Theresa to think he only enjoyed being dominated.

To Rebecca's amusement, Theresa proved awkward when using the latex whip and it had taken her several attempts before she was able to flick sufficiently gently at Christopher's straining erection. The slight grimaces of pain that had crossed his handsome features when she got it wrong amused Rebecca. It also increased her sexual excitement because she knew that it increased Christopher's as well. She could see the uncertainty of what was going to happen while Theresa was in charge was a great turn-on for him.

For Theresa, the entire evening was an astonishing revelation. At first she looked uncomfortable, as if she could hardly believe some of the things that Rebecca was telling her to do to the great Christopher Wheldon. Gradually, though, she seemed to get into the spirit of things; when she was told to instruct Christopher to kneel on the floor while she stood over him, legs wide apart, and ordered him to use his mouth on her, she looked more powerful and sexy than ever before.

After asking her permission, Christopher circled each of her legs with his fingers and ran his hands slowly up her calves as he tongued the insides of her knees and thighs before finally fastening his mouth between her legs. When he slid his long tongue between her outer sex lips and began to lap hungrily at her, she shivered as if she were in almost unbearable ecstasy.

Rebecca was watching the couple very closely and when she saw Theresa's body start to tense she stepped forward and pulled Christopher roughly away. 'You weren't doing that right,' she said angrily.

'Yes he was,' protested Theresa, who hadn't yet grasped the rules of the game.

'Of course he wasn't,' said Rebecca, giving a hard look at the other girl. 'I think I'm the best judge of that, Theresa.'

'Sorry,' mumbled Theresa, who looked as if she were longing for Christopher to resume his attentions.

'That's all right,' said Rebecca, softening her tone as she saw the look of anxiety on Theresa's face. She didn't want to worry the girl; she was simply trying to make certain that neither Theresa nor Christopher had a climax this early in the proceedings.

Christopher was made to kneel back on his haunches and wait several minutes. Ostensibly this was as a punishment for him and, while he knelt there, Theresa trailed her whip down the length of his spine, causing him to breathe more rapidly. In fact, the rest was in order to let Theresa's body come down from its high state of arousal so that, when Christopher did begin tonguing her again, her body would have to resume its climb to orgasm from the beginning.

At last, to Theresa's obvious relief, Rebecca allowed Christopher to continue licking her. Once more, Theresa spread her legs wide and again Christopher slid his hands up her legs, only this time he used his fingers to open her up more fully and his tongue probed the entrance to her vagina, flicking lightly around the inner rim until she was squirming with delight. Rebecca knew from long experience of these games that it would take Theresasa a while to return to the moment just before her climax, and so she allowed herself to join in. As Christopher worked busily between Theresa's thighs Rebecca started to massage the other girl's voluptuous breasts.

Theresa turned her head and looked at Rebecca wide-eyed then, as prickling sensations began behind her nipples, she decided to let Rebecca proceed. She wished that she could see herself with the tall slim dark-haired girl licking and kneading at her breasts while the handsome fair-haired actor knelt on the floor giving her some of the most exquisite oral sex she'd ever been lucky enough to receive. The very realisation of what was happening to her increased her excitement and, suddenly, she began to shake as deep within her a strange coiling sensation began and she felt a pulse begin to beat behind her clitoris.

Immediately, Rebecca let go of her large, rapidly swelling breasts and again she pushed Christopher roughly away. This time Theresa gave a small cry as his clever tongue withdrew from her opening. She ached with the need to feel it back inside her again.

In the adjoining room, Mary Fuller was watching through George's spy hole. It was certainly the most exciting and unexpected thing she'd ever seen and her legs felt weak with desire. Since the three of them were relatively silent at the moment it was difficult for George to know what was going on. He had to rely on Mary to give him a whispered commentary. This she did but every now and again she was so overcome by excitement that she stopped whispering and he had to imagine it all for himself. Despite this he was as hard as Christopher and Mary knew he'd need release by the end of the evening.

After about fifteen minutes, Theresa's whole body felt hot and swollen. It wasn't just her breasts; she felt as though she had grown too large for her skin and, at one point, when Christopher licked carefully between each of her toes, she was sure that she was going to climax from that alone, so sensitive was every inch of her body. What she couldn't understand was why Rebecca kept interrupting the proceedings because it never occurred to her how much satisfaction both Christopher and Rebecca were gaining by continually thwarting her needs.

Eventually, Christopher decided that the time had come for things to change. As he stood up, his grey eyes looked deep into Theresa's green ones and she felt her knees start to buckle. Reaching out, Christopher grasped her firmly round the ribcage, splaying the fingers of his hands so they cupped the undersides of her magnificent breasts. She felt as though she were in some kind of wonderful erotic dream, but it was a dream that was threatening to turn into a nightmare as her moment of release was constantly being delayed.

'I hope you've enjoyed dominating me,' said Christopher, his voice cold.

'Yes, that is, I . . .' Theresa wasn't sure what answer was expected of her; after all, she'd only been doing what she'd been told.

'I think it's time you had a taste of your own medicine,' said Christopher, and there was something about his voice that made the red-haired girl shiver.

Out of the corner of her eye, Theresa saw Rebecca arranging a pile of pillows in the middle of the bed. Once they were in place Christopher removed the mask from Theresa and hooked a finger inside the leather collar around her neck. This ensured that she followed him as he drew her across the room and then laid her face down over the pillows, making sure they were placed directly beneath her stomach. The sensation of the pillows against her needy flesh was exquisite and Theresa started to press her sex against them, hoping that somehow she would manage to gain the last bit of stimulation needed in order to push her over the edge and reach her climax.

'Stop that!' said Christopher at once. 'I'm in charge now. You have to do what I say.'

'And what I say,' added Rebecca.

Theresa's entire body was trembling. She should have been afraid but instead she was incredibly excited. To be at the mercy of two such clever people, to have her body so aroused, frantic and needy, and to know that eventually her pleasure was going to be allowed to spill over, was magnificent. The tiny edge of fear that the situation was engendering in her only added to the piquancy of the situation. She was aware that her bottom was now raised high in the air with her vulva fully exposed.

'Part your legs more,' said Rebecca.

It never crossed Theresa's mind to disobey; indeed, she was suddenly very anxious to do as she was told and she understood why Christopher had been such a willing slave for a short while. It was wonderful to have all responsibility taken away from her.

'Do you promise to keep face down?' asked Christopher. 'Or do we have to blindfold you?'

'I promise,' whispered Theresa.

'Excellent,' said Christopher with satisfaction. 'Now, let's continue, Rebecca.'

Theresa had never felt so exposed and she waited tensely to see what would happen next. Suddenly, she felt hands rubbing oil into her bottom and she jumped instinctively. As she did so she heard Rebecca's soft and unmistakable laugh. The larger pair of hands continued kneading her buttocks and Rebecca's smaller, slimmer hands gently applied the oil around her sex. Christopher made large circular sweeping motions on her buttocks and thighs, keeping up a light and yet insistent motion in the whole area. At the same time Rebecca started to massage Theresa's vulva, and her fingers worked hard between the girl's legs.

Gradually, Christopher and Rebecca increased the tempo, although not the pressure, and then, for one brief blissful moment, Rebecca moved her finger and started to gently massage Theresa's aching clitoris.

For Theresa the sudden rush of warmth into the whole of her lower torso and the incredible tightness of all her muscles was too much. 'Please, please let me come now,' she begged them, but the moment she'd spoken the hands stopped moving and she was left nearly sobbing with frustration while once again Rebecca laughed softly.

In the adjoining room Mary and George glanced at each other and, emboldened by this, George positioned himself behind Mary, putting his arms around her so that he could cup her breasts while he rubbed his erection against her buttocks. To his great relief she didn't voice any objection and they both resumed listening and watching the three in the bedroom.

Theresa knew Rebecca could feel how aroused she was. After all, no one knew a woman's body better than another woman. Because of this it seemed to Theresa that the cruelty was far greater on Rebecca's part than on Christopher's, but she guessed that Rebecca was only doing what pleased Christopher. Somehow, pleasing Christopher was no longer Theresa's main objective. What her body was screaming for now was total satisfaction and she was beginning to grow frantic, wondering if she was ever to be allowed it.

'Just be patient,' whispered Rebecca, her voice kinder now. 'We won't keep you waiting much longer. I don't think we can, Christopher,' she added as Theresa became more slippery beneath Rebecca's clever fingers. Theresa realised that Rebecca was alternating between using her fingers and the palm of her hand between her thighs and this only served to heighten all the sensations for her. She could feel her clitoris enlarging and, as it did so, Rebecca gradually spent more time caressing it, only occasionally moving her finger away for a few brief seconds.

Soon, driven almost out of her mind by this constant titillation, Theresa began to cry out, constantly screaming at the couple to allow her the moment of ultimate release. Christopher was still kneading at her buttocks and she realised that, while Rebecca was sliding two fingers into her vagina, Christopher was carefully easing two well-lubricated fingers into her rear opening. This sensation of fullness was very satisfying but it still didn't provide sufficient stimulation for her to climax.

Rebecca continued to directly stimulate Theresa's clitoris, making occasional breaks just as Theresa hoped that she was reaching the point of no return. With her free hand Rebecca began to caress inside Theresa's vagina.

Theresa had never had this done to her before. She was astonished when Rebecca eased her fingers deeper inside her, searching until she located her highly sensitive G-spot. Gradually, the combined stimulation drove Theresa into such a frenzy of excitement that she began to quake and shout unintelligibly. It was then that Rebecca used her fingers in a thrusting movement, increasing the tempo all the time as though they were a penis.

Theresa pressed her breasts down on to the bed, lowering her arms so that she could move her upper torso and stimulate her highly sensitive nipples. For a brief moment she was terrified that this would make Christopher and Rebecca stop what they were doing but, glancing round at them, she knew they realised that they couldn't force her to wait any longer. A knowing glance passed between the couple and they allowed her to continue, taking obvious pleasure from her small whimpering sounds as she desperately climbed towards her long-awaited climax.

Theresa felt the pulse that had begun so long ago between her thighs start to increase and there was a frantic drumming sound in her ears as the pressure mounted within her. At the last moment, just as Theresa reached the blissful point of no return, Rebecca began very delicately to touch the incredibly sensitive clitoris itself. Theresa screamed with gratitude and delight as her long-delayed orgasm finally crashed over her. At that moment Christopher grasped her hips and thrust himself into her second opening, moving swiftly and urgently, using the violence of Theresa's internal contractions to assist him in reaching his own climax.

The intensity of the whole experience was so great that for a brief moment Theresa lost consciousness. When she regained it, and felt Christopher still inside her thrusting so fiercely, to her astonishment she felt her body begin to climax again. This time Rebecca slid beneath her and used her tongue where her fingers had previously been, licking at the moisture seeping from Theresa's opening and inserting her tiny pointed tongue where, earlier, Christopher had inserted his.

The thrill of feeling Theresa quaking, shaking and shuddering above her, and the knowledge that Christopher was inside the other girl, filling her between her slim buttocks, was so exciting that even without any physical stimulation Rebecca too was able to climax.

Finally, when it was all over, Christopher and Rebecca quickly dressed and left so that half an hour later Theresa was lying in an exhausted heap on her bed wondering if it had all been an incredible dream.

The next morning when Esther came downstairs she was surprised to see a message on her fax machine. As she picked it up she realised from the heading at the top that it was from America and her eyes instantly went to the bottom of the message where she saw Marcus's familiar signature scrawled across the page. Suddenly her heart began to beat rapidly as she wondered if he'd decided that he'd made a terrible mistake. The message quickly disillusioned her.

Have just heard you've joined Christopher Wheldon's People's Theatre. I can't believe you'd do this. You're a TV and film actress not stage. Have you really thought it through properly? C.W. may have his own reasons for taking you on.

Esther's initial excitement was immediately replaced by sheer fury. She couldn't believe that after such a long silence, after totally neglecting to tell her their affair was over, he should now start interfering in her career. Slowly, though, the fury ebbed away as she realised with considerable pleasure that he would never have faxed her unless the news had disturbed him, which was – after all – what she'd intended. Quickly she sat down and scribbled a reply.

Have just heard we're no longer an item. I assume you have your own reasons for dumping me without warning. Have you thought it through properly?

She then signed it and faxed it. Pausing only for a cup of coffee she then dashed off to the rehearsal room feeling very pleased with herself.

She hadn't been needed until eleven that morning and when she arrived Theresa and Michael

were in the middle of rehearsing. Theresa was
playing what was probably her biggest scene
opposite Michael. Although it had never been brilliant it had so far been passable and Esther sat
quietly on a chair at the side of the room to see if
any progress had been made since she'd last
watched it. She couldn't believe her eyes. For some
extraordinary reason Theresa was playing the
down-to-earth, no-nonsense, socialist Madge as
some kind of sex siren. Michael, playing the solicitor, Gerald, looked stunned – as well he might,
thought Esther. This was nothing like anything
Theresa had done before; neither was it anything
like the way Madge was meant to behave.

Noel sidled up to Esther. 'Perhaps this is
Michael's lucky day,' he whispered in her ear.
'Maybe she's trying to tell him something. What do
you think?'

'I thought she was keen on Christopher,' Esther
whispered back.

'Then why the hell's she playing the vamp?'
asked Noel.

Esther shrugged. She couldn't understand it and,
by the look on his face, neither could Christopher.
He looked cross and very slightly embarrassed,
which Esther assumed must be due to the fact that
he'd cast Theresa against type in the first place.
Maybe he was beginning to have second thoughts.

Theresa appeared blissfully unaware of how
badly she was doing and it was only when the
scene ended and Christopher began in no uncertain
terms to tell her that her eyes lost their sparkle.
She looked stunned as he attacked almost everything about her performance, and Esther decided it

117

would be kinder if she disappeared. She was sure that Theresa didn't want anyone around.

There weren't many places to go. Deciding she could do with another cup of coffee Esther headed for the kitchen. As she walked in she was surprised to see Nicholas Maxwell and Rebecca jump apart, both of them looking guilty.

'Nick was helping me with my lines,' Rebecca explained swiftly.

'Good idea,' said Esther, wondering why Rebecca felt that an explanation was necessary. 'Perhaps you'd like to help me, Nick, once you've finished with Becky.'

Nicholas nodded but he didn't look exactly delighted. It occurred to Esther that Nicholas spent a lot of time hanging around Rebecca. At first it had seemed that Rebecca was simply intercepting him on Christopher's behalf, making sure that the great actor and director wasn't disturbed by someone who didn't even have a part in the ongoing play. Now she wondered if there were other motives – if Rebecca could possibly be attracted to Nicholas.

It didn't seem very probable. He was so different from Christopher and Esther had no reason to think that Rebecca wasn't still totally besotted with her famous, fair-haired lover. On the other hand, possibly the contrast between the two men was in itself an attraction. Esther herself wasn't drawn towards men like Nick but she could see that he had a kind of rough and ready magnetism and his refusal to be in the least bit lovey-ish was a refreshing change. If he hadn't had quite such a large chip on his shoulder Esther would have found him a reasonably pleasant companion, but he was forever com-

118

plaining about the system, as though he were the only actor in the world who was finding it difficult to make his mark.

'I think that'll probably do for now,' said Rebecca. Nicholas looked very disappointed. 'We could have another go this afternoon,' continued Rebecca and he gave her a rare smile. For once Rebecca smiled at Esther and this made Esther even more suspicious about what had really been going on in the kitchen before she'd joined the pair of them. After Rebecca had gone Nick fiddled awkwardly with his coffee cup.

'She's bloody attractive, isn't she?' he said at last.

'Rebecca? Yes, she's very striking,' agreed Esther.

'Wasted on that fair-haired streak of piss,' continued Nicholas. 'She needs a real man.'

'Someone like you?' suggested Esther, trying to suppress a smile.

'Why not?' Nicholas demanded aggressively. 'Why shouldn't she like me? I may not be as famous as him but I might be a damn sight more interesting. Not that you'd know; you've only got eyes for him – him and Damon.'

Esther felt hot. 'I've no idea what you're talking about,' she said irritably.

'I've no idea what you're talking about,' mimicked Nicholas.

Esther glared at him. Actually his imitation of her had been quite good but that didn't make it any more pleasant. 'What have I done to offend you?' she asked.

'Nothing,' Nicholas muttered. 'It just bugs me when people like you imply Rebecca's too good for me.'

'I wasn't suggesting anything of the kind,' said

119

Esther. 'All I was trying to point out was that she and Christopher are fairly inseparable.'

'That's not what I've heard,' said Nicholas. 'Now and again I think someone comes between them.' He laughed, although for the life of her Esther couldn't imagine why.

Rehearsals didn't go well for anyone that day and the rest of the week proved a hard grind for them all. Slowly and remorselessly the clock was ticking away and Esther couldn't help but compare the unstoppable passage of time in their situation with that of the Conways. She was horrified at how little progress she herself was making, especially since some of the others were really beginning to shine. Rosie was excellent, far better than anyone could have anticipated, and Damon and Christopher performed with effortless ease. Rebecca was also doing better than expected but Esther was quite relieved that Theresa, like herself, continued to struggle.

It was Mary Fuller who was really holding them all together as Mrs Conway, head of the Conway family. Even when on stage with Christopher, she more than held her own and there were times when Esther could see that Christopher resented this. Nevertheless, it was the making of the play because without a strong Mrs Conway nothing would make sense.

Eventually they were down to the final week's rehearsals. At the end of the week, on the Saturday, the company was to hit the road. They were to open at a country house in Leicestershire called The Small House. The performance was to be indoors, which was lucky considering it was only early spring, in a venue that had been used for world-famous opera singers as well as less well-known touring theatrical companies. It was recognised as a centre of excellence where the Arts were concerned and there was no doubt that they were all expected to give a good performance from night one. According to Christopher the opening night was already sold out and he'd invited the national press along to take some photographs of the final dress rehearsal on the Friday before they left London.

True to his word, Christopher had spent a lot of time giving Esther extra tuition in the part but she still didn't feel that she'd really got to grips with it. On the surface, yes, but inside she didn't feel that she was Kay. She didn't understand Kay and the part simply refused to come alive for her. Despite this Christopher was extremely charming and considerate with her and she began to think that he was far more sensitive than she'd at first believed. He gave up spare time in the evenings, although it clearly annoyed Rebecca, and, despite the fact that he made it clear he'd like further intimacy, he never pressed for it. This had the effect of making him even more attractive to Esther, especially after the fax that she'd received from Marcus.

She knew that Damon was well aware of how badly she was performing. She could see it from the expression on his face every time he watched her. When they were on stage together he seemed to find it difficult to look at her, as though he was afraid that her poor performance might affect his own. Esther still fancied him, but his lack of sympathy and his refusal to mix with the company meant that her feelings didn't develop. It was Christopher who was being kind to her, and

Christopher who made it clear he found her attractive. Damon looked as though he wouldn't care if he never saw her again for the rest of his life.

She also knew, because it was impossible to keep anything secret in such a small group, that Damon and Ellie were lovers. Not that he was particularly agreeable to Ellie during rehearsals, but he was certainly more talkative with her, and since Esther herself loathed Ellie this was another mark against Damon.

On the Thursday, the penultimate rehearsal day, everyone had been asked to arrive at ten. Noel, Michael and Rosie arrived together at the same time as Esther. Esther was aware that Rosie was spending a lot of time at Noel and Michael's flat. What she didn't know was which of the two men Rosie was actually having sex with. Some days Esther was sure it was Michael, on other days certain that it was Noel. Whenever she asked Rosie all she would do was laugh and say: 'Can't you work it out, Esther?' The truth was, Esther couldn't.

Once they were all gathered together Christopher gave them a brisk chat, assuring them that he was quite confident the opening night was going to be a huge success, but adding that that was as long as one or two members of the cast managed to raise their level of performance a little. Theresa and Esther glanced at each other when he said this. They knew that they were the two he meant.

In the morning they had a straight run-through, working out scenery changes, make-up changes – ageing was necessary for the middle act – and costume changes. As was always the case at times like this they over-ran horrendously but nobody was too bothered. When they broke for lunch

Christopher told them that in the afternoon he wanted them to do another run, this time treating it as though it was a performance. After that they would have another short break and then he'd give them notes. On the Friday they would come in in the morning, go over parts that had caused them problems, and then in the afternoon do another run-through. At the end of that some of the press would be allowed in to take photographs and chat to them.

When it came to the lunch break, Esther was so shattered that she didn't feel she wanted anything to eat. She certainly couldn't face the pub, so when Rosie asked her if she'd like to go back to Noel and Michael's flat with her Esther agreed, especially when Rosie promised her that Noel and Michael wouldn't be there.

'Have you got a key, then?' enquired Esther.

'Yes,' said Rosie, waving the key in the air. 'I've had one for ages now. I got it soon after we all met. It means I can pop in there any time.'

The flat was in total chaos, as usual, but this was the first time that Esther had seen it. 'God, what a tip,' she remarked. 'Don't you ever tidy it up for them, Rosie?'

Rosie shook her head. 'I think I make a bigger mess than they do,' she confessed, scooping up some underwear and stockings from the back of the sofa and stuffing them behind a cushion so that Esther could have a seat. 'Shall I make us a sandwich?' she continued. 'You ought to eat something; it's going to be a bloody long day.'

Esther wondered what on earth the inside of the fridge looked like. Somehow she didn't think she fancied eating much there but when Rosie offered scrambled eggs she agreed. Once they were eating Esther decided to take her courage in both hands. 'Come on, Rosie, tell me the truth. Is it Noel or Michael you're having an affair with?'

'Both,' mumbled Rosie, her mouth full of scrambled egg and toast.

Esther nearly choked. 'Both! Not at the same time, surely?'

'Yes, at the same time,' confirmed Rosie. 'It's fantastic, it really is. They utterly spoil me. In fact, I don't think I'll ever be happy with just one man again.' And she laughed.

'But you must prefer one of them,' remarked Esther.

'Why must I?' asked Rosie. 'I think they're both lovely. Anyway, it's only a bit of fun. Once the tour's over we'll probably never meet up again. You ought to have a bit more fun. All you seem to do is work and I don't believe that you're having an affair with anyone, are you?'

Esther shook her head. 'No,' she admitted. 'I think I'm probably the only one who isn't, apart from Mary, but there we are. I suppose it's too soon after Marcus.'

'That's not true,' said Rosie. 'You've been making eyes at Christopher for the past two weeks.'

'God, is it that obvious?' asked Esther. 'Well it doesn't seem to be getting me anywhere.'

'I think it is,' said Rosie. 'He watches you all the time when you don't realise it. I reckon he's just waiting until rehearsals are over and we're on the road. Probably he felt it would get in the way of his directing at this stage.'

'Are you sure?' asked Esther eagerly.

'Absolutely certain,' confirmed Rosie. She paused

for a moment. 'Do you mind if I ask you something?'

'I can hardly object after what I asked you, can I?' Esther replied.

'OK, then. Do you fancy Damon as well?'

Esther hadn't realised that she was so transparent. It didn't say much for her acting abilities. 'Yes,' she admitted quietly. 'I fancy him something rotten, but don't try and tell me that he's interested in me. Anyway, he's pretty busy with Ellie, isn't he?'

'They've certainly got a thing going,' agreed Rosie, 'but I don't think it's very serious. After all, Damon's got more important things on his mind at the moment than sex.'

'You mean his acting?'

'No, not his acting,' said Rosie. 'Esther, I know something about Damon but if I tell you do you promise to keep it secret?'

'Of course,' agreed Esther quickly.

Rosie stared at her. 'You've got to mean that, because it would be dreadful if it got out. You see Michael told me but he swore me to secrecy.'

'Then perhaps you'd better not tell me,' said Esther.

'I think I should, especially as you like him so much. It will help explain to you why he seems indifferent. Besides, I happen to think he'd be much better for you than Christopher.'

'I do wish people would stop trying to choose my partners for me,' Esther said crossly. 'Anyway, what's the secret, Rosie?'

'Well,' said Rosie lowering her voice, 'it seems that Damon has a half-sister called Suzie. I forget what her surname is; Michael did tell me. Suzie was apparently a promising young actress at the

RSC while Christopher was there and they had a really long, intense affair. She was absolutely besotted with him and Christopher told her that they were going to get married. According to Michael, Damon believes that Suzie has the talent to be the next Maggie Smith or Judi Dench.

'Anyway, Suzie and Christopher were in *Much Ado* together; she was playing Beatrice to his Benedick. It was a wonderful production and got rave reviews. The problem was Suzie's reviews were better than Christopher's. He couldn't take that and he dropped her immediately. Michael says that when Christopher told her it completely destroyed her. She left the RSC and now she's not even acting. I think she's working in advertising or telephone sales, something like that.'

'That's absolutely dreadful,' said Esther, totally stunned. She could imagine only too well how the poor girl must have felt.

'Yes, well according to Michael, Damon's dislike of Christopher is the reason that he's here. Christopher doesn't know that Damon is anything to do with Suzie. They don't share the same surname and Suzie never used to talk about Damon because she was afraid that people would think she was trying to use his name to get on. Damon must be planning some kind of revenge on Christopher but Michael can't imagine what it is.'

'So that's why he isn't an admirer of Christopher's,' said Esther. 'Everything makes much more sense now. You'd think that Christopher would have found out though, wouldn't you?'

'No reason why he should,' said Rosie. 'After all, Damon Dowden is extremely well known. This Suzie girl wasn't, and really Beatrice was her big

126

breakthrough. Obviously she never introduced Damon to Christopher and there's never been any connection between them mentioned in the press.'

'I wonder what he's planning to do,' mused Esther. She was intrigued because this meant that both she and Damon were in the company for personal reasons unconnected with their acting. What it didn't explain was why Damon was having an affair with Ellie.

'So you see,' Rosie continued eagerly, 'he might well fancy you but at the moment he's got other things on his mind.'

'Including Ellie,' Esther pointed out.

'I'm sure Ellie's just lust,' said Rosie. 'Let's face it, no man in their right mind would turn her down but she's not exactly the kind of girl you'd make a long-term commitment to, is she?'

'I don't think actors and actresses are looking for long-term commitments, are they?' asked Esther.

'You were with Marcus, weren't you?' asked Rosie.

'That hurt,' said Esther.

'The truth often does,' Rosie pointed out. 'Just be careful, Esther. Don't let Christopher hurt you too.'

'How can he?' asked Esther. 'I'm not in love with him. I suppose it's more like the reason Damon is with Ellie – I lust after him. You have to admit he's gorgeous.'

'Mm, but not my type,' said Rosie. 'I can't imagine that Christopher takes much trouble with his partners, unlike Michael and Noel.' She stretched slowly and sensuously with a soft sigh and Esther laughed.

'You're incorrigible, Rosie! Mind you, it seems to be doing you good. You're really brilliant as Joan.'

127

'Well I do have the advantage of playing most of my scenes opposite Christopher; some of his brilliance is probably brushing off on me,' said Rosie with a mock modest air.

By the time they returned to the rehearsal room Esther was feeling better. She was also intrigued by the gossip that she'd heard. She hoped that at some time during their tour she'd get the opportunity to know Damon better. Since both he and Esther were trying to use Christopher it might be helpful if they were able to get together. On the other hand she didn't want him to know that she was in on his secret. At least now she'd be more tolerant of his snide remarks and his continual putting down of Christopher. It was also rather touching to think that he was so fond of his half-sister that he was willing to go to all this trouble to avenge her. She wished that she had someone who cared that much about her. Apart from Lydia there was no one who seemed to feel that Marcus had done her any great wrong. On the contrary, she knew that many people in the acting business felt that she'd been lucky to be with him for as long as she had.

That afternoon they did a complete run-through trying to stick to the right times and performing to the best of their ability. At the end they took their carefully choreographed bow and then scattered around the room waiting for Christopher's comments.

'That wasn't at all bad,' he said with a half-smile on his face. 'To be honest, it was far better than I'd anticipated. Of course, it's quite difficult for me to judge because I'm on stage so much but George here tells me that it went very smoothly and most of the time he was thoroughly absorbed. There are still one or two problems that need to be ironed out but I'd rather talk to the individuals concerned on their own. In general let's just say that I'm pleased with the way things are going and if you keep this up then the opening night next week in Leicester-shire should be very good indeed.'

'Is that it?' asked Damon from the back of the hall. 'No notes at all?'

'Certainly none for you, Damon,' Christopher said brightly. 'You were very good and extremely powerful. Just be careful not to overshadow Rebecca. I know she's the downtrodden wife in the middle act but we don't want her to look like the victim of some kind of abuse, do we? You could possibly tone it down a fraction; otherwise it's absolutely fine.'

'Serves you right for asking,' said Ellie, who was sitting next to him resting her head on his shoulder.

'I hate to be ignored,' drawled Damon.

Esther, who was sitting near enough to hear, wanted to laugh but she didn't because she knew only too well that she was going to be taken to one side and talked to about her performance. If any-thing, she'd been worse this afternoon than in the morning.

As she'd anticipated Christopher quickly ap-proached her once the group began to break up to leave. 'Esther, darling, I think there are still a few problems, don't you?' he said.

'Yes,' she admitted.

'Look, how about if I came round to your place this evening and we worked really hard on it for a couple of hours? Would that suit you?'

'I think it would be very helpful,' agreed Esther. 'Are you sure you can spare the time?'

'I don't think I've got much choice,' said Christopher.

Esther blushed. 'I didn't realise I was that bad,' she murmured.

'It isn't a question of being that bad,' Christopher explained carefully. 'The truth is, Esther, you're surrounded by some very good actors. I want you to do yourself justice, to really get the best out of you, and I don't mind how much time I spend in order to get you to do that.'

'You know where I live?' queried Esther.

'Of course. I'll be there at eight,' promised Christopher before moving off to speak to Theresa.

Esther quickly grabbed her coat and hurried to the tube station. She needed to tidy up a bit and make sure she'd got some drink in. Not that she'd be drinking, but she guessed that Christopher would want to. She couldn't help wondering if this might be the opportunity she'd been waiting for. Once they'd finished discussing her acting then surely there would be a chance of something more intimate occurring between them, she thought to herself. She decided to change when she got home so that she was looking a little more feminine than she usually did for rehearsals. It wouldn't hurt to give Christopher a nudge in the right direction and, if what Rosie had said was the truth, a little nudge might be all that he needed.

Chapter Six

*E*llie was highly relieved that Damon had agreed to come back to her rooms with her. Although they'd been conducting a torrid affair for some time now, she could never be certain of him. This didn't trouble her too much. Ellie wasn't into long-term commitment; what she wanted was regular and good sex, which Damon certainly provided. However, because of her sexual skills, she'd always found that once men became involved with her they tended to dance to her tune, at least in the beginning. Damon had made it clear from day one that he had no intention of dancing to anyone's tune except his own. At first Ellie had tried to change him, cancelling arrangements at the last moment or hinting of other love affairs, but when it became clear that this didn't trouble Damon she stopped doing it. There was no point if it wasn't going to have any effect.

Tonight she'd half expected him to say that he was tired after the rehearsals and wanted to go back to his own house. She'd never been invited there and knew that she never would be. As far as she was aware no one was invited to Damon's private sanctum. He was the most secretive actor she'd ever come across. Actors and actresses were, by the very nature of their profession, garrulous and outgoing. They loved to gossip and exchange hospitality and even if the friendships were only surface deep, or sometimes false, they were usually quickly forged. Damon appeared to feel no need to make any friendships and before he and Ellie had first got into bed he had made his terms very clear to her. No emotional involvement, no talking about the affair with other members of the group and, above all, no questions.

Ellie didn't know what kind of questions he thought she might ask him. The truth was, she was far too self-absorbed to want to know very much but she hadn't expected such utter silence from him when it came to talking about his family. She wondered if they'd disapproved of his choice of career and cut him off. Since he never gave inter-views there were no cuttings that she could look out to see if she was right.

Because the sex between them was so good she was quite upset that Damon seemed able to take it or leave it. Today, as was always the case with her when the adrenalin was flowing after work, she was quite desperate for him. When he'd allowed her to sit next to him at the end of the day, and to rest her head on his shoulder, she'd guessed that she was going to be lucky. On a bad day he was more than capable of ignoring her in front of the rest of the company, or even going off on his own to have a drink, like the time she'd found him in the pub with Esther. That had annoyed her because she had a sneaking suspicion that Damon was attracted to Esther, although she had no real grounds to support this theory. Just the same she was sure that she was right – a woman's intuition was usually the best guide.

Once they were in her flat, Ellie immediately put the kettle on. She'd have liked something stronger but Damon rarely drank unless he was out. Again this was not like most actors she knew and she wondered if for some reason he was continually watching himself, making sure that he had himself fully under control. It was as though there was a side of him that he was determined to keep from her and from everyone else.

The only time that he really let himself go was in bed and Ellie supposed that this was the only time that should matter to her. If she was honest, she was quite surprised that he'd bothered with her. He was considered one of the best-looking actors in the country and could have had his choice of almost any of the women in the company. Of course, the same could be said of Christopher, but it was accepted that Christopher and Rebecca were already an item which rather counted him out. Damon, though, had approached Ellie within the first two days and as far as she could tell had made no advances towards anyone else. She had twice tried to get him to confess that he liked Esther but he'd become so annoyed the second time that she'd realised it was a subject she'd better leave alone.

Damon sat down in an armchair, stretching his long legs out in front of him and crossing his ankles. 'Only one more day to go in that godforsaken rehearsal room,' he grumbled.

'Do you think we're really ready to open?' queried Ellie, handing him a mug of strong sweet tea.

'As ready as we're ever going to be,' said Damon.

'Esther and Theresa are the weak links, aren't they?'

'You can say that again,' said Damon with feeling. 'It isn't really their fault though. I can't think what Christopher was doing when he cast them the way he did. Casting Theresa as Madge is a total joke. As for Esther, well she was born to play Hazel.'

'He must have had his reasons,' said Ellie. 'He's very experienced.'

'I can't work them out,' said Damon. 'It isn't as though they're making him look good; in fact, quite the contrary. I've got a feeling he gave Esther the part of Kay because he thought she wanted it. From what I've heard he did mention it to her at her audition and she, stupid girl, didn't like to say that she didn't feel right for the part. As for Theresa, perhaps it was a bribe.'

'A bribe?' asked Ellie. 'Why does he need to offer her a bribe?'

'You'll have to ask her,' said Damon.

'Well, OK, but why would he want to please Esther then?' queried Ellie.

'Because he wants to show Marcus what a fool he was going off to America and leaving Esther behind. Surely you know that Christopher's as jealous as hell of Marcus. Think what a coup it would be for him if he showed the world that Marcus had been preventing Esther from showing her true talent.'

'I'd have thought he'd have been better off just sleeping with her,' said Ellie.

'No doubt he's got that in mind as well,' said Damon. 'He'll probably succeed too. She's been making cow eyes at him most days.'

'Well, you know where I think her affections lie,' giggled Ellie.

Damon stared coldly at her. 'If you talk about that one more time,' he said quietly, 'then you and I are finished. Is that understood?'

Ellie's eyes widened in mock innocence. 'I'm really sorry, Damon,' she said. 'Why do you get so annoyed if you don't think there's any truth in it?'

'Just shut up,' Damon said wearily. 'It's been a bad enough day already. I came back here for some relaxation not an argument.'

'I never argue,' said Ellie, 'it's a waste of time. Are you hungry?'

Damon put his head on one side and eyed her thoughtfully. 'For what?' he asked seductively.

'Anything,' said Ellie, standing provocatively in front of him with her hands on her hips.

'I could do with a toasted sandwich,' he said at last.

Ellie was furious but she didn't dare show it. She hated anything connected with domesticity, and must have made Damon more toasted sandwiches in this rehearsal period than she'd made in the rest of her life prior to their meeting. Despite this, she still managed to burn it.

'I shall quite miss these singed sandwiches when we get on the road,' drawled Damon. 'You're going to make somebody a dreadful wife, Ellie.'

'I'm not going to be anyone's wife,' said Ellie. 'I'm going to be a superstar.'

Damon laughed, but not unkindly. 'You don't mean that, do you?' he asked.

'Why not?' asked Ellie, pouting a little.

'You're a competent actress,' Damon assured her, 'but hardly star material. You're not another one who's aiming for Hollywood, surely?'

'Of course not,' said Ellie, her annoyance beginning to show in her voice. 'That doesn't mean that I don't want to get on here, though. You might be surprised to learn that there's quite an important director in the West End who's very interested in me.'

'I'm not surprised,' said Damon. 'I hope he's got enough energy to cope.'

'He's big in musicals,' said Ellie. This was something she'd intended to keep secret but Damon's words had goaded her so much she found it impossible not to tell him.

'Big in what way?' asked Damon with a smile.

'He's got a lot of influence. He's said that he can put me up for a part in *Phantom of the Opera*.'

'I didn't know you could sing,' said Damon. 'Isn't that a necessity?' He hesitated for a moment. 'Maybe not, though,' he continued. 'Many an actress has succeeded despite a lack of proficiency.'

'You can be really vile sometimes,' said Ellie. 'I sing very well. Actually, I think singing and dancing are my two strongest assets.'

'Then what the hell are you doing touring with Christopher Wheldon and his People's Theatre Company?' asked Damon.

'It's good stage experience,' said Ellie. 'I haven't done much stage work before and my friend, this man I've just been telling you about, wanted me to have some stage work on my CV. He said that would make it easier for him to put me forward.'

'I see,' said Damon. 'Is there anything else you

136

have to do, not necessarily something that goes on a CV, before he puts you forward?'

Ellie shrugged. 'There might be, but he hasn't mentioned it yet. I don't care. Plenty of girls have got on that way and I know I've got talent. It might not be the kind of talent that you're interested in, Damon, but it's got popular appeal and, contrary to what you may think, there's nothing wrong with popular appeal. Do you know who makes the most money these days?'

'No idea,' said Damon in a bored voice.

'It's the stars of soaps, sit-coms, TV presenters, personalities,' said Ellie.

Damon thought for a moment. 'I've no doubt you're right, but that's an indictment of society in general not a commendation for you personally.'

'You're an artistic snob aren't you?' said Ellie.

Damon frowned. 'I don't think so, I just happen to have a love of great acting.'

'Do you mean you think you're a great actor?'

'No, of course not,' said Damon quickly. 'What I meant was, I like to watch great acting and I like to aspire to it. It's no different from you aspiring to be in *Phantom of the Opera*; we're just going in different directions.'

'I hope we're going in the same direction tonight,' said Ellie, suddenly losing interest in the discussion and wanting to feel his hands on her.

'Well, at least we're in the same room,' said Damon.

'Why do you like me?' asked Ellie.

Damon laughed. 'That's a strange question! I'd have thought you knew the answer by now.'

'But I'm not your type, am I?' persisted Ellie.

'I don't have a type,' said Damon.

'Have you ever had a serious relationship with anyone?' Ellie asked him.

'No,' said Damon. He put his plate down on the carpet and glanced at Ellie. Her clothes were different today. Usually she wore traditional rehearsal clothes but, because it had been such an important run-through, she'd decided to dress in a younger way, to help her feel more like the sixteen-year-old Carol. She was wearing a blue and stone gingham checked dress. It was shirt styled and came down to her ankles, although the last button ended just above her knees. On her feet she had a pair of canvas lace-up deck shoes and the overall effect was certainly one of a much younger girl. It also meant that she'd be far easier to undress than normal and she saw, from the look in Damon's eyes, that he was just beginning to realise this.

When he stood up Ellie turned to go towards the bedroom but Damon caught hold of her arm and held her back. 'Let's stay here,' he said, his voice deeper than usual.

Ellie felt a surge of desire for him. At times like this she was putty in his hands, and she only wished that they were going to be in London a little longer because once they were on the road it would be far more difficult for them to carry on their affair discreetly.

'What have you got on under that?' he asked her.

The corners of Ellie's mouth turned up in a mischievous smile. 'Not a lot,' she said, 'and what there is is fairly easy to get rid of.'

'I'm very pleased to hear it,' said Damon, reaching out and running his hands through her short, light-brown hair. She let her head fall back a little and his fingers continued to move over her scalp, massaging it firmly until she closed her eyes at the sheer sensual pleasure. As soon as she closed them his mouth descended and she felt his lips hard against hers.

His hands were moving across her shoulders, down her arms, and then over her breasts until at last he was able to start undoing some of the buttons. Now that her head had been freed Ellie was able to look up at him. Because he was so much taller than her she always felt wonderfully small and feminine when he was making love to her, despite the fact that she was as sexually voracious as he was.

Damon's fingers were now busy unfastening her bra. She'd deliberately worn one which had a clasp at the front and this made it much easier to undo. He uttered a sound of delight as the material parted and his hands were able to cup her small tight breasts. As usual his fingers were firm and she pressed her upper body against them. She liked intense stimulation of her breasts and Damon had quickly grasped this. For a few moments they stood there, Damon's mouth moving over her lips and neck while his hands continued to knead and arouse her breasts. Then, as he felt her nipples start to swell, he sat back in the chair, pulling her down with him so that she was sitting astride his left thigh. His right hand moved up her legs and encountered the crotchless panties that she had put on in the hope they would be having some sex. He gave a tiny chuckle. 'My word, we are well prepared, aren't we?'

'Don't you think Carol would dress like this?' asked Ellie teasingly and then she gave a gasp as he swiftly thrust two fingers inside her vagina before starting to move them vigorously in and out.

'I think Carol would have been in serious trouble if she'd behaved like this at sixteen, particularly in 1919,' said Damon between heavy breaths.

'It's lucky I'm not really Carol then, isn't it?' teased Ellie.

'Can't you stop talking for five minutes?' gasped Damon, sliding his thumb between her outer sex lips until he located her clitoris and began to massage that too. At last Ellie was silenced and she began to tremble. Suddenly Damon withdrew his hand, leaving her feeling utterly bereft.

'Grip your thighs round mine,' he suggested. 'I want to see you make yourself come.'

Ellie reached forward with her hands until they were resting on his shoulders and then she moved her lower body frantically along his well-muscled thigh, gripping tightly with her own leg muscles and jerking her hips backwards and forwards until, at last, she felt the first tremors of an orgasm. Damon's dark eyes were fixed on her face and as she shuddered she looked straight into them and saw the expression of delight there.

'I love watching you come,' he said.

'I want to come again,' said Ellie swiftly.

'I'm sure you will,' said Damon, and then she felt his fingers returning to the place where they'd been earlier. Once more his two fingers were inside her while his thumb played unceasingly around the tight bud of her clitoris. She always came quickly and fiercely when he did this, and within seconds she was climaxing once more and again she saw him watching her with an expression of utter contentment.

When she'd finished, he helped her off his knee and then pushed her down on to the floor as he slowly unzipped his chinos. Ellie reverently removed his straining penis from the confines of his tight underpants and then, lowering her head, she drew the tip into her mouth and slid her tongue over the soft silky flesh. Damon let his head fall backwards against the top of the chair. Ellie knew better than to let him come this way: he always liked to come inside her, but she was now expert at judging exactly how far she could go. Just as his hips began to twitch she drew her mouth away and then very lightly ran a finger round the underside of the ridge of flesh at the base of the glans, causing him to draw his breath in sharply.

'I want you now,' said Damon suddenly and Ellie knew from past experience that he meant that quite literally. That was one of the most exciting things about their lovemaking – the swift urgency that seemed to come over him, resulting in some of the most exciting couplings she'd ever had.

For some reason the fact that both of them were fully clothed added an extra piquancy to the whole scenario. When Damon stood up, Ellie reached out and led him across the room until she was standing with her back against the wall. Then, she put her hands out flat on either side of her as she moved her hips seductively against the hard surface. It didn't take Damon more than a few seconds to work out what she wanted and, with a look of excitement in his eyes, he gripped her round the waist and lifted her up, taking care to make sure that her back was still supported against the wall. He lifted her slightly above his waist level at first and then lowered her down on to his massive erection. She felt the pressure of the wall behind her and Damon positioned her carefully so that her shoulderblades were fully supported, which meant that she was free to move her buttocks as much as she wanted.

Damon's hands were gripping her beneath the tops of her thighs and she wrapped her arms around his neck as she began to bounce slowly up and down on his straining erection. Damon's mouth fastened on to the sensitive flesh at the base of her throat and she felt the tip of his tongue licking lightly, flicking here and there as he nuzzled her, his breath hot against the side of her neck.

Somehow, he managed to move so close to her that as she bounced her breasts rubbed against the roughness of his white cotton T-shirt, which meant that she was being stimulated in all the areas she needed in order to come once more.

'I can't wait much longer,' gasped Damon suddenly as she continued to thrust her hips vigorously up and down.

'It's all right,' gasped Ellie, 'I'm nearly there too.'

She sensed that Damon was right on the brink but, as usual, his self-control was incredible and veins stood out in his arms and neck as he strained to wait for her to catch up with him. Suddenly she felt her whole body pulling in on itself and the dreadful tension that always preceded the wonderful warmth of release descended on her. Her movements grew frantic and she heard herself gasping and shouting. Damon's fingers dug hard into the flesh of her upper thighs and this proved the trigger which precipitated her third orgasm. With a shout of triumph she toppled over the edge of the abyss and felt the gorgeous contractions flood through her. As she cried out she heard Damon utter a strange gutteral sound and he threw his head back and shuddered violently with the force of his own release.

Although it had been quick it had been incredibly exciting and when Damon released Ellie, allowing her to slide slowly to the ground, she felt totally sated. She half expected him to pick her up, carry her over to the sofa and sit with her for a little while, possibly even bringing her to further climaxes later in the evening. However, it was quickly clear that this was not going to happen. Once he'd helped her to her feet and pulled her dress down again, Damon readjusted his own clothing and then turned to pick up his script.

'Are you going already?' asked Ellie, wondering what it was about him that meant that no matter how much he satisfied her she still longed for even more.

'I think I'd better,' said Damon. 'After all, we meet the press tomorrow. I don't want to look as though I've been up all night, do I?' And he laughed.

Ellie hid her vexation. Instead, she went over to him and wrapped her arms round his waist, resting her head against his chest. This time though, Damon clearly didn't want her to do it. Gently but firmly he pushed her away from him. 'Sorry, Ellie, that's it for tonight,' he said. 'It was great, as usual.'

'It certainly was,' agreed Ellie with a bright smile.

After he'd gone she curled up on the sofa and thought about him at length. She'd known right from the beginning that there was no future in it. What she hadn't expected was for her body to get so used to him and to need him so badly. 'Never mind', she told herself consolingly. 'We'll be on the road for several months; you won't be losing him just yet.'

It was some comfort to her, especially when she thought about the West End director and what he'd probably expect from her if she was to get the coveted role he'd promised her. Still, it was all part of the business and at the end of the day Ellie was a professional through and through. Sex with Damon was fantastic, but the dream of holding a West End audience in the palm of her hand was even better.

Chapter Seven

Christopher arrived at Esther's house in North London full of eager anticipation. Although he'd left behind him a very irritable Rebecca and a somewhat confused Theresa, he was in no doubt that he'd done the right thing. If he was to make Esther his full-time girlfriend by the end of the company's tour then he had to start soon and tonight seemed the perfect opportunity. He hoped that Esther would be as eager as he was, and when she opened the door to him wearing an ankle-length tight-fitting black wool skirt coupled with an ivory, long-sleeved crepe blouse with a long strand of false pearls round her neck and deliciously high-heeled black shoes on her feet, Christopher felt certain he was right. He smiled admiringly at her. 'You look great.'

She smiled back at him, albeit a little awkwardly. 'I thought it might help to keep me in the character of Kay,' she explained. 'It's rather like costume drama: once you get into these tight skirts you walk differently and hold yourself differently and it does make me feel in the period.'

'I couldn't agree more,' said Christopher enthusiastically. 'In Acts I and III, when I'm wearing my uniform, I really do feel like a soldier. I find the middle act far more difficult though.'

'That's because it isn't really you,' said Esther. 'You do it brilliantly but really and truly it's hard to think of you as a seedy drunk, let alone a total failure.'

Christopher was not immune to any kind of flattery, in fact he lapped it up. 'That's very kind of you. I certainly do my best,' he said, strolling round the living room and examining the books on the shelves. 'Are all these yours?'

'No, most of them belong to Marcus,' explained Esther.

'I thought so. He's very into Stanislavski, isn't he?'

'He certainly uses parts of Stanislavski's theory; he calls himself a Stanislavskian purist. According to Marcus, modern-day drama teachers have distorted Stanislavski's original theories.'

Christopher yawned. 'Well, don't let's get bogged down talking about what Marcus likes or doesn't like. We're here to discuss *your* acting.'

'Before we begin, would you like a drink?' asked Esther.

'Sounds a good idea,' agreed Christopher. 'Got any whisky?'

Esther didn't have much whisky and hoped he wasn't intending to drink it steadily throughout the evening. 'Of course,' she said quickly. 'What do you like with it?'

'Nothing, unless it's a very inferior one,' Christopher retorted.

'No it's a good malt. Someone gave it to Marcus, only he's not that keen on whisky.'

'Fine, then I'll have it as it stands.'

'Not even ice?' asked Esther.

'No, nothing with it at all thanks. Now then,' he continued as she handed him his drink, 'I've been trying to work out exactly where you're going wrong. In Acts I and III you're not too bad and I'm sure that once you get an audience you'll be fine. It's the middle act that's really giving you trouble, isn't it?'

'Yes,' confirmed Esther. 'I suppose I find it difficult to understand what's really happening. Is Kay's vision the truth or is it simply a foolish dream brought on by overexcitement, as her mother suggests at the end of the play?'

'I believe you've got to leave that to the audience to decide,' said Christopher.

'But what was the playwright's intention?' asked Esther.

'We can't ask him, can we?' laughed Christopher. 'He's dead and gone.'

'But what do you think it was?' Esther persisted.

'What I think doesn't really matter,' Christopher explained. 'It's what you believe that's going to make the difference. Tell me, why is it such a problem to you?'

'I suppose because Kay is a realist. She comes across as sensible and intelligent.'

'In that case it isn't likely to be an hysterical piece of girlish nonsense, is it?'

'No, but I do have a problem with this vision. It's all so bleak. Not only does everyone fail – apart

147

from Ernest Beevers – but poor Carol dies. It does seem that this family are going to have rather more than their share of bad luck.'

'I think what it represents,' said Christopher carefully, 'is how things are going to change for everyone, not just the Conways. Clearly Priestley uses the Conway family to epitomise the changes that the next twenty years are going to show and if you analyse it then, yes, they probably are more unlucky than it would be reasonable to expect. But if it's done well no one's going to think that. They should, hopefully, just feel a terrible sense of impending tragedy, especially since Act III ends on a high note with Kay desperately hoping that it has all been a dream. That gives the audience a chance to hope if they want to, doesn't it?'

'So what I talk about in Act II,' said Esther slowly, 'is the truth. Ernest Beevers *is* going to get rich and treat Hazel abominably. Carol *is* going to die. Robin's going to become a hopeless alcoholic who never does anything, they're going to lose their family money, Alan will become some kind of weird recluse, and Madge will end up a frustrated school teacher. As for Gerald, well he becomes so pompous and unpleasant he's hardly recognisable from the agreeable young man in the first act.'

'But that's what life does to people, isn't it?' said Christopher, surprisingly gently. 'Just think about your own life, Esther. Think of yourself at say fifteen and how you imagined you'd be at the age of twenty-four. Has it turned out the way you expected? Is this where you thought you'd be?'

Esther thought hard for a moment. 'No, of course not. At fifteen I was madly in love with a boy I played tennis with. I was sure that we were going

148

to get married, have three children and live happily ever after.'

'What an old-fashioned little thing you must have been,' said Christopher. 'Weren't you passionately in love with some pop group?'

'No,' confessed Esther. 'I suppose I was horribly conventional.'

'And are you still?' asked Christopher meaningfully.

Esther's eyes met his and her heart began to race. 'Not in the least,' she assured him.

'Well, there you are then, my point exactly. Life doesn't go the way any of us expect, and although the changes in the Conways' lives are perhaps overdramatic that shouldn't prove such a big problem for you as it is at the moment. When I was going through the text I decided that, if you can manage to tie Act II into Act III better, then the sense of tragedy will be all the stronger.'

'Tie it in where?' Esther asked.

'It's very near the end. Look, here you are.' They were sitting side by side on the sofa and Christopher leant across her to turn the pages of the play. She was acutely aware of his physical nearness. 'See here, the next to last page. It's when Kay wants Alan to comfort her, the way he did in her vision. You know, you're almost willing him to do it so that you get proof that what you think you saw is going to happen.'

'Yes, I've got it here,' said Esther.

'Right, now you have to quote a piece of Blake and I think that when you quote it you should take a little longer over remembering the words because, let's face it, it was in the previous act that

Alan said it and you're struggling to remember, right?'

'Agreed,' confirmed Esther.

'OK, then, so you take longer than you have been to think about it and then when you do quote it, break it up more. I don't mean the verse; I mean let your voice break slightly at the terrible sorrow of it all. I'd like to hear you give it a go. Start with just the two lines: "Joy and woe are woven fine, a clothing for the soul divine."'

'Do you want me to stand up?' asked Esther.

'Perhaps you could stand in the middle of the room facing me. Imagine that Alan is slightly to your right so you turn that way, but only a fraction of a turn. Remember, I'm the audience and we need to get a good look at you as well.'

Esther obeyed him and said the lines. She said them the way she'd been saying them at rehearsals but here, after listening to Christopher, she was absolutely aghast at how dead they sounded.

'Right, that's the way you have been doing it. What I want you to do now is break it up so that after "joy" you have a break and then perhaps you could say "and woe are" and then look away or let your voice crack slightly before you say "woven fine". Then you could almost rush through "a clothing for" and then stop and search for the last few words before ending with "the soul divine". Try it like that.'

Esther obeyed and instantly it was totally different. It was the first time that she'd felt any true emotion when she said the words and, after she'd finished, a smile spread over her face.

'Great,' said Christopher, 'a big improvement. Now let's tackle the last two lines: "And when this

we rightly know, safely through the world we go."'
Try and break that up in your own way now that
you've got the hang of it.' Esther did, and after a
couple of false starts was delighted with the result.

'Excellent!' exclaimed Christopher. 'OK, now
when you've finished that, if you remember, you
have to repeat the last line: "safely through the
world we go". Now, considering the way you're
doing the first part, let me hear how you think you
should deliver that final line.'

'Do you think it would be all right if I went
through the whole thing?' queried Esther. 'I think
if I do the first four lines and then repeat the last
one I'll get the feel of it much better.'

'Anything to make you happy,' said Christopher.

Esther was so caught up in her part that she
didn't seem to realise quite what he was saying,
but Christopher still felt quietly confident about the
evening. He watched with interest as she delivered
Blake's verse and, when it came to the repetition of
the final line for the very first time, he felt genuinely touched by what she was saying.

'That was a huge improvement,' he said
enthusiastically.

'It felt quite different,' said Esther with delight.
'Perhaps I can do this after all.'

'I never doubted that you could. It was only your
own inhibitions holding you back,' said
Christopher.

'Well, I'll make sure I discard them for the rest
of the evening,' said Esther, and she gave him a
tiny smile.

For the next half-hour they continued to work on
the play and by the end of that time both of them
knew that Esther's performance was now entirely

151

different. 'Let's take a break,' Christopher said at last. 'I think I'd like a coffee, how about you?'

'That sounds great,' agreed Esther. She was already on a high from the excitement of finding out exactly what she could do with the part now that she felt artistically free. She made them both coffee, put some chocolate biscuits on a plate and took them back into the lounge. She went to sit in an armchair but he patted the seat next to him. 'What are you doing going over there?' he queried.

'I don't know,' confessed Esther.

Christopher wondered if she was deliberately playing hard to get or whether he'd been wrong, but then, as she cast a quick glance at him from beneath lowered lashes, he decided that his original thoughts had been the right ones. Esther was definitely attracted to him. As he tried to wonder what she'd be like in bed he felt his excitement growing.

After they'd drunk their coffee Esther reached for the play again but Christopher put a hand over her wrist. 'I think we've done enough work on that for the evening,' he said quietly.

'Are you sure?' asked Esther.

'I think I'd like to spend some time getting to know you better,' said Christopher. 'It's been pretty hectic these last few weeks.'

'It certainly has,' she agreed, settling back into the sofa.

Christopher turned towards her and then he started to unfasten the buttons of her V-necked blouse. He did it very slowly, and Esther held her breath when he reached the final one. With exquisite care, he eased the blouse off her shoulders and down her arms before draping it over the side of the sofa. She was now sitting in the long, tight black skirt and high-heeled shoes but, incongruously, the only things that she had on her upper body were a cream satin camisole and a long strand of pearls, which ended just at the start of the cleft between her rounded breasts.

Christopher, who was wearing a pair of jeans and a heavy cotton shirt, quickly began undressing. He turned around and carefully lifted the lower edge of Esther's camisole until the top of her stomach was revealed. Then, he very lightly drew the palm of his hand over the exposed flesh, drawing the hand backwards and forwards in a way that was somehow hypnotic.

He watched as Esther's eyes closed and her head went back. Emboldened by this Christopher, while continuing to massage the tiny piece of exposed flesh, moved closer and allowed his lips to travel around the sensitive points of her collarbone. Then, very slowly, he allowed himself to lick the skin within the circle of pearls.

He moved very carefully and could tell by the small sighs she was uttering that this was to Esther's liking. Next, he began to kiss her nipples and the surrounding areolae but he did it through the satin of the camisole, licking and blowing alternately until she was squirming helplessly beneath him.

For Esther it was not only a triumph but sheer delight as well. For some reason she'd expected him to be a more hasty lover and this incredibly slow build-up was highly erotic. Eventually, after further stroking and licking, Christopher helped her to remove her skirt and then slid a hand beneath the wide leg of her French knickers. To her surprise, he didn't go anywhere near her pubic mound but instead concentrated on stroking the flesh of her groin and then moving upward to draw tiny circles on her hipbones. It was all so delicate and unexpected that it had the effect of heightening her desire even more. She could hear herself uttering tiny whimpers of pleasure and knew that she was wriggling, desperately trying to get him to touch her more intimately but, instead, he continued his slow steady arousal in his own way.

It seemed to her that this provocative stroking and touching, which was heightening and strengthening her desire with every second, was never going to end but, eventually, she heard him mutter in her ear, asking where the bedroom was. He was careful to keep one arm tightly round her as she led him through to the room where she and Marcus had shared such passionate times.

There was no chance for her to dwell on this thought, though, because Christopher immediately removed the last items of her clothing and then, very gently, he stepped away from her for a moment and removed his own so that at last they were both naked. Together they moved on to the bed, and Esther positioned herself above him as he wrapped his arms around her and kissed her deeply, occasionally pushing her back from him a little so that he could stare into her eyes. He felt as if his own were full of affection and desire.

'I want to know every part of you,' he whispered. 'I want to lick you all over. I want to drive you mad with desire.'

'You have already,' gasped Esther.

It was the truth but, although she half-wished for him to hurry up and enter her, there was another part of her that wanted this teasing to go on even longer. It was clear that Christopher was in no rush and that he enjoyed tantalising her in this way. Suddenly he wrapped his arms about her and started rolling around on the bed. Such close physical contact was bliss and Esther felt her arousal reach an even higher level. Her breasts felt swollen, her cheeks were flushed, and there was an ache between her thighs. Eventually Christopher positioned Esther on her back, raised her knees and then parted her legs so that he could kneel between them. Then he put his hands beneath her waist and lifted her up so that he could use his tongue on her stomach and ribcage while his fingers kneaded softly down the sides of her body. Esther was reaching such a peak of physical longing that she wasn't sure how much of this gentle foreplay she could stand. She hadn't realised how many nerve endings there were in her skin. Clearly, Christopher did know and was determined to stimulate them all.

After what seemed an eternity he finally allowed his mouth to move between her thighs and then used his hands to part her sex lips. Suddenly his tongue was moving much more firmly as he ran it in long strokes along the moist inner flesh. When he first touched her clitoris in this way, Esther gave a groan of relief and her hips jerked upwards as she tried to press her pubic mound against his face. She desperately needed some kind of pressure there and Christopher, clearly understanding this, used the palm of one hand and pressed firmly against her pubic bone. After a few seconds he began to rotate the palm of his hand so that beneath his slippery tongue the clitoris itself was moved and the combination resulted in a sudden shockingly abrupt climax that took Esther by surprise. The moment it had ended Christopher continued to lap around the entrance to her sex, not even giving her a short breathing space, and Esther uttered a small sound of protest.

'It's all right,' said Christopher, 'I know what I'm doing.'

Esther felt so unbearably sensitive between her thighs that she wasn't sure he was right. All at once though, she felt her flesh start to tighten again and her belly quaked as he inserted the point of his tongue into her moist opening. He ran it delicately around the inside while with one hand he pressed hard on her lower abdomen. Again, because all her senses were at feverpitch, Esther was startled by a short sharp climax that was so intense it was almost painful. She could hear herself breathing rapidly now and at the same time she was uttering tiny mewling sounds which she'd never done before. She wanted to ask Christopher to stop and yet, perversely, she longed for him to continue, to see exactly what would happen if he carried on this way.

For Christopher it was incredibly exciting. He knew that Esther really wanted him to stop but he could also tell by her responses that she was capable of more orgasms in this way before he even started to penetrate her. Very gently he drew back the hood that was covering the clitoris and allowed his lips to fasten around it. Then he sucked very gently while at the same time his hands firmly massaged her abdomen. Again the result was spectacular and he felt her heaving and shaking as her muscles rippled with the force of her climax. She was uttering strange animal-like sounds and, even when the last ripples of her orgasm had died away, her hips continued to move slightly, which he knew meant she was capable of more.

Eventually he decided that the time had come for him to have an orgasm as well, so he slid himself slowly up Esther's sweat-drenched body, making sure that he kissed every possible inch of her skin as his head travelled upwards until it was resting next to hers on the pillow. His hands entwined with hers and for a few moments he continued to kiss her cheeks, forehead and the corners of her mouth before raising himself up on his arms.

To Esther's surprise Christopher didn't immediately enter her. Instead, he used his penis to continue caressing her clitoris, and all the soft moist tissue around it, driving her half crazy with need. 'Please, I'd like you inside me now,' she whispered.

'In just a moment,' Christopher promised her.

'I don't want to wait any longer,' Esther begged him.

Christopher ignored her and continued thrusting between her outer labia until he felt her body writhing beneath his and knew that he'd managed to give her yet another orgasm before penetration.

For Esther, this climax was more intense than the previous ones but the ache between her thighs was growing steadily worse and she knew the only thing that would ease it would be the fullness that would come when Christopher finally entered her. Unable to stand it any longer she wrapped her legs around his waist and tilted her pelvis upwards so that Christopher was sliding into her, even though she knew he'd intended to wait a little longer. For Esther the bliss was indescribable. At last she felt really full, and as he moved slowly in and out of her, his own pleasure mounting, she felt him adjust his upper body slightly until he had freed his right hand, which he then used on her left breast. He cupped it carefully from beneath and then, using his fingers, squeezed it rhythmically in time with his pelvic thrusting.

The shards of pleasure seemed to be all over Esther now and she felt that at any moment she would explode. Christopher was an expert at prolonging the build-up to final release and she was becoming quite frantic. She heard herself begging and moaning for him to hurry up and let her come but still he continued to move slowly and easily while his hand continued the matching pressure on her breast.

Then, suddenly, the rhythm changed. Christopher's breathing became harsh and gutteral and his hips moved faster and faster. He had positioned himself so that every time he moved his pubic bone was stimulating Esther's clitoris and she knew that she was only seconds away from reaching yet another orgasm. For Christopher the point of no return came suddenly and she heard him give a gasp and then, just as she was afraid that she would be left behind, his fingers gripped her breast almost cruelly. At his moment of orgasm he tweaked her nipple fiercely and caused a searing burst of pleasure to shoot through her and she too convulsed in an ecstasy of release.

As soon as it was over Christopher withdrew from her but he made sure they remained physically close, wrapping his arms around her and gently stroking her back and buttocks for a long time until she had finally come down from the excitement of it all. 'There,' he said with a charming smile, 'I don't suppose that's how Kay would have behaved but it was fun, wasn't it?'

'It was fantastic,' Esther assured him truthfully.

Christopher glanced at the clock on the bedroom wall. 'God, is that the time? I shall have to be going or Rebecca will kill me,' he said.

Esther didn't mind; it had been wonderful and she knew that it would happen again. Furthermore, it was exactly what she'd planned from the start and it was merely an additional bonus that it had proved so highly enjoyable.

'You don't mind if I stay in bed I hope,' she said with a laugh.

'Not at all. I take it as a compliment,' Christopher assured her.

When she heard the front door slam Esther gave a small sigh of contentment and promptly fell asleep.

Christopher was feeling very cheerful as he made his way home. If only Marcus could know, he thought to himself, and then he smiled as he realised that by the end of the tour, when he and Esther would hopefully be a permanent fixture, Marcus would know and would have to imagine for himself what the pair of them had been doing during their weeks together.

Chapter Eight

*T*he final rehearsals on the Friday went well. Both Esther and Theresa gave their best performances so far, and Esther in particular felt very pleased with herself. At last she really was coming to grips with the character and she felt that all she needed now was an audience to make her performance a realised success.

The company's meeting with the press had also gone well and, although Christopher had done most of the talking, each of the members had been allowed to talk to one reporter. Esther had been careful to praise Christopher's dedication and stressed how much time he had given to all of them in order that everyone performed to the best of their ability. She spoke about the happy company atmosphere and how all of them were 'united in their ambition to take the plays to the people'.

Unfortunately, while Esther was talking, she couldn't help noticing that Damon was listening to her and the expression on his face nearly made her lose her train of thought. It was utterly sardonic and she sensed that he totally despised her and all the rest of them who were gushing forth praise – both about the project and Christopher himself. She did see that Damon exchanged a few words with a reporter but wasn't able to hear what he said. When she asked him later he said that, as he felt Christopher and the company had already received more than its fair share of praise, he'd talked about what he hoped people would enjoy most if they came to see them.

On the Saturday the whole company got on the move. As usual there were numerous complaints that the women had brought too much luggage and that it would be quite impossible to fit it into the car and mini bus. Nevertheless, and this was a miracle that regularly occurred within the acting profession, everything was finally safely stowed on board and they set off for Leicestershire. They arrived at four in the afternoon and Esther was astonished at how imposing the estate was.

All that any of them had known about it before was that it was called The Small House and this had conjured up a vision of a rather cosy house with sufficient grounds and space to accommodate visitors winter and summer. In fact, it was a total misnomer. It was only called The Small House to distinguish it from the original big house, which had been demolished in the 1950s. The estate had been in the same family for over 500 years but the owner at that time, following a fire, had decided to adapt two large stable blocks and form a new country seat for his family's future.

The result was very grand indeed. Quite apart from the sheer size of The Small House there were over five acres of ground and, as they drove along the side of the west wing in their somewhat battered mini bus, Esther and Rosie exchanged glances.

'It's a good job I bought a posh frock for meeting the local press tonight,' commented Rosie. 'This doesn't look a leggings and tunic sort of place, does it?'

'It certainly doesn't,' agreed Esther. 'I wonder what on earth it looks like inside.'

All the company had assumed that they would be living in cottages in the grounds but this didn't turn out to be the case. As soon as they drew up outside the main entrance a man of about thirty emerged. Christopher leapt down from the driving seat of his car and went across to shake hands with him. Watching through the windows of the mini bus Esther deduced that this man must be quite important because Christopher was being both charming and slightly obsequious – highly unusual for him. After a short conversation he strolled over to the mini bus and Damon wound down the passenger window.

'It appears we're staying inside the house,' said Christopher, looking quite excited at the prospect. 'Apparently the family live in the north wing and shut up the rest. When they've got people here they open up the rooms in the south-east corner and those are the rooms we'll be using.'

'And where do we perform?' asked Damon.

'That's on the south side too. It's a converted orangery tacked on to the side of the house. It seems there's a ballustraded gallery, so it will be quite like olden days.'

'Do you mean the days when you first started

162

acting?' asked Damon with apparent sincerity. Rosie giggled.

'I meant Elizabethan theatres,' Christopher said coldly. 'They'd like us to park our vehicles round the back, out of sight of any visitors because the grounds are open all the year round. Once we've done that, one of the maids will show us where to take our things.'

'And are we still meeting the local press tonight?' asked Esther.

'We certainly are,' confirmed Christopher. 'From what Sir Michael said it seems that it's going to be quite a smart do so all you girls had better put on your gladrags and full war paint. I'm sure you won't mind,' he added with a smile. 'It's what ladies like doing best, isn't it?'

'I've heard it isn't just ladies,' said Damon in a low voice.

Christopher turned smartly on his heel and walked away from the mini bus. 'What do you mean by that?' asked Esther.

Ellie, who was sitting next to Damon, smiled. 'Damon's just being horrible as usual. Last year Christopher developed this nervous rash and apparently he used to wear make-up even in the day when he was giving interviews and things, to hide it. Then he decided that it suited him so much he'd always wear it.'

'But he doesn't, does he?' asked Esther.

'I think he uses what we would call a tinted moisturiser,' said Ellie. 'Not that I think there's anything wrong with that. I like a man to look as good as he can.'

'I suppose so,' Esther agreed doubtfully. She knew that in theory there wasn't anything wrong

163

with it but she still felt it was excessively vain even for an actor.

Fortunately there were plenty of rooms for them, all large and incredibly plush with highly expensive pictures, gorgeous drapes at the windows, and magnificent four-poster beds. The entrance hall had enchanted Esther; it had an iron staircase balustrade copied from an eighteenth-century Irish design and a beautiful crystal chandelier hanging from the high ceiling. According to Christopher there were originally two libraries in the house although the second one had been converted into a drawing room in the past year. All in all, the surroundings were so sumptuous that the entire company felt uneasy. It was an incredible contrast to their rehearsal room in London.

Esther was relieved to find that she wasn't expected to share her room with anyone. She knew that Christopher and Rebecca were sharing, as were Ellie and Damon and Noel and Michael. Both Mary and George had their own rooms but Theresa and Rosie had doubled up. Esther felt utterly spoilt. Her room was so vast that it could have slept three since it contained a double bed and a chaise longue large enough for any of the company to use.

After she'd unpacked she joined the others on their official tour of the house but, like all the rest of them, it was the converted orangery that really interested her. All of them were relieved to find that they were acting on a proper raised stage. The acoustics were good and the lighting excellent. The room probably seated about 200 people, possibly 250 at a push, which meant that they really needed to play to full houses for most of the week if they were to make a good profit.

'According to Sir Michael the tickets are selling very well,' Christopher told them. 'That doesn't mean that we haven't got some work to do still. Remember, while we're here we're not only doing *Time and the Conways* but two potted Shakespeares.'

'That's rather lucky,' said Nicholas. 'If we weren't, I can't imagine what *I'd* have to say to the press.'

'Where are you sleeping?' asked Rosie.

Nicholas hesitated. 'He's sharing with me,' George said quickly.

'George has asked me,' admitted Nicholas. 'I suppose I might as well – it seems a bit greedy to take up a whole room to myself,' and he looked meaningfully at Esther.

'I can't remember, which other Shakespeares are we doing while we're here?' asked Rosie.

'My dear, we're doing *Macbeth* and *Lear*!' exclaimed George. 'I'm not just here to admire you all, you know; this is going to be my finest hour.'

'I hope so, George,' said Christopher. 'Make sure you remember which night you're doing it and stay off the bottle that day.'

'It's Wednesday, isn't it?' asked George.

'No it isn't; it's Thursday,' said Christopher irritably. 'For God's sake at least get that right when you talk to the press. Now has anyone got any questions?'

'What time do we meet up tonight and where?' asked Damon.

'Seven thirty for eight in the drawing room,' said Christopher. 'If you get lost just ask one of the servants; there seemed to be plenty of them around.'

'I think I could get used to living like this,' said Ellie.

'Well I'm sure your friend in the West End will do his best to allow you to,' said Damon, rather too loudly for Ellie's comfort.

After that they all went back to their various rooms and had a rest before the evening's events. Esther couldn't decide what to wear. She finally settled on an outfit that she'd bought for one of Marcus's opening nights. It was an incredibly expensive trouser suit, dark beige in colour with a silk and wool jacket that had a high Mandarin collar and black double-button fastenings across it. They were a fiddle to manage but the effect was very striking. The jacket was long-sleeved and tight-fitting as far as the waist where the buttons ended and the jacket then fell loosely to just above her knees. The matching tapering trousers had a black seam down the outside of each leg and beneath them she wore a pair of opaque tights with satin-heeled loafers on her feet.

Just before she went down to join the company she looked at herself in the mirror and was delighted with the overall effect. Her blonde hair, freshly washed and blow dryed, flicked up perfectly on her shoulders and she'd swept the front back slightly to give herself a more sophisticated look. She'd also taken extra care over applying her make-up, accentuating her eyes but playing down her mouth to allow her bright-blue eyes to have maximum impact. The tight-fitting jacket accentuated her voluptuous figure and she knew that she should certainly appear in any photos. Wondering what the other girls had decided to wear, she finally left her room.

She was one of the last to arrive in the drawing room and the Clifford family, the owners of the house, were all there mixing with the rest of the group. It was impossible not to notice Ellie, who had decided to play the vamp and was wearing a highly seductive evening dress in black velvet with a satin ribbon tied in a bow around her waist and a frothy chiffon skirt that ended well above her knees. The dress was sleeveless and the deep plunging V of the neckline was highly impressive, although it would have been more so if she'd had the right figure for it, thought Esther. As it was, it rather emphasised the fact that she was relatively slim. Nevertheless, with her dramatically scarlet mouth and long silver earrings worn with a matching necklace she certainly made an impact. Rosie was wearing a fairly simple long skirt and blouse, as was Mary Fuller, but Rebecca couldn't fail to catch the eye.

She was standing next to Christopher – who was resplendent in a dinner suit – and had swept her raven hair back off her face but allowed one long strand to fall behind her left ear and down over her shoulder while the rest was pulled back into a sleek, tight chignon. Her dress was very unusual. The top of it was rich black satin; around her waist there was a highly dramatic jewelled translucent panel, rather like a cummerbund, while the bottom half of the dress was dark-blue satin cut at an angle in a wrap-over style which, considering that it was above her knee at its lowest point, meant that she showed an incredible amount of extremely attractive and slender thigh. There were a lot of men gathered around her and Christopher, and Esther suddenly wondered if her own outfit was too taste-ful and not dramatic enough.

This thought was confirmed when a young woman sidled up to her awkwardly. 'Excuse me, but can you tell me who any of the actors are?' the woman asked. 'I'm new on one of the local papers and I haven't a clue who anybody is. Are you a reporter too?'

'No, I'm one of the actors,' said Esther with a smile.

The reporter went scarlet. 'I'm so sorry,' she said quickly. 'To tell you the truth your face looked a bit familiar so I thought you must be from round here.'

Esther shook her head. 'No I'm Esther Reid and I play Kay Conway in *Time and the Conways*.'

The reporter quickly got out her notebook but then, as she was about to begin writing, she sud-denly looked Esther straight in the face in astonish-ment. 'You're Esther Reid? That's why I recognised you! You used to go out with Marcus Martin, didn't you?'

Esther wondered if this was ever going to end or if she'd spend the rest of her life being known as the woman who once went out with Marcus. 'That's right,' she said with a strained smile.

'So, why are you here?' asked the reporter tact-lessly. 'It's a long way from Hollywood isn't it?'

'It certainly is,' agreed Esther. 'The truth is that Marcus and I are following rather different career paths now. Basically, I've always felt that I'm a stage actress at heart and that's why I was so delighted when Christopher invited me to join the company.'

She continued chatting to the reporter in this

vein for some time but was extremely grateful when at last Damon crossed the room to rescue her. 'Esther, there you are,' he said with unusual warmth. 'There's someone who's absolutely dying to meet you. Do excuse us,' he added with a smile at the reporter, and then, putting one hand beneath Esther's elbow, he guided her to the side of the room.

'You looked as though you were getting a bit tired,' he said, his tone unusually gentle.

'I was,' said Esther. 'Do you know, I don't think I'm dressed quite right for this evening.'

Damon's eyes moved slowly up and down her figure and she felt her cheeks starting to go hot. 'You look great to me,' he said at last. 'Classy too, not like some over-dressed tart.'

'I'll take that as a compliment,' said Esther.

'It's certainly the nearest I'll ever get to one,' Damon conceded. 'Have you eaten anything yet?'

Esther confirmed that she hadn't and together they went across to where the buffet was laid out on a long table. Unfortunately, just as they'd started talking, Rebecca arrived and led Damon away to meet someone who was 'anxious to talk to him'. Esther was bitterly disappointed. It was the first time that Damon had been even remotely civil to her and she had definitely seen admiration in his eyes when he'd looked at her. Despite the incredible sex that she'd recently had with Christopher, she knew that it was still Damon she really desired, but she also felt certain that they were never going to get together.

Eventually the evening came to an end and shortly after midnight all the actors returned to their rooms. The next day was their final run-

169

through, so each of them knew how important it was that they got a good night's sleep. Because it was important, Esther found it more difficult than usual to drop off and at three in the morning was still wide awake. In the end she picked up a magazine from the bedside table. It was mainly about agricultural developments in the twentieth century and this finally proved sufficiently boring to send her to sleep. However, when she awoke in the morning she still felt tired and thoroughly unrefreshed.

They worked hard all day Sunday. They had to get the set up, test the lighting, work out where they were to change and in addition give their first performance on a stage since they'd begun rehearsing. Even the ever cheerful Rosie was subdued by the time they finished at eight o'clock and when Christopher said that they'd been invited to join the Clifford family for an evening meal there were groans all round.

'I'm certainly not going to sit there and eat for their entertainment like some kind of tame monkey,' snapped Damon. 'I'm going into town and having something in a local pub. Does anyone want to join me?'

Esther felt very tempted but then Christopher looked over at her. 'You'll join us, won't you, Esther?' he asked anxiously.

'Of course,' she said brightly, inwardly fuming at her own weakness but knowing that it was important that she still remained close to Christopher if she were to achieve her goals. She saw a fleeting look of distaste cross Damon's handsome features and then, without another word, he was gone.

By eleven o'clock that night, Esther knew that Damon and Ellie had made the right decision. Mary and George had also gone with them, which left the other eight to be bright, cheerful and optimistic. Esther was beginning to wish that she'd never heard of *Time and the Conways* as she explained for the third time that evening to one of the other guests exactly what the play was about while at the same time trying to disguise the twists and turns that were meant to make it entertaining. At this stage she was beginning to wonder if it was actually entertaining at all and if anyone would gain any pleasure from it. She knew, however, that was the way actors usually felt just before they opened in a play.

At last they were all free to go back to their rooms and it was with a sigh of relief that Esther, slipping on a short satin nightshirt, slid between the thick damask sheets and laid her head back on the soft pillows ready for a good night's sleep.

Esther wasn't certain what it was that woke her; what she was certain of was that she had been asleep for some considerable time. As she started to drift back into consciousness she was startled to realise that there was someone else in the large double bed with her. Just as she was about to scream she felt a hand cover her mouth in the darkness of the room and then Christopher's familiar voice was whispering in her ear.

'It's all right, it's only me.'

As he withdrew his hand Esther gave a sigh of relief. 'You really frightened me,' she said accusingly.

'Sorry,' apologised Christopher. 'I had this

sudden irresistible desire to make love to you while
you were asleep. Unfortunately, you woke up
before I could.'

'I prefer to be awake,' said Esther, still feeling
less than happy.

'Well you are now so that's OK, isn't it?'
responded Christopher, and she felt one of his
hands start to slide up her leg until it reached the
hem of her satin nightshirt. To her annoyance her
body instantly started to respond to him and she
turned on her side to allow him easier access.

Christopher gave a low laugh and drew her
closer to him. 'It will help relax you before
tomorrow,' he promised her as his hands continued
their upward movement and began to softly stroke
the undersides of her breasts.

At his words Esther remembered that tomorrow
was the big opening night and suddenly she wasn't
sure that this was a good idea. He seemed to sense
her doubts because immediately he started to carefully massage each of her breasts in turn while at
the same time pressing his erection between her
parted thighs, allowing it to brush across her pubic
hair before easing its way between the cleft at the
bottom of her buttocks.

Esther's pulse was quickening now and suddenly
tomorrow didn't matter – tonight was all that
counted. She started to reach out for the bedside
lamp but Christopher quickly stopped her. 'It's
exciting in the dark,' he whispered.

Esther had to agree with him. There was something very arousing about feeling his hands moving
over her and having his lips trail across her neck
and face without there being any eye contact
between them. It enabled her to feel even less

inhibited than she had the first time they'd made love. Reaching down, she started to caress the head of his penis before letting her hand slide lower to begin to massage the root of his erection. Christopher's response was to start nibbling at her earlobes and then they were rolling around in the double bed together until finally they finished up with her pinned beneath him.

Esther was longing for him to remove her nightshirt and she was just about to say so when, all of a sudden, the room was flooded with light. With a startled exclamation Esther pushed herself upright and stared over Christopher's shoulder to see Rebecca framed in the bedroom doorway.

Rebecca's eyes were blazing but what astonished Esther the most was the other girl's outfit. She was wearing thigh-length leather boots and a figure-hugging micro dress, also in black, which ended about an inch above the top of the boots so that a tiny area of flesh was exposed. In her hand she carried a riding crop and, as Esther continued to stare, Rebecca closed the bedroom door behind her and walked further into the room.

'What does she think she's doing?' asked Esther in astonishment.

'She's come to join us,' replied Christopher, his beautiful voice almost a caress in itself.

'I'd rather she went,' said Esther firmly.

'Don't be so narrow-minded,' said Christopher. 'You'll enjoy yourself, I promise.'

'Not if she intends to hit me with that riding crop,' said Esther.

'Don't worry,' said Rebecca, 'the riding crop isn't for you. It's for Christopher later on.'

Esther frowned, bewildered, but, before she

could ask any more questions, Rebecca strode across the room and pulled the duvet off the pair of them. Again, Esther gave a cry and attempted to grab the duvet back, but it was no use. It was beyond her reach. Christopher was now crouching over her unfastening the buttons of her nightshirt and peeling it off her, just as she'd wanted earlier, only now the whole atmosphere in the room had changed.

Christopher too had changed. He no longer seemed the gentle caring lover that he'd been the first time they'd had sex together; instead there was a strange kind of frantic excitement about him and Esther felt that it was Rebecca who was controlling the whole situation.

'Did you bring everything we needed?' Rebecca asked Christopher, totally ignoring Esther as she lay naked and exposed on the bed.

'Yes, it's all in the box over there,' replied Christopher. 'The trouble was I woke her up before I could get properly started.'

'It doesn't matter,' said Rebecca. 'You're not going to make a fuss are you, Esther?'

Esther, who was now pinned to the bed by Christopher's hands gripping her shoulders, didn't quite know how to reply. 'I might do,' she said defiantly.

'I doubt if anyone would hear,' said Rebecca, 'and, anyway, what on earth would Damon Dowden think?'

'Why should I care?' asked Esther, but the uncertainty in her voice gave her away.

'It's all right,' Christopher assured her again. 'We're all going to have a great time, I promise you.'

174

Then he straddled Esther's prone body and, still keeping her fixed to the mattress with his hands, began to move his buttocks so that he was caressing her with his lower body and the tip of his penis. As he pushed himself higher up her body he moved his hands and pressed her breasts together so that they surrounded his glans. She could feel his velvety flesh between her soft round globes. Despite herself she was becoming aroused and was both alarmed and excited when she felt a hand between her thighs.

'You're getting very moist,' said Rebecca with amusement. 'It seems Christopher's right and you are going to enjoy this after all.'

Esther wished that she could deny it but her treacherous body was already betraying her and her excitement was mounting rapidly.

'These white damask sheets are perfect,' Christopher remarked to Rebecca as his lover placed a large cardboard box beside him on the bed. He then turned to look into Esther's blue eyes. 'You're going to be our picnic table,' he explained.

'Picnic table?' asked Esther, totally out of her depth.

'That's right. Think of yourself as an enormous plate. Rebecca and I are going to spread the food around on your body and then we're going to eat it. But we aren't going to use knives and forks, just our lips and tongues. It should be delicious for all of us but you have to keep quite still or else the food will fall off. Anyway, tables don't usually move around when you're eating off them, do they?' He laughed with obvious delight.

Esther allowed the other two to spreadeagle her and then she lay there fascinated as Rebecca carefully began to spread various types of food on different areas of her body. She spread some special body chocolate across Esther's belly and, above that, slices of fruit: pears, bananas and small segments of satsuma. Then, as Esther fought to stop herself from trembling in her excitement and so dislodging anything, Rebecca spread some soft cream cheese over Esther's swollen breasts, taking care to cover the nipples entirely.

'Remember now,' said Christopher, 'you must keep absolutely still, which means of course that you mustn't have an orgasm.'

Esther was unbearably excited by his words, which she knew were designed to make everything even more difficult for her, and once again she fought to subdue the treacherous trembling and quaking of her muscles as she became more and more aroused.

The true depth of the exquisite torture, however, only became apparent when Christopher and Rebecca began to eat. Rebecca chose to lick the body chocolate from her stomach while Christopher bent his fair head next to his lover's dark one and, with almost unbelievable delicacy and precision, slowly nibbled at the segments of fruit. Every now and then his teeth would graze Esther's soft white flesh beneath and she would catch her breath as hot darts of pleasure spread through her erogenous zones.

It was when the other two parted and sat each side of her, slowly starting to lick and suck at the cream cheese that was covering her nipples, that her orgasm really threatened to take over. As she tightened in anticipation Christopher, sensing the danger, nipped sharply at the soft underside of one of her breasts to remind her that it was forbidden.

As the cream cheese was slowly removed, so the sensitive flesh of Esther's nipples was freshly aroused by the touch of the cool air in the room. They stiffened and extended and she heard Rebecca's soft laugh as the other girl, sensing the huge struggle that was consuming Esther, took hold of her left nipple and very lightly tickled it with the end of one finger. Immediately, Esther flinched and Christopher swiftly slapped her lightly with the back of his hand across her belly so that she was still once more.

'We haven't finished eating yet,' he reminded her. 'What on earth would our host and hostess think if they found food all over their damask sheets?'

'I can't help it,' murmured Esther. 'Not when Rebecca does things like that.'

'Leave her alone, Rebecca,' said Christopher. 'You're only meant to eat food, not touch her in any other way.'

'I couldn't resist it,' confessed Rebecca. 'She looked so hot and needy. Is that how you feel, Esther?'

Esther groaned in acknowledgement and Rebecca pretended to be sympathetic. 'You poor thing,' she said sweetly and then, to Esther's horror, she took a small jar of honey and very slowly and deliberately poured the liquid between the crevice of Esther's thighs. Esther could feel the sticky substance trickling over her sex. The honey slid between her buttocks and formed a small pool on the sheet beneath her.

It was a blissful sensation and she gave a tiny

cry of pleasure. Christopher and Rebecca began to lap at the honey, both licking and sucking on her at the same time until finally it was impossible for Esther to follow their instructions. The bottoms of her feet flattened against the mattress. She felt her legs bend at the knees, almost against her own volition, and then she was thrusting her pelvis upwards, trying to force their insidiously gentle tongues to stimulate her harder. As she moved, the first wave of her climax began to ripple through her, building to a huge crescendo until suddenly her whole body was racked by a spasm of release that went on and on while Rebecca and Christopher watched in silent appreciation.

When Esther was finally still, Rebecca disappeared into the adjoining bathroom and then came back with a sponge and towel which Christopher used to wash and dry Esther's body. When he'd finished, she fully expected the pair of them to leave but, instead, Christopher pulled her upright until she was in a sitting position and then very softly he stroked the side of her face.

'You did enjoy that, didn't you?' he asked her earnestly.

Esther nodded, unable to admit out loud how delicious it had really been.

'That's good,' he continued, 'because now I want you and Rebecca to really please me. Will you do that?'

'Of course,' said Esther in some surprise.

'Does she know what it is that you like the best?' Rebecca asked abruptly.

Christopher shook his head. 'No, I thought I'd leave you to explain that.'

'I rather imagine my outfit's already done it,'

said Rebecca, looking Esther directly in the eyes for the first time. 'Have you got the picture, Esther?'

Esther frowned. 'Well, I . . .'

'Oh come on,' Rebecca said irritably, 'Christopher likes to be dominated. I don't wear this for my own amusement, you know, although it is quite a turn-on in the end, as I'm sure you'll learn.'

Esther swung her legs over the side of the bed and watched in some surprise as Christopher suddenly threw himself down on the bedroom carpet. Rebecca stood over him, her hands on her hips and her legs on either side of his. He was entirely naked and propping himself up slightly on one arm, looking up at her with an expression of submission on his face.

Esther could hardly believe her eyes. This wasn't the Christopher Wheldon that she'd seen on the stage, or the man who'd shared her bed a few nights before. This showed an entirely different side to him, and one that she found far less appealing.

'Come on,' said Rebecca. 'We're in this together you know. It's a pity there's nothing you can wear that's suitable, but you could blindfold him. Have you got anything that would do?'

'I've got a scarf,' Esther suggested.

'That'll be fine,' said Rebecca. Christopher turned his head to see where Esther was going and Rebecca swiftly grabbed hold of his hair, pulling him into a sitting position. 'Stay right there,' she said angrily, pressing the hard leather riding crop firmly against the naked skin of his spine as he remained with his head between her parted thighs, his mouth level with the hem of her mini dress.

As Esther returned with the scarf she saw that

Christopher's tongue was busy trying to lick at the flesh of Rebecca's inner thigh. Rebecca realised this at the same moment as Esther, and she swiftly raised the riding crop and brought it down with considerable force on Christopher's shoulder. 'Don't you dare do anything unless you're asked,' she hissed.

As Esther stood over the prone actor in order to blindfold him she saw that he was already fully erect and there was a tiny drop of clear fluid hanging on the tip of his penis. He was clearly very excited and this gave Esther the courage to tie the scarf over his eyes. She tugged hard at the knot, taking a perverse satisfaction in the grunt that he gave as she did so.

'I think you could get quite good at this,' drawled Rebecca.

Esther rather doubted it but, nevertheless, when Rebecca ordered her to tip Christopher's head back and then start kissing him, she did enjoy the sensation of power, especially when he twisted and turned in her grasp and she had to press her hands firmly against his ears before lowering her mouth and then thrusting her tongue deep inside his mouth. It was clear that he was delighted by her action. She felt his tongue clash with hers and then their lips were almost glued together, only there was nothing soft and sensual this time. Esther realised that it was like having a male sex slave and the sheer thrill of this realisation was an aphrodisiac in itself.

For the next half-hour she and Rebecca forced Christopher to kneel, crouch, grovel and even crawl around the room. Every time he was too slow to respond to their instructions, or if Rebecca considered that he was too close to coming, he would be struck firmly on each of his buttocks in turn with the riding crop.

Eventually, Rebecca left Christopher in a totally submissive position, kneeling but bending forward with his forehead on the carpet and his hands bound loosely behind him. His knees were spread apart and it was then that Esther had the brilliant idea of sliding her naked body beneath his face so that, although he couldn't see her, he could feel her breasts pressing against him. In a voice that she scarcely recognised as her own, she ordered him to start licking and sucking at each of her breasts in turn.

Rebecca applauded silently and as Christopher busied himself obeying Esther's instructions Rebecca carefully lubricated the middle finger of her right hand and then very gently eased it into his rectum until her knowing fingers located his prostate gland. 'I'm going to massage this for three minutes,' she told him in a clear voice. 'I don't expect you to come until the three minutes are up, do you understand me?'

'I can't last that long,' whimpered Christopher in a plaintive voice.

'If you don't, you'll be punished even more severely,' Rebecca promised him.

Esther realised that this had only served to heighten his excitement. 'You've stopped licking my breasts,' she complained, and she heard the riding crop rise and fall as Rebecca punished him for this omission. Immediately Christopher started to lick and suck frantically and suddenly Esther's whole body shook with a tiny orgasm which she hadn't even realised was imminent but which had been triggered by his absolute submission to the two women.

Christopher continued to do as Esther had ordered him while Rebecca remorselessly massaged his highly sensitive prostate gland. It was only then that Esther realised what a long time three minutes was because Rebecca counted the seconds out aloud and, with every one that passed, Christopher groaned and gasped more helplessly. Esther stretched out her right hand and let her fingers brush the purple glans. 'No! Please don't do that,' Christopher begged her. 'I can't stand any more. I'll never last.'

Esther hadn't meant to arouse him further; she'd only wanted to see exactly how near to coming he was, but she realised that he was having to use incredible self-control to endure what Rebecca was doing to him.

Finally, Rebecca was down to the last ten seconds and Christopher was gasping like a man in agony. Despite this Esther could tell that he was more excited than she'd ever seen him. She thought that he wasn't going to make it as his tongue worked faster and faster on her aching breasts but, finally, the three minutes were up. At the very last second, as Rebecca massaged even more firmly, Christopher came in a series of shuddering jolts. Esther cupped a hand round the end of his erection so that she could catch the hot sticky white fluid.

When his climax was over Rebecca swiftly removed the binding from around his wrists and Esther removed the scarf that had covered his eyes. He rolled on to his side, sweat pouring down his face, and stared up at the pair of them. 'You were both fantastic,' he said enthusiastically. 'What a night!'

Within ten minutes he and Rebecca had departed, leaving behind the sexually satisfied but highly confused Esther. She'd never experienced anything like it in her life, and still wasn't certain that it was something she would want to do again, although it had been incredibly arousing. Unfortunately, the resulting confusion of emotions meant that sleep proved very elusive and, when she awoke the next morning, she knew that she was going to find it very difficult to get through the important opening night.

Chapter Nine

As Esther made her way towards the theatre the next morning she met Rebecca on the landing. The other girl gave her a sideways glance but there was no smile or any acknowledgement of what had passed between her, Esther and Christopher during the night. Esther slowed her pace, allowing Rebecca to go on ahead of her. She felt incredibly tired and was reluctant to arrive and begin rehearsing. Suddenly she heard footsteps on the stairs behind her and turning round saw Christopher approaching. He waved and smiled happily at her. Unlike Esther he seemed totally refreshed and full of energy.

'The big day then,' he said, reaching out and squeezing her round the waist.

Esther stiffened slightly and Christopher looked at her in surprise. 'What's the matter?'

Esther couldn't explain. It would be ridiculous for her to try to pretend that she hadn't enjoyed last night and yet now, in the cold light of day, she knew that what she had witnessed meant that she was no longer particularly attracted to the golden boy of acting. Esther enjoyed equality during sex but she'd never felt any desire to dominate and, although last night had been a highly arousing experience, it wasn't one she wanted to repeat. Neither had she particularly liked having Rebecca there witnessing her in her most intimate moments. What did surprise her was how quickly her body had responded to what had happened. She wondered if her sexuality was more complex than she'd previously imagined.

'You enjoyed last night, didn't you?' continued Christopher as they walked through the beautiful hallway.

'I'd have thought that was obvious,' said Esther.

'It certainly was!' Christopher agreed. 'I thought it would be a great way to celebrate when tonight's over. Perhaps this time you'd like to come to our room. We've got more gadgets and things there and could make it all much more complex this time. What do you say?'

Esther didn't know what to say. The truth was that she had absolutely no intention of joining him and Rebecca after the performance. On the other hand she knew that it must appear she was still keen on him if her plan was going to succeed. Quite apart from anything else she needed Christopher to continue helping her with her role, and she also wanted the outside world to think that the pair of them were close. For a fleeting moment she wondered if Marcus was really worth all this effort. Certainly she wanted to prove to him that she was a good stage actress but was it necessary to include a personal relationship with Christopher as well? Finally deciding that it was, that this would hurt

Marcus even more than any success she might achieve as an actress, she forced herself to smile back at the waiting Christopher.

'I'm sorry, I'm a bit distracted this morning,' she confessed.

'First-night nerves,' said Christopher briskly. 'You'll be fine once you get going. Don't worry, I've got every confidence in you.'

During that morning's run-through Esther thought that Christopher probably had a lot of time to regret those words because her performance felt flat and stale. Luckily she wasn't the only one, but they all knew that this was common. For a start, each of them was saving their energy for the evening. There was no point in going for broke when they'd got a full performance to give to a fee-paying audience in a few hours' time. All this was really just a form of reassurance both for them and for Christopher and George, who had undertaken the role of deputy director since Christopher was on stage for such a great deal of the play.

When they broke up for lunch Christopher gave a few final notes but they were only minor ones. He told them all that they were marvellous and that he just knew it was going to be tremendous. They were free to do what they liked until six that evening, by which time they had to be in their dressing room.

Rosie asked Esther if she would like to join her, Noel and Michael at the local pub and she agreed because she didn't want to be alone with Christopher and Rebecca. Just as they were setting off, since it was within walking distance, Theresa suddenly barred Esther's path.

'I hope you're satisfied,' said the red-haired girl

angrily. 'What's your problem? Are you trying to prove that Marcus made a mistake or something?'

'What's all this about?' asked Noel in surprise.

'You'd better ask Esther.' Theresa spat out the words.

'No, I'm asking you,' said Noel.

'It's only that Esther's become very friendly with our director,' said Theresa. 'His private tuition extended beyond the play, didn't you know that?'

'Did it really?' asked Michael, raising an eyebrow in some amusement. 'Good for you, Esther. That explains why he talked so gushingly about you to the local press.'

'Did he?' asked Esther in surprise.

'Sure, I overheard him telling them that you were the most exciting discovery he'd made for years. He was saying that you were going to be one of the great actresses of the next generation.'

'That's gilding the lily a bit, isn't it?' said Rosie, and then she looked apologetically at Esther. 'Sorry, but you must admit it's a little over the top.'

'It's a nightmare,' said Esther in horror. 'The way I acted this morning they'll think he's off his head.'

'He probably is,' said Theresa shortly. 'What did you do to ensnare him?'

'I really don't see what business it is of yours,' said Esther, trying to push past the other girl.

'Don't lie,' said Theresa angrily. 'You know perfectly well that he and I have been lovers.'

'Darling,' drawled Noel, 'we honestly aren't that interested in who you're sleeping with. It could have been anyone, except me that is.'

'You or Michael,' said Theresa spitefully. 'You always share a girl, don't you? What's the matter, can't one of you satisfy a woman on your own?'

Rosie giggled. 'Yes they can,' she said enthusiastically. 'It's just that they're so generous they like to give double helpings of pleasure.'

'I'm sure you know,' retorted Theresa.

'Oh yes,' Rosie readily agreed. 'I know and it's totally delightful. You're just jealous, that's your trouble. Anyway, Rebecca's Christopher's full-time girlfriend so you can only ever have been a bit on the side.'

'Well, what does that make Esther then?' Theresa demanded.

Rosie and the two men glanced at Esther, waiting for her to answer. 'I haven't a clue what you're talking about,' said Esther, and at last she managed to push past the angry girl and continue walking down the long drive of The Small House.

Once they were in the pub she knew that she was going to have to say something to the other three. Rosie had been totally honest with her and, although they didn't particularly like Theresa, none of them would think she'd have said what she had if there wasn't any truth in it.

'Here you are,' said Noel cheerfully, placing a large plate of assorted sandwiches in the middle of the table while Michael handed round the drinks. 'Eat as much as you can; you won't feel like eating tonight.'

Esther knew this was true. She always felt horribly sick before performing. It was only afterwards that she became starving. 'About what Theresa said,' she remarked awkwardly.

'Oh yes, do tell,' said Michael eagerly, not making any pretence at lack of interest.

'It's true that I'm having an affair with Christopher,' Esther confessed.

188

'Good for you!' said Rosie. She exchanged a knowing glance with Esther, remembering how Esther had told her that this was one of her main aims in joining the company.

Noel pulled a doubtful face. 'Are you sure he's the right one for you? I'd have thought he was far too self-centred, and he's never faithful to anyone. Let's face it, Rebecca's meant to be his girlfriend and it looks as though he's been knocking off Theresa *and* you behind her back.'

Esther didn't like to tell them that it wasn't exactly behind Rebecca's back. 'I know it isn't anything serious,' she assured him. 'It's just one of those things.'

'Well as long as it keeps you happy,' said Michael. 'I did think your performance had improved a lot.'

'But not today,' said Esther, the corners of her mouth turning down.

'Today doesn't count,' Rosie assured her. 'We were all hopeless today, even Christopher. He fluffed his lines several times and that's never happened before.'

'It won't happen tonight,' Noel said firmly. 'Both he and Damon are far too professional to allow that.'

'What I'm nervous about,' said Michael, 'is Theresa's performance as Madge. I'm the one who's on stage with her when she's ranting on about socialism and equality, and if the main thing on her mind's really Christopher and who he is or isn't bonking then I hardly think she's going to deliver one of the greatest performances of all time. If she starts vamping me again I don't know what I'll do.'

189

'Cut and run,' suggested Noel with a laugh. 'The audience will probably sympathise with you.'

They all laughed and after that the conversation became more general as they discussed what kind of an audience they might get, whether the local press reviews would be kind to them, and how the following night's potted *Macbeth* would go.

'I think *Macbeth*'s going to be very interesting,' said Noel as they got ready to return to The Small House. 'Nicholas is playing Banquo as though he were Macbeth and Christopher's going to have to pull out all the stops to match him.'

'That's because Nick feels he ought to have been given Macbeth,' explained Esther. 'He is rather being left out of things. Christopher must have taken him on for a reason but he isn't going to have much to do. Apart from the Shakespeares he isn't in anything.'

'You could hardly put him in anything by Coward, could you?' said Michael. 'The trouble with Nick is he doesn't accept his own limitations. He's very good indeed at the things he's good at, if you get my meaning. The problem is he wants to be brilliant at everything and it just isn't possible for him. Personally, I know my place only too well. Parts like Gerald I can do standing on my head. I look right, I speak right, and the way I see it I should be able to maintain a steady if not spectacular career for a long time in these kinds of roles.'

'What about when you get old?' asked Rosie.

'I shall retire gracefully and set up an agency,' said Michael. 'Then I shall concentrate on gorgeous nubile young actresses and finding them parts. I shall take great pleasure in that and with any luck so will they!'

'I'm sure there are rules against agencies like that,' said Esther with a smile.

'By then there won't be any rules about anything,' said Michael. 'The whole country will be flooded with young actors and actresses coming out of drama school and they'll be so desperate for an agent they won't care if I'm legit or not. Seriously though, I do think I shall set up as an agent in the end once I've made enough contacts and the parts start drying up.'

'The parts start drying up much sooner for women,' said Rosie. 'It really isn't fair but men improve with age and women get discarded, certainly as far as films and television are concerned. As for the stage, well there just aren't that many parts for older women.'

'You poor thing,' said Noel, patting her on the head as though she were a dog. 'I'm sure it won't matter to you, Rosie. You'll be married with about half a dozen children by then.'

'I don't want half a dozen children!' said Rosie in horror.

'Well, you're so dizzy you'll probably have them anyway,' laughed Noel.

Having lunch with the three of them lifted Esther's spirits considerably and she felt much more cheerful. She was grateful that she didn't meet any of the rest of the cast as she made her way back to her room. Once there she lodged a chair firmly under the door handle and then lay down for a rest. When she awoke at four thirty she had a bath in the old-fashioned enamel bathtub and then started to prepare herself mentally for the evening that lay ahead.

It never ceased to surprise her how the hour

from six to seven before a play would go very slowly but then the last half-hour, when you could hear the audience taking their seats and the hum of their voices rising steadily, flew by so that one minute you had endless time ahead of you and then suddenly you were expected to go out there and start performing.

She'd exchanged first-night cards with all the members of the cast and particularly liked her one from Damon. It was a picture card of an old-fashioned music hall singer, blonde and not dissimilar in appearance to Esther. It was titled A Bird in a Gilded Cage and Esther smiled to herself. She didn't keep all her cards but collected the few that she found particularly unusual or striking and decided that this was definitely one for her collection.

All too soon came the call for beginners and Esther made her way slowly to the wings. She wasn't the first to go on; Ellie and Rebecca had to open the play then Noel joined them within the first page and Esther was only a few minutes after that. The palms of her hands were damp and her stomach was churning incessantly. She couldn't wait to begin now, because until she did she knew that her nerves would continue to overwhelm her. All at once she heard Theresa as Madge give her her cue line: 'Look here, we ought to be starting. Kay, we ought to be starting.' By the time she'd finished the second sentence Esther was on stage as Kay and the play was finally under way for her.

Afterwards she could never quite believe just how great a disaster her performance had been. It was probably her worst ever and the reason was that every time her eyes met Rebecca's or Christo-

192

pher's she was catapulted back to the events of the night before. She could even feel the pair of them, feel their lips taking food from her naked flesh, and Rebecca's fingers insinuating their way between her thighs. She couldn't understand why it was impossible for her to drive these thoughts away and concentrate instead on the play, but she simply couldn't and the result was mortifying.

In the intervals between the acts Esther noticed that everyone carefully avoided speaking to her. They weren't being unkind. It was the only thing to do in the circumstances and, as she'd already had three prompts, she knew that even the most unsophisticated member of the audience would be well aware of the fact that she wasn't doing well.

As she staggered through to the end of the final act her spirits began to lift slightly. At least once it was over the nightmare would end for tonight, if not for the whole tour. She heard Noel as Alan say, 'No, I don't ... understand,' and knew that now she was coming to the quotation from Blake. She tried to remember what Christopher had told her and, at last, a little passion crept into her voice as, being careful to let it break dramatically now and again, she started to recite. She thought that it was going well, and that at least the audience would remember something good at the very end, but then disaster struck. As she came to the last two lines she got the end words of the lines transposed and, to her horror, heard herself saying, 'And when this we rightly go safely through the world we know.'

The moment the words were uttered, Esther broke out in a sweat. She simply couldn't believe

that she could have done something so unpro-
fessional. After that her mind went blank. Luckily
there were only a few moments of the play left and
for several of them Esther was positioned with her
back to the audience looking out of the window,
meant to be lost in her own reverie. In actual fact
she was perilously close to tears, and at the very
end of the play, when she had to turn towards her
brother, Alan, while the lights dimmed around
them until only a spotlight was left on the pair, her
tremulous smile was not an act.

When she came off stage Esther felt as though
she were in a waking nightmare – one which would
never end. She was so distracted that if Damon
hadn't caught hold of her by the hand and pulled
her back on stage she would even have forgotten
to take her bow. She managed to smile prettily at
the audience and the applause was tumultuous but
she knew that none of it was for her. She'd been
diabolical; there was no other word for it.

Finally, Christopher stepped forward from the
line and spoke to the people at the front. As he
began to thank them for their appreciation there
was a spontaneous burst of applause that went on
for at least a minute and he smiled modestly and
charmingly with a humility that, to those who
knew him, was probably the best performance he'd
ever given. At last it was all over, and the audience
trooped out into the night and the actors returned
to the dressing room to remove their make-up and
costumes and return to their everyday selves.

All around Esther people were congratulating
one another: 'Darling you were wonderful.' 'Terrific, the audience loved you.' The words reverber-
ated in her head non-stop but no one spoke to

Esther. In a way she was grateful because she would hate to be given false compliments.

Forcing herself to enter into the spirit of the thing a little, she congratulated Rosie and Rebecca on their performances because they'd both done very well. Rosie smiled her thanks but didn't offer false congratulations in return. Rebecca merely shrugged, as though Esther's words were of no significance to her whatsoever.

As Esther was standing in her slip removing the very last vestiges of make-up with cold cream she saw in the mirror that Christopher was standing a couple of inches behind her and their eyes met in the glass. Christopher's were cold.

'What the hell was all that about?' he asked angrily.

'I'm really sorry,' Esther said quietly. 'I know I was dreadful and there's just no excuse.'

'Was it nerves? Did you panic or something?' Christopher demanded.

'I don't know,' persisted Esther. She couldn't possibly tell him because she needed him to believe that she still desired him if she was to carry her plan through to fruition.

'Well, don't let it happen again,' said Christopher. 'I told all the reporters at the press night how wonderful you were going to be. You've made me look a complete fool.' At that he turned and walked angrily out of the room.

'At least you saved him the trouble of doing it himself,' said Damon quietly.

Esther glanced over her shoulder across the room to where Damon was sitting in front of his mirror. 'What do you mean?' she asked.

'You know perfectly well what I mean. He can

make a fool of himself at any time without help from you.'

Esther laughed nervously. 'That's not very kind and he was extremely good tonight.'

'Sure, he was OK but he wasn't exactly challenged, was he?' said Damon.

'You were good too,' Esther added. 'I think you were more powerful than you've been in rehearsals. Rebecca seemed quite taken aback.'

'Did she?' queried Damon. 'I imagine it would take a lot to disturb Rebecca.'

'She was still good,' Esther murmured. 'I thought everyone was good except me.'

'You've got to put it behind you,' said Damon. 'It's fatal to dwell on nights like this. We all have them, you know,' he added more gently. 'It's probably your lack of stage experience showing. I expect it'll be a completely different story next time. Maybe you'll outshine us all.'

'Right now I don't care if there isn't a next time,' Esther exclaimed passionately. 'I think perhaps I'm better off in television where you get a chance to do re-takes.'

Damon's eyes narrowed. 'Somehow I've never pictured you as a quitter, Esther,' he remarked. 'What you need is a drink and a quiet chat. I know there's some kind of a party going on but I don't imagine you feel like going, do you?'

'I certainly don't,' she said.

'Then let me take you into the village. There's a really nice little restaurant where we can get something decent to eat, have a civilised glass of wine and talk about things.' He saw the expression on Esther's face. 'Not the play,' he promised her. 'Other things.'

196

She was very touched by his kindness, especially since no one else in the cast had taken the trouble to say anything in the least sympathetic to her. 'That sounds nice,' she agreed.

'I'll meet you outside. We can easily walk, then it doesn't matter how much we drink,' said Damon.

Left alone, Esther hurried to dress. Suddenly she was beginning to feel better. It was the first time that Damon had been in the least bit agreeable towards her and the prospect of an evening alone in his company was very attractive. She realised once again that it was Damon she really fancied. The trouble was, Damon wouldn't make Marcus jealous. Their paths had simply never crossed and it wouldn't matter in the least to Marcus if the pair of them were having an affair. Nevertheless, she knew instinctively that she was going to have an enjoyable evening and hoped that it would help take away the memory of the night before: a night that she couldn't deny had been a valuable experience but not one she wished to repeat.

'Where the hell's she going?' Christopher demanded as he saw Esther and Damon disappearing into the night.

'To enrol at drama school?' suggested Rebecca.

'I suppose you think that's funny,' said Christopher.

'It is quite,' laughed Rebecca. 'Mind you, I wasn't the one praising her to the skies and making her sound like the next Vanessa Redgrave.'

'I can't think what was the matter with her,' said Christopher. 'I really did think she'd got to grips with that part, you know.'

'Perhaps she didn't get enough sleep last night,' said Rebecca.

'Well, if I have my way she won't get a lot tonight,' said Christopher with a smile. 'I thought it would be fun to repeat the experience. In fact I've suggested to her that she should join us in our room. Not that I knew then that she'd be going out with Damon Dowden for the evening. God, she's got appalling taste, first Marcus and then him.'

'Why do you want her to join us again?' queried Rebecca. 'Aren't I enough for you?'

Christopher ran a hand through her long dark hair. 'Of course you are,' he reassured her. 'It's just that it's so much more exciting when there are three. Maybe we could get Theresa to join us if Esther's going to be late back. What do you think?'

'You're wasting your charm on me,' Rebecca pointed out. 'I know you're an actor, remember? And since you ask, no I don't want Theresa to join us. I'd like it to be just the two of us.'

Just then someone called Christopher's name. 'Look I've got to go to this damn party,' said Christopher, irritably. 'You know I promised them that I would. You're coming, aren't you?'

'I'll be along in a minute,' said Rebecca, a weary tone to her voice.

'I hope you're not going to prove tiresome,' said Christopher. 'I hate it when women play games. I just haven't got the time for it.'

Rebecca watched him go and bit on her lower lip. His charm was definitely losing its appeal for her and she was beginning to grow tired of his need to be dominated or be joined by another woman. It had been fun at first but she wanted him to start spending more time alone with her. She

198

was still very keen to have plenty of experimental sex but didn't see why they needed a third person for that. She could think of lots of things they could do on their own. She was also getting rather tired of pandering to his professional ego.

She knew that she could give a better perform-ance than she had tonight but she was deliberately toning it down a little because she was due to play Lady Macbeth opposite his Macbeth the next night. Rebecca knew that if he thought for one moment that she was going to be too good he'd have replaced her without a second thought – probably with Ellie Ford.

As she wandered disconsolately in the darkness Rebecca suddenly bumped into Nicholas. 'Are you going to the party?' he asked her.

'Yes, in a minute,' confirmed Rebecca.

'What's the matter?' asked Nick. 'You sound a bit low.'

'Tired I guess,' said Rebecca.

'You were absolutely brilliant, you know,' enthused Nick. 'I couldn't take my eyes off you.' He paused for a moment. 'To tell you the truth I never can,' he said in a low voice.

Rebecca took a step nearer to him. He'd already made his feelings for her plain, and once or twice during rehearsals in London they'd come very close to having an affair, but she'd always drawn back at the last moment because of Christopher. Now, sud-denly, Nick was becoming more attractive to her and she moved her body so close to his that their hips were touching. 'Isn't there somewhere we could go?' she suggested. 'Somewhere quiet where we could be alone?'

'Sure,' said Nick. Then he stopped for a moment.

'Aren't you going to the party? It's back at The Small House.'

'I promised Chris I'd meet him there later on but I'm not his exclusive property, you know,' said Rebecca.

'I didn't imagine you were,' said Nick, 'but I can't afford to upset him at the moment. None of us can, come to that.'

'It doesn't matter. How could he find out?' asked Rebecca. 'Neither of us are going to tell him, are we?'

'Of course not,' Nick laughed.

'Where shall we go then?' asked Rebecca.

Nicholas thought for a moment. 'I know. If we go along the gravel path by the west side of the house there's a secluded spot near the wall with a long bench where we can sit. No one goes there; it doesn't lead anywhere.'

'Sounds perfect,' said Rebecca.

Nicholas took her by the hand and as they walked together round the building she felt his thumb caressing the inside of her palm. Even before they reached the seat they began kissing, and Rebecca found his firm strong grip and demanding mouth very arousing. It was also nice to be the object of such adoration because when she was with Christopher she was always aware that the person Christopher most admired was himself.

As they reached the seat, Nicholas's hands found the gap between Rebecca's black palazzo pants and silver lurex top. Sliding them upwards he made a sound of appreciation as he realised that she had nothing on underneath. Immediately his hands started to caress her breasts. 'You're wasted on him,' he muttered thickly, his mouth close to Rebecca's ear.

Privately Rebecca was beginning to agree but she didn't respond because she was trying to concentrate solely on the sensations. Nick was less gentle than Christopher but there was no doubting his enthusiasm and within a few seconds he was easing Rebecca back on to the bench until she felt the ivy that clung to the walls of the west wing of the building tickling her hair.

The night was cool but her body felt hot and she made no protest when Nick started to remove the lurex top. When the air hit her hot flesh she felt her nipples grow instantly erect and uttered a tiny cry of delight as Nick's tongue started a slow descent from the base of her neck down between her breasts. At the same time his hands were on her hips, tugging at the palazzo pants and forcing them downwards until they finally fell around her ankles. Rebecca quickly kicked off her shoes and then managed to remove the trousers as well so that she was lying sprawled in a semi-reclining position, her upper body totally nude and with only the protection of her flimsy, pink silk bikini pants to protect her from the night.

Nick was also sprawled on the seat but he was positioned above her with one hand taking his weight at the base of the back of the seat and the other insidiously working its way through her pubic hair. In the distance Rebecca could hear the sounds of people chattering and laughing and this added to her excitement.

She felt Nicholas's fingers wandering through her dark pubic hair. Suddenly he pulled lightly on a few strands and when she jerked in response he laughed softly before repeating the procedure several times. To Rebecca's surprise this had the effect of bringing her very near to the point of orgasm and, as her body gathered itself together, she let out a soft sigh of contentment. Immediately Nick stopped what he was doing and instead knelt down on the path, leaving her feeling momentarily very exposed.

Then his hands were parting her knees and she felt them on her inner thighs but, instead of stroking them, he used his nails to scratch very gently at this highly sensitive area. Rebecca's hands reached down and she tried to pull his head upwards so that he would use his mouth on her but he refused to do what she wanted. Instead he gently drew a piece of skin at the top of her left thigh into his mouth and then with great deliberation closed his teeth on it.

The result was an increase in desire that had her moving more and more restlessly on the seat. He then resumed his gentle scratching, only this time he allowed his hands to wander over the crotch of her panties until he located her swelling clitoris beneath the material and rubbed it very lightly.

Rebecca knew that the silk panties were becoming very damp. She could feel them sticking to her, moulding themselves to every nook and cranny. As he started to use his tongue on the material, her flesh beneath swelled rapidly and she thought that she had never been so desperate to come. Her sex was hot and throbbing and when he carefully grazed her clit through the panties with his teeth Rebecca's body spasmed as it prepared for orgasm again.

Once more, Nicholas changed position, easing

himself back up on to the seat so that he could pull Rebecca's upper body against his chest and allow her to stimulate her nipples against his jumper. His right hand pulled her panties to one side and then, at last, he straddled her upper thighs and she felt his thick penis moving up and down the moist channel of her inner lips. She thought then that she was finally going to orgasm but, for some reason, her body let her down and she realised she desperately wanted him inside her; wanted to be taken for a change instead of having to be in charge, as was so often the case with Christopher.

'I want you inside me,' she gasped to Nicholas as his glans continued to slide up and down her sex, slowing in pace when it was near the shaft of the clitoris.

'Are you sure?' he asked, teasing her.

'Yes! Yes!' she shouted, quite forgetting that they were out of doors and that her well-trained voice would carry easily on the night air.

'All right, then,' said Nicholas and suddenly he thrust into her with such force that her body was slammed back against the seat. She gasped aloud, and he seemed to be lost in his own world as he pumped furiously, his hips moving faster and faster while his hands gripped her round her upper body, his nails digging into her flesh.

She was amazed at how well he filled her, and also delighted at how long he was able to continue thrusting. At last the fire that he had kindled was allowed to take light and spread. Rebecca's whole body came alive before the sensations drew inwards, centring in that one vital spot set behind her clitoris. She was so excited now that she couldn't control herself and, reaching round him she tried to slide a hand down the back of his jeans, which he hadn't bothered to remove, in order to stimulate him, but he moved his body slightly so that she had to draw her hand back again.

'I'm in charge tonight,' he reminded her.

'Yes! OK!' gasped Rebecca, hoping that her body hadn't lost its rhythm. She needn't have worried because Nicholas now proceeded to launch an erotic onslaught on almost every part of her body using mouth, lips, tongue, teeth, hands and fingers while all the time he continued to thrust fiercely. At last Rebecca felt her belly tighten, and her internal muscles quake, and then she exploded into orgasm with a scream of delight that sounded more like a wild animal than a human being. The moment she'd come Nick came too, still thrusting fiercely into her and calling her name over and over again as his body spasmed and the veins on his neck stood out like whipcords.

When he finally withdrew, Nick helped Rebecca to dress and then pulled her roughly against him. 'Wasn't that great?' he asked.

'Terrific,' Rebecca agreed breathlessly.

'Are you sure you've got to go to that party?' asked Nick.

Rebecca thought for a moment. 'I suppose so,' she conceded. 'I don't want to, but like you said we really can't take any chances with Christopher right now. The tour's only just beginning.'

'When can we meet again?' asked Nicholas.

Rebecca hesitated. 'I don't know, but I'll make sure we don't have to wait long,' she promised him.

'You will be watching me tomorrow night in *Macbeth*, won't you?' he asked anxiously.

'I'll be watching you all the time from now on,' Rebecca promised him with a smile.

Taking her hands, Nick drew her to her feet. 'I think we're more alike than you imagine,' he said.

Rebecca suspected that he was right but she wasn't going to tell him as much right now. 'I don't know what you mean,' she said.

'I think you do,' he replied. 'You need a real man.'

'And you don't think Christopher's a real man?'

'Not if what I've heard's true,' said Nicholas.

'Well you mustn't believe all the gossip you hear,' laughed Rebecca.

'You mean I'm wrong?' persisted Nicholas.

'Did I say that?' Rebecca asked him and then, before he could question her any further, she started to run down the path and away to the party.

When Rebecca got to the main entrance of The Small House she stood for a moment checking that her clothes were in order and trying to cool her hot cheeks. Her skin was still tingling and she could remember only too clearly how Nicholas had felt as he'd thrust so savagely, almost primitively, in and out of her, satisfying her far more in those few moments than Christopher ever did with their long, complicated sex sessions. Nevertheless, Nicholas couldn't help Rebecca get on in her profession and, for the moment, her body would have to be satisfied mainly with Christopher. Just the same, she was going to make sure that she and Nick were able to enjoy each other again before too many days had passed.

When she finally felt composed enough she walked into the house and quickly found the party.

'Sorry I'm late,' she said to Christopher as he frowned at her.

'Where did you disappear to?' he demanded.

'I needed air and then I met some fans.'

Christopher's eyes lit up. 'You talked to some of the audience?'

'Yes,' Rebecca lied.

'What did they say?' he asked.

'They thought it was terrific and they particularly liked your performance,' she said with a smile. She knew that this would take Christopher's mind off where she'd been.

'Great!' exclaimed Christopher. Then he tried to hide his self-satisfaction. 'I mean, it's great for the whole company, isn't it?'

'It certainly is,' agreed Rebecca.

After that they mingled with the other guests for a while and Rebecca made sure that she hung on to Christopher's arm and gazed at him adoringly every time a camera was near. This was what he expected and it was also what would help her. She was very pleased to realise that in general the first night had been a success. It seemed that despite Esther's failure the play had caught the audience's imagination and lots of people were promising to tell their friends to make sure they came on the Wednesday night.

It was one in the morning by the time she and Christopher were able to go back to their room and Rebecca's body now felt utterly exhausted. As she started to undress she saw Christopher staring at her. 'What's the matter?' she asked.

'You've got red weals all over your back and there are bruises at the top of your left leg on the inner thigh, look,' said Christopher.

Rebecca glanced down at her thigh and realised that it was where Nick had bitten her. As for the marks on her back, they must have come from where she'd been pressed up against the back of the wooden seat. 'I was standing leaning against the wall when I was talking to those fans,' she said casually. 'It must have grazed my back.'

'Well it couldn't have bruised your leg,' said Christopher.

'I've no idea how that happened,' said Rebecca. 'Do I have to account for every bruise that appears on me?'

'I think you owe me some kind of an explanation, especially when you've disappeared for half the evening,' he retorted.

'That's an exaggeration,' said Rebecca, trying to stifle a yawn. 'Most of the evening we were performing the play, remember? The play in which you were such a success.'

'I was, wasn't I?' said Christopher, the smile returning to his handsome face. 'No,' he said suddenly to Rebecca, 'don't put your nightdress on. I'd rather you put those on instead.' Rebecca's eyes followed the movement of his hand and, when she saw the leather boots, riding crop and black-leather mini dress laid out on the bed, her heart sank. Just the same, she knew that the sensible thing to do was go along with him. If she didn't he'd be even more suspicious and, on the plus side, she'd be sure to have another orgasm.

She did eventually but, as she came, standing astride Christopher while his tongue busied itself between her thighs, she couldn't help remembering how it had been with Nicholas. She knew then that sooner or later she was going to leave this golden-haired boy of the theatre.

Normally Rebecca never thought about anyone else but as she finally fell asleep that night she did wonder what on earth Esther Reid could have found to talk about with Damon Dowden after they disappeared that night. She hoped that Damon hadn't been too hard on her because, if he had, it certainly wouldn't help her next performance. She was pleased that he'd taken Esther out, though, because it had saved Rebecca from having to endure another long session which involved them both.

In the early hours of the morning Rebecca awoke to find Christopher lying on top of her, his penis deep inside her as he moved slowly and silently in and out of her body. He was often like this when he was riding high on success and she sleepily allowed him to bring her to a gentle but pleasurable climax. But this didn't make her change her mind; she was beginning to realise that her sexual tastes were no longer the same as Christopher's.

Chapter Ten

While Rebecca had been enjoying herself with Nick, Esther and Damon were also getting to know each other.

'Where's Ellie tonight?' she asked Damon once they had been served their food. She'd ordered a lasagne and side salad and Damon had chosen a mixed grill. The restaurant was small but beautifully furnished with dark wooden beams and highly polished brass ornaments. There were only two other couples eating there and it provided exactly the kind of calm and peaceful atmosphere that Esther needed after the debacle earlier that evening.

'I'm not sure,' said Damon. 'I think she said she was going to the party with Mary and George.'

'Mary and George?' Esther couldn't keep the surprise out of her voice.

Damon smiled. 'They both adore her, didn't you know? It will suit Ellie down to the ground to have two admirers.'

'But she's already got you,' Esther blurted out.

Damon frowned. 'No one "has" me, Esther,' he said softly.

'That's not what I meant,' said Esther. 'The two of you are lovers, aren't you?'

'On and off,' he conceded.

'So why does she need George and Mary's admiration?'

'Because I don't provide everything she needs, I guess,' laughed Damon. 'Besides, I think our affair's nearly run its course.'

'Well, surely she isn't planning on an affair with Mary?' retorted Esther.

'Not Mary, no,' agreed Damon. 'George, however, is a different matter.'

'Don't be ridiculous!' said Esther. 'George is old enough to be her father. He isn't rich and he isn't particularly attractive. Why on earth would she want to have an affair with George?'

'Because George adores her and Ellie can't resist adoration,' he explained. Then he shrugged. 'The truth is, Esther, I've no idea who she'll be sleeping with next or why and quite frankly I'm not a bit interested.'

'Oh,' said Esther in a quiet voice.

'Are you feeling any better yet?' Damon asked after a short pause.

'Not really,' she replied. 'It's not just that I messed that piece of poetry up; I was awful all through the play. I was never Kay; I was always me dressed up in Kay's clothes, and I'm furious with myself. I wish I could go back and do it all again. I'm capable of doing it so much better.'

'Agreed,' said Damon. 'You did very well at one

of the rehearsals recently. I expect it was Christopher's private tuition,' he added.

'I expect it was,' she agreed. She wasn't feeling calm but she had no intention of letting Damon know what was going on in her mind. As she sat opposite him she was beginning to wonder how she could ever have been attracted to Christopher when Damon was around.

It wasn't just that he was incredibly good-looking – that was fairly common in their profession – but he had tremendous character in his face. Also, the fact that he was quiet and secretive made him far more interesting than the majority of actors she'd met. Most of them would tell you their life story within the first five minutes of meeting you, whether you wanted to hear it or not. She only wished she knew what Damon felt about her.

'Why did you join the company, Esther?' he asked.

'Because I was invited,' she explained.

Damon raised his eyebrows. 'You mean he approached you?'

'No, but he invited me to join.'

'Hardly the same thing, is it? Perhaps I should have been more precise. Why did you decide to audition to join the company?'

'Because I wanted a change,' said Esther. 'I wanted to get away from the spotlight; away from the photographers and all the gossip about Marcus and me.'

'So you chose to join a high-profile touring company starring a man with an ego second only to Marcus's, right?' asked Damon.

'Put that way it does sound a bit odd,' Esther

agreed. 'But like a lot of things it seemed a good idea at the time.'

'I don't think you're telling me the whole truth,' said Damon.

'That's your privilege,' retorted Esther. 'Since we're on the subject, why did you join? It's perfectly obvious you loathe Christopher and I don't think you particularly like the plays. Besides, you could have had far better roles in other companies. After your Iago you must have had loads of offers.'

'Not necessarily,' said Damon. 'You know what it's like in our business: you can do really well at something and then be out of work for a year.'

'So you didn't get any offers?' asked Esther.

'A few,' he admitted.

'Then why did you join Christopher Wheldon's company?' Esther persisted.

'Perhaps I had a burning desire to bring the classics to the people,' drawled Damon.

'Yes, and perhaps you didn't,' she remarked.

'It seems,' said Damon slowly, 'that both of us are telling lies. Perhaps we'd better change the subject.'

Suddenly Esther was overwhelmed by a desire to tell Damon the truth. It was clear that he already suspected her motives and suddenly she wanted everything to be above board with him, at least on her side. It was up to him whether he chose to confide in her or not. She rather suspected, however, that no matter how frank she was with him he wouldn't spill the beans. All the same, she decided to take the plunge.

'Do you honestly want to know the truth about why I joined?' she asked.

Damon sat up straight in his chair. 'Yes, I do,' he admitted.

'I joined to get my own back on Marcus,' said Esther. 'He hated Christopher. Well, he probably still does, and he also tried to keep me off the stage. He used to tell me that I was better suited to television but at drama school they wanted me to try and pursue a stage career.'

'You aren't being strictly fair to him. Maybe he thought that TV was a good stepping stone to the stage,' Damon pointed out. 'These days it often is done that way round.'

'You're playing devil's advocate, aren't you?' said Esther.

Damon nodded. 'It's a habit of mine,' he confessed.

'You could be right but I don't think so,' she said. 'Anyway, I wanted to get back at him and this seemed the best way. I thought that if I did really well as an actress, and if my name was linked with Christopher, however tenuously, then when the news got back to Marcus he'd be furious. Jealousy was one of his big weaknesses.'

'I don't wish to be unkind,' said Damon, 'but if Marcus isn't in love with you any more do you really think it will bother him if your name's linked with Christopher's?'

'Yes,' Esther said firmly. 'The thing about Marcus is, he isn't really that confident. Oh, he is when it comes to acting, but not in other respects. If he thought that Christopher Wheldon liked me, that we were what I call "an item", he'd start to question whether he'd done the right thing in dumping me. Be honest, Claudine isn't anyone really; she's just an extremely pretty face and –'

213

'She's certainly that,' Damon interjected.

Esther sighed. 'Are you trying to make this more difficult for me?'

'Sorry,' he said swiftly. 'I didn't mean to interrupt.'

'I expect it all sounds very petty and boring to you,' said Esther, a trifle curtly, 'but it matters to me. At least it did in the beginning. Now I'm not quite so sure. Anyway, if I'm an utter flop on the stage, then the plan isn't going to work, is it? I'll have done all this for nothing.'

'Not exactly for nothing,' said Damon.

'What do you mean?' she asked.

'You've managed to become linked with Christopher. Perhaps that will be enough on its own to infuriate Marcus.'

Esther felt a little uncomfortable. 'I haven't read anything about us being linked together,' she said swiftly.

'I wasn't talking about the press,' explained Damon. 'No doubt that will follow but it's generally accepted within the company that the pair of you have been sleeping together. Are you going to tell me that's not true?'

Esther hadn't expected him to be so direct. 'It's true,' she muttered.

'Well I hope it's worth it for you,' remarked Damon. 'Does Rebecca know?'

Esther was highly relieved that Damon didn't know anything about the threesome she'd had with Christopher and Rebecca. 'She probably guesses,' she said, 'but I don't think she's too bothered at the moment, particularly after tonight.'

'And is that it?' Damon asked her.

'Yes,' said Esther.

'I'm in no position to make any comment at all really,' said Damon. 'As you rightly suspected my motives for joining aren't exactly as pure as the driven snow. I happen to think Christopher Wheldon's acting ability is vastly overrated and I think this whole tour is going to be a disaster. However, like you, I joined for more personal reasons.'

'Do you want to talk about them?' asked Esther.

'I think perhaps I do,' said Damon, obviously surprised at himself. 'I've got a half-sister, Suzie, and she was at the RSC with Christopher. She's incredibly highly strung and only twenty now. She's also beautiful. One of the most beautiful girls I've ever seen. Naturally Christopher fell madly in love with her and although she was only a junior they became lovers. Probably partly because of this, but also because she's got amazing talent, they were cast opposite each other as Beatrice and Benedick. They both got good reviews only, sadly for her, Suzie's were even better than Christopher's.

'About two days after the reviews appeared she went back to the house they'd been sharing in Stratford and found he'd changed the locks. That was how she discovered she'd been dumped. After that he made her life absolute hell there. Suddenly she was relegated back into the ranks and although she had offers from other companies she didn't take any of them up. All she could think about was Christopher. It was Christopher morning, noon and night and when she wasn't talking about him or trying to ring him up then she was sitting sobbing her heart out.

'In the end she had to get some counselling and at the moment she's given up acting completely. I wish you'd seen her. She really was something very special, and he's ruined her. I decided that I was going to make him pay for what he did to her and that's why I'm here.'

'But how are you going to get your revenge?' asked Esther.

'That's the problem,' admitted Damon, 'I haven't worked it out yet.'

'Perhaps we ought to join forces,' suggested Esther.

Damon looked at her intently and she found herself wondering once more what he'd be like in bed. 'That might be a good idea,' he conceded.

'What would hurt Christopher the most, do you think?' asked Esther as they waited for their desserts to arrive.

'I suppose failing as an actor,' said Damon, 'but I can't see that happening.'

'I think you could out-act him,' she said. 'You're just as talented, you've got more stage presence and a far stronger role as Ernest Beevers. I know Christopher doesn't like the middle act of *Time and the Conways* when he's playing Robin as a weak drunkard. If you could really dominate that scene then he might not pull himself together for the third one.'

'I know something else that would hurt him,' said Damon.

'What?'

'If his ability to assess true talent is called into question. I know he's been boosting you to the skies but after tonight he's going to dump you very smartly and I imagine that he'll go back to pushing Rebecca, who was accepted as his protégée before your arrival on the scene.'

'But Rebecca is good,' said Esther.

'She's good, but she isn't brilliant,' said Damon. 'If she was, Christopher wouldn't have her around him, not after what happened with Suzie.'

'Rebecca's also clever,' explained Esther. 'She knows what she wants and where she's going and she knows that she needs Christopher to achieve it all. She isn't going to make the same mistake as your half-sister.'

'I know that,' said Damon. 'Obviously she isn't going to out-act her own boyfriend, particularly if it's going to ruin her career, but since he's promoting her, think how wonderful it would be if she failed. Not only failed but failed in front of a really big audience – an audience who mattered.'

'I don't see how we could make that happen,' said Esther. 'It's a brilliant idea but it isn't feasible.'

'I think you're wrong,' said Damon. 'We do have one advantage.'

'What's that?' queried Esther.

'It's the fact that I'm playing Rebecca's husband in the middle act. I have to show that I'm a bully who dominates her, and that's a dreadful contrast between the way things are at the beginning and end of the play. The audience are meant to be shocked to realise that this pretty girl with the whole world at her feet is quite probably going to end up married to a man who treats her appallingly and doesn't even love her. They're meant to feel really sorry for her, and at the moment they probably do.

'The thing is, I could be far more dominating than I have been and I could also play things slightly differently in the first act so that Rebecca will already be on edge by the time the second act starts. She's the sort of person who has to feel in full control. It will only take a couple of fluffed lines and she'll totally lose her cool. I think that if I manage to make her feel I *am* dominating her, that she's paling into insignificance, then she'll start to fall apart. Christopher warned me not to over-shadow her before we left London, remember?'

'That's true and I suppose it's possible,' conceded Esther. 'If you are successful, where are we going to get a really big audience who matter?'

'Haven't you heard?' asked Damon.

'Heard what?' asked Esther.

'About the grand finale,' explained Damon. 'At the end of the tour we're giving an open-air per-formance of *Time and the Conways* in Regent's Park. Christopher's been pulling strings all over the place and he's got loads of agents coming along with a couple of American talent scouts. Obviously he's invited them there to see him and, presumably, either you or Rebecca, too. I imagine that at the time he hadn't decided which of you it would be. Now, if Rebecca and Christopher both give poor performances on that night but you and I give strong ones then we'd feel that we'd really got our revenge, wouldn't we?'

'I imagine so,' said Esther, although she was slightly doubtful.

Damon's eyes narrowed. 'Of course, I forgot, you wanted to be sleeping with Christopher.'

'Not necessarily sleeping with him,' said Esther quickly. 'Quite honestly I'd rather I didn't any more, but I'd quite like people to think that I was.'

'Even if he's going to fail?' asked Damon. 'If you and I are going to shine you'd be better off if people thought you were sleeping with me!' He laughed and Esther wished that he hadn't.

'Do you really think we could manage it?' she asked anxiously.

'Yes, if we work bloody hard between now and then,' said Damon.

'I shall have to string Christopher along a bit,' said Esther. 'I'm going to tell him that I'm channelling all my energy into rehearsing my part. That way I can avoid sleeping with him without denting his pride.'

'Good thinking,' said Damon. 'One possible thing that could bring us down is if you and I don't perform well enough. Have you thought of that?'

'I've thought about it with regard to myself,' said Esther, gloomily. 'You won't have any problem but heaven only knows what I'm going to do.'

Damon leant closer to her across the table. 'Listen,' he said softly, 'I'm more than willing to give you as much tuition as you need. We can work on all the parts you'll be playing as often as you like but we've got to do it in secret. Neither of us must give any suggestion of how well we're going to act until that last performance. I shall continue playing Ernest Beevers the way I have been all along, and as long as you give a reasonably competent performance both in that and as Ophelia, when you play opposite the great Christopher's Hamlet, then no one will get suspicious. We'll only pull out all the stops on the final night.'

'It means we're going to have to spend a lot of time together,' said Esther.

'I'll try and make it as painless for you as possible,' Damon said dryly.

'I didn't mean I wouldn't enjoy it,' said Esther.

'Don't worry, I'm not like Christopher. I don't

219

expect you to sleep with me as well. In fact I'd rather that you didn't.'

Esther's heart sank. Even as he'd been telling her of his plan she'd been plotting how she could use this to her advantage in getting Damon's attention directed at her. Now he was making it perfectly clear that he didn't want her. And yet she was sure that she wasn't mistaken when she sensed that he was attracted to her.

'Don't worry,' she replied. 'I'm as anxious as you are to keep this thing platonic.'

'Good, then we understand each other,' said Damon.

'Presumably Ellie will be relieved as well,' she said.

'I told you, that affair's nearly over,' he replied.

'There's a difference between nearly and completely,' Esther pointed out.

'I do have to watch my words with you, don't I?' said Damon. 'OK, I admit it. I probably will keep on sleeping with her, and why not? We both enjoy it and we know it isn't a permanent thing.'

'Won't she object to the amount of time we spend rehearsing with each other?' asked Esther.

'I don't particularly want her to know,' said Damon. 'If she finds out she'll probably tell the entire company and then Christopher might start to get suspicious. I shall have to work out what I'm going to say to her, but she's used to me having odd moods and disappearing. She doesn't question where I am every moment of the day and night, thank God.'

'Lucky you,' said Esther. 'What a very accommodating girlfriend she is.'

'Yes, she is,' agreed Damon with a weak smile.

Esther decided that she wanted to leave. She wondered why he was so firm in his resolution not to become involved with her. Perhaps it was because he knew she'd already slept with both Marcus and Christopher. However, in their profession, the number of partners you'd had wasn't normally a problem. Whatever his reason he'd made it perfectly clear, and she decided that for the sake of successful revenge she would just have to put her sexual feelings for him to one side and concentrate on her acting. Given her performance tonight it was going to take a hell of a lot of hard work to produce anything approaching a stunning performance by the middle of June.

As they were going, Damon helped her on with her coat and suddenly he caught her face between his hands and looked carefully into her eyes. 'Tell me, Esther, are you professionally ambitious for yourself or just for revenge?' he asked softly.

Esther thought hard about the question. 'Both,' she said at last. 'I've always been far more ambitious than anyone realised.'

'That's good because you've got a lot of talent, only somewhere along the way you've forgotten how to use it,' said Damon, releasing her. Striding out into the car park, he started to walk home. 'Don't worry about it, though, it's nothing I can't put right.'

'You're not very modest, are you?' said Esther, hurrying to keep up with his long strides.

'I don't believe in false modesty,' said Damon. 'I know what I can and can't do.'

'I wish I did,' muttered Esther, half to herself.

'When you work it out then you'll finally realise your full potential,' said Damon.

Back at the house they slowed their steps and Damon suggested that Esther went in ahead of him. 'I'm sure people saw us leave together,' he remarked, 'but just the same, we don't want to make a big thing of it, so you go on ahead of me. I'll follow in a few minutes.'

'All right,' she agreed. 'I take it you'll let me know when we can start rehearsing.'

'Sure,' agreed Damon and then, to her astonishment, he pulled her fiercely towards him and kissed her directly on the mouth. The kiss was a long one, but just as Esther's knees started to buckle he released her and, with a muttered curse, walked away into the darkness of the grounds. Esther felt a tiny surge of triumph. She was right and had been right all along. Damon did care for her but for some reason he didn't want her to know. Well that was something she could cope with. If she had anything to do with it they would become lovers before the tour was over.

Altogether, Esther felt far more cheerful than she should have done when she retired to bed that night. The memory of her appalling performance was already beginning to fade and she was looking forward to her private rehearsals with Damon. She looked forward to the end of the tour when the pair of them would finally get their revenge on Christopher.

'Where's Damon tonight?' Mary Fuller asked Ellie as the pair of them left the room where the first-night party was just ending.

'I've no idea,' said Ellie.

'You aren't bothered?' said Mary in some surprise.

222

'Damon likes to go off and do his own thing,' explained Ellie. 'If he thought I was trying to keep tabs on him he'd soon lose interest.'

'It went very well tonight, I thought,' commented Mary.

'With the exception of Esther, yes,' agreed Ellie. 'It must have been a nightmare for her. Once she had to have a prompt in the first five minutes I knew she was in trouble.'

'I don't know what was the matter with her,' said Mary. 'She's been doing so much better lately. I was really quite impressed and then suddenly she just fell apart.'

'Perhaps she's still missing Marcus,' said Ellie. 'Anyway, for all our sakes let's hope she can pull herself together.'

'What are you going to do now?' asked Mary, looking thoughtfully at the petite, elfin-faced girl standing next to her.

'I've no idea,' said Ellie. 'I shan't be able to sleep; the adrenalin's still flowing.'

'Mine too!' Mary laughed. 'Isn't it terrible? You know you ought to sleep after a play because you're going to be on stage again the next day but you never can because you can't get rid of that buzz.'

'I'm not on stage tomorrow,' said Ellie. 'Christopher wasn't silly enough to put me in his potted *Macbeth*.'

'Oh, of course, I'd forgotten it was that,' said Mary. 'I am in it. I'm the gentlewoman attending Lady Macbeth, but it doesn't entail much work.'

'So what shall we do?' asked Ellie.

Mary glanced at her. 'Any ideas?'

'I've always got plenty of ideas,' said George,

coming up behind the two women and putting his arms around them. 'The problem is no one wants to join in.'

Ellie looked provocatively at him. 'Why don't you tell us one of your ideas,' she suggested. 'Maybe I'd be interested.'

George's eyes lit up. 'That sounds exciting. The trouble with my ideas is that they always require a large cast.'

'Do you mean one large lady or more than one member in the cast?' enquired Ellie with a grin.

'Two average-sized ones would suit me nicely,' said George.

Ellie glanced at Mary. 'I imagine that would suit you, too,' she said.

Mary nodded. 'It would suit me down to the ground.'

'I've got an idea, then,' said Ellie. 'Theresa's been mooning around all evening. For some reason Christopher's ignoring her. Why don't I go and see if she'd like to join the three of us.'

'Join us where?' asked Mary.

'I'm sure we could find an empty bedroom in a house this size,' said Ellie.

'Do you think she'd agree?' asked George in some surprise.

'I think she might,' said Ellie. 'She's been dropping quite a few hints lately and I think her sexual tastes are fairly broad.' With that she disappeared back into the party leaving Mary and George standing in the hall looking expectantly at each other.

'Could be our lucky night, Mary,' said George.

'It looks like it,' she agreed. 'I must say, I think Theresa is delicious.'

'I prefer Ellie,' said George. 'I love girls who are

small and boyish and yet incredibly feminine at the same time.'

'It's Theresa that drives me wild,' said Mary with a sigh. 'Ever since I saw her that night in London I haven't been able to forget her. Let's hope Ellie's successful.'

Ellie was, and within ten minutes the four of them had found an empty bedroom in the guest wing. It was large, beautifully furnished and – much to their relief – it even had a lock on the door. As soon as they were inside George turned the key. 'Don't want to be disturbed, do we?' he said.

'Definitely not,' agreed Ellie.

Theresa looked slightly hesitant. 'What exactly is it that we're going to do?'

'I'm not going to do anything,' confessed Mary. 'I'm afraid I'm rather lazy. I shall just sit in this comfortable chair here and watch anything you two girls choose to do.

'What about you, George?' asked Ellie. 'Are you going to be a participant or a voyeur?'

'I'll start out by watching,' said George, 'but I might join in later.'

Ellie smiled prettily at him. 'I hope you do.'

After George and Mary had settled in their seats, Ellie moved closer to Theresa. 'Why don't we start off by just dancing together the way we do at the beginning of the play,' she suggested to the red-haired girl. Theresa nodded in agreement and, for the next few minutes, the pair of them danced slowly and sensuously in the middle of the room. It wasn't really the way they danced in the play but it was far more exciting and very soon both of them were anxious to proceed further.

Ellie made the first move. Very, very slowly she began to unbutton Theresa's blouse and then stepped back so that Theresa could remove it herself, which she did, turning it into a kind of striptease, moving her body and arms around all the time so that her full breasts, trapped in a tiny half-cup bra, were displayed to their full advantage to the watching couple. When she'd finally thrown the blouse carelessly across the room, Ellie undid the other girl's skirt, pulling it down so that Theresa could step out of it, leaving her standing in her black bra and G-string with black hold-up stockings and black high-heeled shoes. Mary Fuller gave a smile of appreciation and George leant forward eagerly in his chair.

Luckily Theresa and Ellie were about the same height, so it was easy for Ellie to nibble on Theresa's ear and plant butterfly kisses on her shoulders before gradually working her way to her breasts. Theresa started to unfasten her own bra but Ellie stopped her and instead signalled for George to step forward. He almost fell over in his haste and then he was standing in front of the red-haired girl, his hands shaking slightly as he unclipped her bra, allowing it to fall forward on to the floor so that her breasts were finally totally exposed. Immediately he reached around to cup the firm orbs but Ellie, with a half-smile, pointed to his chair.

'You're meant to be watching this, George,' she reminded him.

Reluctantly George returned to his chair and now Ellie was able to resume her ministrations on Theresa's body. She, like the two watchers, was fascinated by the size of Theresa's breasts with their large rosebud nipples and she closed her mouth over one, rolling it between her teeth and drawing her tongue over the rapidly hardening tip while she caressed both breasts with her hands.

Theresa's breathing quickened and her whole breast area swelled as her excitement mounted. The silence in the room was a heavy one, full of sexual expectation. For Theresa it was a very exciting moment. With Christopher and Rebecca she always felt that she was the least important person but here she suddenly felt centre stage and this enhanced her natural sexuality.

She watched as Ellie knelt on the carpet before beginning to kiss her feet and then, very carefully, felt her lift one foot and suck on the toes. It was a delicious sensation but it meant that Theresa's breasts were unattended. Without thinking, she put her own hands on them and started to stroke them softly before suddenly squeezing them hard. Ellie moved her hands and slid them between Theresa's legs, pushing her G-string to one side. Theresa's head fell back a little and her long hair caressed her naked shoulders. When she felt Ellie's hands opening her outer sex lips to reveal the swollen bud within, Theresa pushed her hips forward slightly so that Mary and George could have a better view.

There was no doubt that Ellie was an expert at using her tongue on another woman. As Theresa's clitoris continued to swell, Ellie circled it lazily with her tongue before taking it prisoner in her mouth, tantalizing it by sucking gently but firmly and then nibbling softly. As she worked on the shaking girl with her mouth she allowed her hands to wander behind the tight buttocks until, at last, she was able to slip one slender finger inside Theresa's rectum, stroking with amazing lightness on the paper-thin skin within.

Without any warning Theresa's hips bucked violently as she suddenly came and Ellie sucked even harder on the other girl's clitoris, keeping it imprisoned firmly in her mouth as it tried to retract beneath its protective hood. The incredible intensity of the sensations drove Theresa wild and she felt sweat trickling down between her breasts and heard herself gasping as the muscular contractions tore though her.

'Sit on the end of the bed,' Ellie whispered the moment Theresa's orgasm had finished. Theresa didn't argue; all she wanted was for this exquisite pleasure to continue. As soon as she'd done what Ellie suggested, Ellie started to tantalise her once more with her fingers and mouth, using her skilful tongue on her until she was just about to come again. However, as Theresa felt her body reaching the point of no return, Ellie stopped for a moment and Theresa uttered a wail.

'For God's sake don't stop now!' she cried.

Mary and George were gathered at the end of the bed. They'd been unable to resist the temptation to get nearer and Theresa didn't care; in fact she wished that they'd join in and stimulate the parts of her body that Ellie was unable to reach. Mary looked into the auburn-haired girl's eyes and read the silent appeal there. Sitting on the side of the bed the older woman reached out and very carefully began to massage the skin that covered those delicious swollen globes that so excited her.

'That's wonderful,' Theresa whispered. 'Would you use your mouth on them as well?'

Mary didn't need any second invitation and

228

within seconds Theresa felt a tongue travelling over her left nipple. Suddenly she was astonished to realise that her other nipple was also being tongued, because George had decided to join them.

Theresa allowed her head to fall back on to the bed. She was more than happy for them all to stimulate her in any way they wanted as long as she was able to keep having intense orgasms at the same time knowing that she was exciting everyone in the room. Such power was a heady aphrodisiac.

Ellie kept bringing the prone Theresa to the peak of orgasm with her tongue and fingers between her thighs before stopping so that the hot tightness would build and build inexorably and then, just as Theresa was about to explode, the feelings would start to fade as the stimulation between her thighs ceased. She cried out, begged and beseeched, but Ellie waited and waited knowing that delay would intensify Theresa's pleasure when it finally swamped her again.

Mary briefly left Theresa's side for a moment and placed her capacious handbag on the floor next to Ellie before returning her attentions to Theresa's breasts. Ellie opened the bag and inside found the perfect toy. After bringing Theresa tantalisingly close to the point of no return she stopped and then, as Theresa began to beg and beseech her again, Ellie stood up and showed Theresa what was in her hand.

'Would you like this inside you?' she asked.

'Please, please,' begged Theresa, almost out of her mind now.

'Not much longer to wait,' said George, and Theresa felt herself start to tremble all over.

Very gently and slowly, Ellie licked Theresa's

juices from around her moist entrance and then eased the sex toy inside the prone girl. It was a long, ribbed vibrator and even as she eased it in Theresa's belly began to heave and her head turned restlessly from side to side as she muttered, 'Yes! Yes!'

At the exact moment that the long-awaited climax began, Ellie switched on the power and Theresa felt as though her body was being torn apart by a series of electric shocks. All her nerve endings responded and her tight tortured muscles were finally released in an explosion of ecstasy.

Within seconds of the orgasm dying away Ellie turned up the power on the vibrator and, as it throbbed within the thrashing girl, she moved her mouth so that she could lick and suck at Theresa's clitoris at the same time. Theresa couldn't believe what was happening to her. Both her breasts were being sucked and massaged, sending shooting sparks of pleasure down through her belly and into the cleft between her thighs. That, coupled with the ecstasy of the vibrator and Ellie's amazingly knowing tongue, meant that she was being stimulated in so many places at once her body hardly seemed able to cope and another climax tore through her as she screamed her pleasure aloud.

She looked so enchanting every time she came that the onlookers were transfixed and unable to resist taking her to the peak of pleasure yet another time. Theresa felt at first that she wouldn't be able to bear it but then, as the pleasure mounted rapidly and her nipples grew hard again, she knew that they were right and she was capable of even greater pleasure.

This time after the last tremors of her orgasm

had died away she opened her eyes and looked up at Mary. 'Not any more,' she whispered beseechingly.

Mary stroked the girl's damp forehead and ran her fingers through her tousled hair. 'What you need,' she said quietly, 'is a nice warm bath.'

Dazed and sated with passion, Theresa was led into a tiny adjoining bathroom. Ellie joined her in the bath and, while George soaped Ellie vigorously, Mary did the same for Theresa. The two girls sat looking at each other, each watching to see how the other responded to the attentions they were receiving. Suddenly Ellie straightened one leg and eased her toes between Theresa's sex lips, then she wriggled them very gently. To Theresa's astonishment her body, now so ready for pleasure that it needed only the tiniest stimulation to cause a climax, responded instantly and, yet again, the wave of hot, delicious pleasure flooded over her.

She was relieved when George and Mary left her alone for a few minutes and turned their attentions to Ellie. Now it was Theresa's turn to watch as Ellie knelt in the bath and was brought to orgasm by George's fingers as he lathered her sex and then worked busily between her legs. Mary contented herself with kissing and caressing Ellie's upper body.

Theresa watched with interest as Ellie's tiny breasts with their almost flat nipples slowly began to swell a little and the nipples finally formed hard little peaks which Mary pounced on with delight. As George continued his work, Theresa saw Ellie's flat belly cave in for a moment and then the muscles began to contract and she knew that the other girl was also going to climax. It was so exhilarating watching Ellie come that Theresa, despite all that had gone before, reached down between her own thighs and rotated her hand against herself. To her great delight, she was able to achieve an orgasm at exactly the same moment as Ellie. The two girls quaked and cried out in unison as their pleasure was allowed to come.

Suddenly Mary glanced at her watch. 'I think we'd better get out of here,' she said quietly. 'We ought to be back in our own rooms; it's nearly one.'

Theresa's body felt so heavy that she had to be helped out of the bath by George. He dried Ellie while Mary did the same for Theresa. To Theresa's delight Mary dried her as sensually as she'd licked her breasts. Wherever her hands moved they caressed and fondled so that despite their gentleness they had the effect of causing Theresa to start to get aroused again.

'There's no time,' laughed Ellie, seeing the expression in the other girl's eyes.

'There'll be plenty of other times,' Mary whispered to Theresa, and Theresa nodded sleepily.

Finally, when both the girls were dressed, they made sure that they'd collected all their belongings and the room was in its original state before unlocking the door and going their separate ways.

When Ellie crept into the bedroom that she shared with Damon he was already there and the light was out. 'Are you asleep?' she whispered.

'Yes,' he said.

'That's all right then,' Ellie said casually, and she clicked on the light.

Damon pulled himself up in bed and stared across the room at her. 'Was the party good?'

'Very good,' said Ellie, starting to undress.

232

'Only just ended?'

'No, it ended ages ago but I went on to an orgy,' she said.

'Hope you enjoyed it,' Damon remarked casually and within a few minutes he was fast asleep.

'I certainly did,' Ellie muttered to herself as she climbed into bed next to him. She'd been very surprised by the way Theresa had responded. It had been a good day and, although she had intended to ask Damon where he'd disappeared to, suddenly she didn't care that much. Whatever he'd been doing he couldn't possibly have had as much fun as she'd had.

Chapter Eleven

*T*he week in Leicestershire proved a great success
and provided an excellent springboard for the
entire tour. As the company travelled around the
Midlands, the North and West Country, and then
made their way towards London via some of the
fringe venues, so their fame grew. A month before
they were due to perform in Regent's Park the
Sunday Times ran a huge feature on them, calling
them 'The success story of the nineties'. It praised
them all but particularly Christopher for his innovative idea and for having the courage of his con-
victions that real theatre wasn't dead and that good
plays properly done were what most people
wanted to see.

Although all the members of the company were
asked at various times to give interviews, only
Christopher gave them. He was careful to make
sure that he stressed the ethos of each member
being equally important but at the same time every
interviewer – whether because of what Christopher

said or not – stressed that but for Christopher the tour would never have been such a success. In general the reviews were good, and as time went on they improved.

Esther and Damon, following their discussion over dinner after the opening night of the tour, began work in earnest and, as the weeks went by, Esther felt herself growing in confidence every time she went on stage. But she was careful not to show it too much. She was never bad, and at times she attracted some good notices, but she always kept part of herself in check so that the true extent of her improvement was hidden from Christopher's watchful eye. She knew that he was watching her because he couldn't understand why she had suddenly stopped letting him make love to her. Again and again she'd explained to him that because of the terrible performance she'd given on the opening night she felt that all her energies must be channelled into her work and that, sad as it was, sex was obviously a distraction she couldn't afford.

Christopher listened, nodded and smiled but she knew that he didn't truly believe her. Rejection was something that he hadn't had to handle before and he was clearly at a loss as to how he should deal with it. Rebecca, on the other hand, seemed delighted at Esther's decision and became far more friendly. On the whole the company atmosphere improved because the longer they were on the road the more they formed themselves into a unit, a group of actors against the world, or so it seemed at times. The odd unkind review where one member might be singled out for adverse criticism would unite them even more deeply and quite often Esther realised that when it all ended she would miss the sense of being a part of a special family.

That was one of the problems with acting; you spent a lot of time with people, became intensely involved with them, and then suddenly parted never to meet again. It wasn't so bad if you had someone of your own to return to but in her case there would be no one. She hoped that the fame which would come about if their plan worked would prove sufficient to satisfy her.

Damon didn't only help her with her role as Kay in *Time and the Conways*; he also coached her extensively for Ophelia in Christopher's potted version of *Hamlet*. This had proved very popular with audiences and because the role suited Christopher so well it was difficult for Esther not to be overshadowed by him. The first few times it was performed she knew that she made very little impact and this was confirmed by Christopher's enthusiasm for her performance. 'I think we ought to do something about this,' Damon said.

'Well, I mustn't look too good,' said Esther. 'We're saving that for Regent's Park.'

'I know, but that doesn't mean you have to look like a feeble bimbo. Ophelia's a wretched part but I'm sure you can do more with it than you are.'

As a result of that conversation they spent a lot of hours working on it, on the nights that *King Lear* was being performed, which neither of them was involved in. 'You know,' said Damon, sitting on the edge of Esther's bed, 'it's the mad scene that we need to crack.'

Watching him, Esther wished that he would give some indication that he fancied her. The problem was she was becoming keener and keener on him

236

while he seemed more and more detached and, although he watched her closely, it was with the eyes of a director, certainly not the eyes of an aspiring lover. He would take hold of her shoulders and move her into certain positions. He would put a hand under her chin and tilt her head to a better angle – but it was all done as though they were total strangers. Esther would feel her body stir with delight every time he touched her but it seemed there was nothing she could do to encourage Damon to reciprocate.

'Let's run through one of your mad pieces again,' he remarked, looking slightly tired.

'We don't have to,' said Esther. She wished that the whole company wasn't staying in one large house and that she and Damon could have a little more privacy but at this particular venue – in Wales – it hadn't worked out that way.

'I know we don't have to but I want to,' said Damon. 'If you really want these scouts from Hollywood to notice you you've got to be able to do more than play Kay convincingly. You do realise that they've probably got people watching us a lot of the time during this tour, don't you?'

'I hadn't thought about it,' confessed Esther.

'Well, you bloody well should have done,' said Damon in exasperation. 'Now then, let's have this line: "So would I ha' done, by yonder sun, An thou hadst not come to my bed." Say that piece again for me, would you?'

Esther did and she saw him frown. 'What's the matter?' she asked anxiously.

'You sound mad enough,' explained Damon, 'but the pathos isn't there. Remember this poor girl's been driven mad by love. She fancies Hamlet something rotten and she knows he fancies her, but for his own peculiar reasons he's decided to reject her. She's like some kind of modern groupie and she just can't cope with it. Try and imagine what it would be like to be desperately in love with someone, certain that they feel the same about you, and then suddenly have them refuse to sleep with you. There's got to be truth in this madness otherwise it isn't sad. It's just watching some pretty girl go batty.'

Esther flushed. 'I did realise that,' she replied angrily. 'I'm not a complete fool, you know.'

'I know you're not,' sighed Damon, 'but even if you do know it, it isn't coming across. Give me that whole verse again and when you come to the end and say those two lines I want to really feel for you, OK?'

Esther looked at his incredibly handsome face and felt a surge of pure lust for him. Realising that if she replaced Hamlet with Damon in her mind then the words would be easy, this was what she did. When she came to the last two lines of the verse she heard her voice crack on the words 'Hadst not come to my bed' and she had a job to fight back genuine tears.

Damon shot upright on the bed. 'That was brilliant!' he exclaimed. 'Why on earth didn't you do it like that before?'

'I don't know,' lied Esther.

'Well do it like that tomorrow and you'll bring the house down,' Damon promised her.

He was right. The following night Esther received an unexpected round of applause after her speech in Act III scene 1 beginning: 'O, what a noble mind is here o'erthrown'. When she'd finished the mad speech that she'd practised with Damon the previous evening, she could sense that she had the audience in the palm of her hand. It was a wonderful moment – the best of the tour so far. When they all took their bows Esther couldn't help but notice that the clapping rose in volume as she curtsied prettily and, although Christopher got his usual tumultuous applause, his smile was somewhat strained.

'You were a bit over the top tonight, I thought,' he said to Esther in the wings afterwards.

Esther opened her eyes wide in feigned astonishment. 'Was I? I'm sorry. I don't know what happened.'

'Nor do I but it wasn't a bit like you,' said Christopher. 'In future, please, I'd rather you went back to playing it the way you have been.'

'I'll try, but I didn't realise I was doing anything different,' said Esther.

Rebecca joined them. 'You were frightfully good tonight, Esther,' she said with a lazy smile. 'Kept you on your toes, Christopher.'

'I've already discussed it with her,' said Christopher. 'There's no more to be said.' After that Esther knew that Damon had been right and that the pair of them were going to be able to pull off the big plan.

The days sped by all too fast and suddenly they were in London. All the fringe venues were sold out in advance and every night was a triumph. 'Be careful,' Damon warned Esther one evening after they'd finished *Time and the Conways*. 'You were a bit too good tonight.'

'So were you,' said Esther. 'Christopher gave you a really nasty look in the middle act.'

'Point taken,' conceded Damon. 'We haven't got long to wait. It doesn't matter if we seem a bit weak for the next few days. We're nearly there now.'

'I'm nervous,' Esther confessed.

'You've no need to be,' said Damon with a rare smile. 'You've surprised me, Esther, and I don't mind admitting it. You deserve to succeed. I'm quite sure you will. In fact, I've no doubt that you'll get everything you want in life.'

'Somehow I don't think that's true,' said Esther softly as she walked away to get changed, leaving a slightly puzzled Damon behind her.

In order to prepare for the open-air performance at Regent's Park the company had left themselves two spare days. By this time some of the relationships within the company had changed. For a start, Damon and Ellie were no longer an item. In fact rumour had it that Ellie was involved with George, although no one really believed this. Theresa had stopped hanging around Christopher and seemed to be more content in the company of Mary Fuller. Most of the cast assumed that Mary was acting as a kind of surrogate mother although the older ones there, who knew Mary's sexual preferences, suspected it might be something altogether different.

Rosie was still thoroughly enjoying herself with Noel and Michael and she kept Esther highly entertained with tales of what the three of them got up to. 'Sometimes, I can't believe my luck,' she told Esther. 'It's wonderful having two men. Obviously they don't both feel like it all the time but I usually do and it's only very rarely that neither of them are up to it.'

'What on earth are you going to do when the tour's over?' Esther asked.

'We've already thought about that,' said Rosie. 'We've contacted this touring company and we're probably going abroad with them. At the moment we're trying to persuade Theresa to join us.'

'Wouldn't that alter the dynamics of your relationship?' asked Esther.

'Yes, but it might add a little something as well and anyway it would be good for Theresa to have something to go on to. She hasn't had a very nice tour really. Christopher seemed to take her up and then he dropped her.'

'Well, according to you that's a habit of his,' Esther pointed out.

'Oh, you mean Suzie,' whispered Rosie, lowering her voice. 'Yes, I suppose it is. I thought he was keen on you for a bit too but he's only with Rebecca now, isn't he?'

'That's really my fault,' explained Esther. 'I need to concentrate on my acting. I found it all a bit of a struggle.'

'You've done very well,' said Rosie. 'One night you were really brilliant in *Hamlet*.'

'Only one night?' queried Esther.

'Oh, you're always good,' said Rosie. 'It's just that for one night you really shone.'

Esther wanted to smile but she didn't. At least Rosie's words proved that Damon had been right about her. When she pulled out all the stops she became the centre of attention, and that was what she had to do when they opened in Regent's Park.

On the final day of rehearsals, as Christopher cursed at aeroplanes going overhead and they battled with the breeze and the threat of rain the

241

following day, as well as the changes necessary in vocal technique for this performance, Rebecca came across to Esther.

'Damon's not his usual self today,' she remarked. 'I think his performances have been dropping off a bit recently. It's a pity when the scouts are going to be here tomorrow.'

'Perhaps he doesn't have the stamina for long tours,' suggested Esther.

Rebecca shrugged. 'Maybe. Whatever the reason, Christopher's delighted.'

'He shouldn't be too pleased,' said Esther. 'We need a strong Ernest Beevers.'

'He'll be good enough,' said Rebecca. 'Damon's never bad; it's just that recently he hasn't been as good.' She hesitated for a moment. 'To tell the truth I thought you'd gone off the boil a bit, too.'

Esther pulled a face. 'Oh dear, I'd better pull my socks up, hadn't I?'

'Don't worry about it,' said Rebecca. 'I'm sure you'll be brilliant tomorrow. Anyway, you've had some really good reviews, haven't you? Joining Christopher's company certainly hasn't done your career any harm.'

'No, but it's done yours even more good,' replied Esther. 'You've had consistently good reviews and, by the look of your performance today, playing in the open air suits you.'

For the first time Rebecca couldn't hide her sense of self-satisfaction. 'That's nice of you,' she said. 'I think that when you act opposite someone like Christopher, and spend all your spare time around them, some of their genius can't help but rub off on you – at least if you've got any talent of your own.'

'And you certainly have that,' said Esther, wondering if she was going too far with the flattery. She wasn't. The other girl loved it.

'I'm glad you've noticed,' she said and then walked away.

That evening all the company dispersed in small groups to relax in any way they chose. There was nothing more to be done and Esther and Damon wandered through the London streets until they reached Damon's favourite Italian eating house. There, over a delicious meal, Esther told him of her conversation with Rebecca. Damon nodded in approval. 'It looks as though we've timed it perfectly,' he said. 'Do you know, for the first time in years I'm really excited about tomorrow's performance. I can't wait to wipe that smug smile off Christopher's face. Every time he takes his bow I want to punch him.'

Esther was surprised. 'Goodness, I didn't realise you felt that strongly about him.'

'I told you about Suzie,' said Damon.

'Yes, I knew you felt strongly about him but not so strongly that you wanted to hit him!'

'Well I do,' said Damon. 'And when tomorrow's over it's Suzie that I shall be thinking of.'

Esther's heart sank. Even at this late stage she'd half hoped that Damon was thinking of her as well as of Suzie but it seemed that she was wrong. 'What's the matter?' asked Damon. 'You look sad suddenly.'

'Just nerves,' explained Esther.

'Where are you staying tonight?'

'I've got somewhere,' said Esther. 'I'm in the same house as Rosie, Noel and Michael.'

Damon pulled a face. 'I've heard that three's

243

company, four's a crowd in their case,' he remarked.

'That's true,' admitted Esther, 'but I don't mind. It's better than being on my own. Where are you?'

'I've got a room in a small hotel,' said Damon.

After he'd paid the bill he got up from his chair and looked thoughtfully down at Esther. 'You really are nervous, aren't you?'

Esther was, but that wasn't the reason for her quietness. However, she thought it better to pretend that it was. 'Horribly nervous,' she murmured.

'I think you'd better come back with me for a nightcap,' said Damon.

Deciding that that was better than nothing Esther agreed and soon they were sitting in his hotel room sipping brandies and talking about how it would be the following day.

Esther was sitting in a large easy chair that was by the window, looking out over London, while Damon sat on a more upright chair next to his bed. Esther wondered what on earth she was going to do when tomorrow was over and she and Damon parted company. Even if they celebrated their success it was now clear that she was unlikely to become involved with him. He'd had plenty of opportunity to make a move if he'd wanted to in recent weeks and he hadn't. A chill ran over her body and she shivered slightly. Suddenly Damon crossed the room and sat on the arm of the chair. 'What's the matter?' he asked very softly.

'Someone stepped on my grave,' said Esther.

Damon put an arm round her and hugged her. 'Don't be silly,' he whispered. 'It's all going to work out brilliantly. You've nothing to worry about and you're going to have an incredible career.'

Esther wanted to shout at him, to tell him that it wasn't just her career that worried her, but somehow she couldn't find the words and she simply stared mutely at him. Then, to her utter amazement, Damon lowered his head and kissed her very tenderly on her forehead. 'I know a good cure for first-night nerves,' he said seductively.

Esther couldn't believe that she was hearing him right. 'You do?'

The eroticism between them was incredible and now she could see desire in Damon's eyes as he held out his hands and drew her towards the bed. He undressed her as tenderly as you would a child and then, when she was naked, gazed admiringly at her while at the same time removing his own clothes. Then the pair of them lay on the bed; Esther flat on her back with Damon propped up on one elbow looking down at her.

'You're incredibly beautiful, but then you already know that, don't you?'

Esther didn't reply. She simply couldn't take her eyes off him and, as he stretched out his free hand towards her breasts, she waited to feel his fingers at last caressing her body. To her astonishment he didn't; instead he moved the palm of his hand in the air about a quarter of an inch above her, circling just above her breasts, then her ribcage and then her trembling stomach. He moved his hand lower so it hovered over her legs and feet. She she could feel the movement of air but never once did he actually touch her skin. All the time he was whispering to her, telling her what he was going to do to her and how it would feel when he did. Esther longed for some direct physical contact but, perversely, at the same time, she wanted this strange

245

caress to continue because it was the most erotic thing that anyone had ever done to her. As his hand continued to move just above her body he gently kissed her eyelids, ears, the tip of her nose and the ends of her shoulders, before letting his tongue trail over the delicate flesh at the side of her armpit.

Everything that he did was soft and gentle and yet Esther's body was reacting as though she was being robustly aroused; as though her breasts were really being manipulated and stroked, and as though his hand was actually touching the skin of her belly and thighs. It was an amazing experience and when, at last, he let his hand move between her parted thighs she was so moist that it was easy for him to slip one finger gently inside her.

At regular intervals he would stop, sometimes just inside her entrance and sometimes further in, and when he stopped he would whisper, 'Would you like to feel me inside you here? Or here?' All the time he questioned her his finger would be moving, touching different parts of her that made her squirm and long for the moment when he did enter her.

After finding out exactly what she liked the most, Damon positioned himself above her and then slid his erection into her. His fingers were gliding across her nipples as he began to pump his hips and find a rhythm which suited them both.

Even as he was moving inside her, positioning and re-positioning himself so that he was stimulating her in the way that he'd discovered she liked best, Damon continued the incredibly arousing questioning. The words themselves became a different kind of caress so that she was totally enfolded in an aura of sensuality which was nothing like anything she'd experienced before.

At last she felt the slow languid pleasure that his skilful foreplay had caused building towards the delicious peak of a climax, and her body began to move beneath his. She arched her hips and thrust her pubic bone up against his to increase the stimulation. Damon, sensing that she was ready now, increased the tempo of his thrusting but continued massaging her breast and, just before she climaxed, he covered her mouth with his own so that when she finally cried out with ecstatic delight her cries were muffled by the delicious firmness of his lips. Then he too was climaxing, and she felt closer to him then than she had ever felt to any man before.

'Was that all right for you?' he whispered urgently as they were lying wrapped in each other's arms a few moments later.

'It was the best ever,' replied Esther.

'I didn't mean it to happen,' said Damon, 'but I couldn't hold back any more. I've been wanting to make love to you for weeks now.'

'Then why didn't you?' asked Esther.

'Partly because I wasn't sure how you felt about me and also because I didn't want to get involved.'

'You don't have to be involved,' Esther assured him.

'I don't have any choice,' said Damon, his voice very quiet. 'You mean a lot to me, Esther. This isn't something I'm going to be able to walk away from, but I know that all you're interested in is your career.'

'Not all,' Esther said with a small smile. 'Didn't you realise how much I wanted you, too?'

Damon shook his head. 'No, I must be blind.

Perhaps I was concentrating too much on your acting.'

They lay together for a little longer and then, as Esther began to caress Damon's taut stomach muscles and tease the paper-thin flesh over his hip bones, she felt him start to harden within her again. Suddenly they were making love once more, only this time it was fiercer and more intense, as they both allowed their sexuality full rein. It was Damon who uttered the loudest cry as he came for the second time that night.

Esther fell asleep in his arms, no longer worried about her performance the following day or even about Marcus. All she could think about was Damon and the fact that she hadn't been wrong about his feelings for her. She didn't want to think about the future too much because it was like tempting fate. For tonight at least she was content.

Chapter Twelve

*L*uckily for Esther the memories of the previous night helped her keep calm all the following day. Most of the cast were racked by nerves and Christopher, in particular, was on edge. Once or twice he lost his temper completely and, although he apologised at the end, Esther knew that this was a sure sign he was worried. Tonight was his big chance; tonight was his opportunity to make a bid for Hollywood where he could meet Marcus on equal terms again, and he couldn't afford to fail.

Although Damon didn't mention what had occurred between them he occasionally caught her eye and on his face she could see both passion and amusement at what was going on around them. The passion excited her so much that when she wasn't on stage she kept replaying in her mind what he'd done to her the previous night. He'd been so extraordinarily tender while bringing her to an incredible peak of satisfaction. She realised that it was this combination of both the physical and the emotional elements that had proved such a revelation. Even Marcus had never made her feel like that.

Suddenly the evening was upon them and the play began. There had been the usual urgent whispers of 'Break a leg' or 'Show them how it's done' between various members of the company but Damon had found time to slip an arm round Esther's waist and whisper in her ear: 'Remember, this is for Marcus and Suzie,' he said urgently.

There was no chance of Esther forgetting that and as she stepped out in front of the huge audience on a wonderful summer's night she felt the adrenalin flowing through her and somehow sensed that this evening she was really going to fly.

Everything went exactly as she and Damon had planned. Both of them gave their roles everything they'd got and Esther knew that she was acting out of her skin. She completely forgot herself and became Kay. Nothing fazed her, not even the minor fluffs and stumbles that were occurring around her. Most of the cast were far more nervous than they'd been before but this only served to inspire Esther even more. Tonight, ensemble acting was forgotten. She intended to shine like a potential star.

It was towards the end of Act II that Damon was able to really set the ball rolling. The scene was the time-warp act where he, as Ernest, was married to Hazel, played by Rebecca, and the audience realised that this once beautiful girl, so full of confidence that she had looked down on the young Ernest Beevers, is now a very wealthy but a very scared wife with an unpleasant and dominating husband.

Esther, who had little to say during the interplay

between Ernest, Hazel and Robin – played by Christopher – was able to watch as Damon took centre stage. This had always been his finest hour but tonight he excelled himself. For a time Rebecca struggled manfully and Esther thought that such intense acting by Damon should have enabled Rebecca to react even better than usual, but it didn't. Because Rebecca always liked to feel in control she panicked as Damon forced her into subjugation, even though it was only in the play.

'I might as well tell you,' said Damon as Ernest, 'while I'm making myself unpleasant that I could lend you the two or three thousand without feeling it. Only I'm not going to. Not a penny.'

This remark was addressed to Mrs Conway and Robin but Rebecca as Hazel had to respond with a mixture of indignation and fear. Her proper line was: 'You make me feel ashamed.' Normally she did this quite well but tonight she looked hot and flustered. 'You make me feel . . .' Rebecca dried up.

There were no prompt – it was too difficult in the open air – and for a moment there was silence.

'Feel what?' improvised Ernest/Damon.

'I don't know,' wailed the distraught Rebecca, getting further and further into trouble.

'Ashamed?' suggested Damon.

'Yes! Yes ashamed!' responded Rebecca, looking genuinely ashamed and also astonished at her own failure.

Damon swung easily back into the play: 'Tell them why I make you feel ashamed. Tell me. Or would you like to tell me later when I'm telling *you* a few things?'

At this point Christopher as Robin had to jump to his feet and shout, 'I never did like you, Beevers,

I've half a mind to boot you out of this house.'
Because Christopher was becoming increasingly
aware that Rebecca was losing her grip on her part,
he was genuinely angry and, white-faced, he leapt
up too fast, stumbled and half fell as he uttered his
line, ending up on his knees at Damon's feet. A
ripple of laughter rang round the audience and
Damon waited for it to end before carrying on with
his next speech.

The cast carried on with the rest of the act but
neither Rebecca nor Christopher gave anything like
their normal performances and, in Rebecca's case,
it was becoming positively embarrassing.

Things didn't improve in the third act and Christopher began to try too hard. He over-emphasised
words and his gestures became huge. Both Damon
and Esther knew that he was stumbling and
watched with secret amusement as he was lured
into the trap they'd set for him. In the middle of
the third act it was Christopher's big romantic
moment. He had a love scene with Rosie, who was
playing Joan, and at the end of the scene had to
end up proposing to her although this had never
been his intention at the start. Normally, because
Rosie was so sweet and touching as Joan, the scene
went well and Christopher's dashing charm – he
was in his army uniform at this point – showed him
at his best. Tonight even that couldn't save him.

As he caught hold of Rosie and started to
embrace and kiss her he accidentally put a foot
behind her ankle so that she almost fell backwards
during a girlish twirl. Then he had to grab at her in
an ungainly fashion, which meant that she was
suddenly so close to him it looked as though they
were about to start having sex.

Rosie, realising this, drew away a fraction but for some reason Christopher tightened his grip. 'Oh, Robin!' said Rosie.

'Oh, Joan!' replied Christopher. He was meant to be mocking her nicely but it sounded snide and bad-tempered so that the atmosphere was all wrong.

'I suppose you've been doing this to dozens of girls?' said Rosie.

At this point Christopher was meant to say, 'Yes, Joan, dozens,' in a light teasing way. Instead, to everyone's astonishment, he said, 'Yes, I have – dozens and dozens!' He made himself sound like some kind of Don Giovanni – and a thoroughly unpleasant one at that. As the audience began to laugh, Rosie too started to lose it.

She struggled gamely through her lines but the shy, almost embarrassed, air proved hard for her to sustain in the face of Christopher's aggressive approach. There was nothing boyishly charming about him now; he looked like a spoilt overgrown schoolboy and sounded thoroughly petulant.

When the romantic interlude was interrupted by the entrance of Mary Fuller as Mrs Conway both Christopher and Rosie looked highly relieved, as though they welcomed this, although they were meant to look decidedly put out.

Off stage, Damon stood and watched, his face devoid of expression. Looking at him, Esther realised that no one would know how delighted he was feeling; no one but her.

After that, almost all of the cast struggled, with the exception of Esther and Damon. They continued to give the performances of their lives and the very end, a part that Esther had never really managed to master, went like a dream.

'I think we'll take our bow in unison,' Christopher said hastily as they started to assemble in the wings.

'Why?' demanded Damon.

'Well the light's beginning to go. It'll speed things up.'

'Don't be so bloody ridiculous,' snapped Damon. 'Everyone should have a chance to go out there and take an individual bow. You know perfectly well the audience is full of agents and scouts. You can't alter things now just because you gave a rotten performance.'

'A rotten performance?' snarled Christopher.

The rest of the company held their breath. No one dared look at anyone else and, instead, they shuffled their feet uneasily. 'Did you think it was all right then?' asked Damon.

'Oh, for God's sake let's just get it over with,' replied Christopher and he pushed Michael out front to take his bow as Gerald.

The audience made their feelings very clear. For Esther the applause was tremendous and as she stood there looking out over the park she finally felt that she was free of Marcus. She'd succeeded beyond her wildest expectations and the audience had loved her. This was what it was all about; this was what every actor and actress aspired to and she knew that, whatever happened in the future, this was a moment that would live in her memory for ever.

If anything, Damon's applause was even better. There were a few 'Bravos' and 'Hurrahs' and cameras were going off all around him as he smiled briefly. Unlike Christopher he didn't attempt the 'you're too kind, I don't really deserve this' approach. Instead he remained withdrawn and dignified but Esther knew that he was fighting to contain his intense emotions.

Wonderful as the applause had been, even better things were to come, for when Christopher strode out to take his bow, head erect, shoulders back and smiling his usual charming smile, the applause dipped horrendously and somewhere a brave soul uttered a quiet 'boo' that carried on the night air so that the entire cast heard it. Christopher's smile wavered for a moment and as the cast took an ensemble bow everyone could see that he was shaking with fury.

Afterwards it was pandemonium. Christopher made it clear that he didn't want to talk to any of the cast. Unfortunately for him the important people in the audience also made it clear that they weren't interested in Christopher. Instead, both Esther and Damon found themselves surrounded by representatives from theatre companies and even – to Esther's incredulous joy – scouts from Hollywood.

Now and again as Esther listened, smiling and nodding in the right places and hugging her delight to herself, she managed to glance over to where Damon was also holding court. For a brief moment the pair of them exchanged a secret smile; a smile of joy and physical longing. Esther wanted the evening to go on for ever. Needless to say, Christopher did not.

'How could you?' shouted Christopher, pacing around the suite of his London hotel. It was a very expensive suite because he'd been expecting to entertain the Hollywood scouts there. Unfortunately for him, and also for Rebecca, they weren't there. Not only weren't they there, there was no indication that they ever would be.

'How could I what?' asked Rebecca.

'Ruin the whole play!' shouted Christopher.

'I didn't.'

'Oh? You mean it wasn't you playing Hazel tonight?'

Rebecca's cheeks flushed with anger. 'I know I messed up but I wasn't the only one.'

'Meaning what?' asked Christopher.

'You don't have to be a genius to work that one out,' snapped Rebecca. 'I'd have thought the audience reaction would have told you enough.'

'But it was your fault,' Christopher reiterated. 'I could tell you were in a state and I tried too hard to over-compensate.'

'And I suppose I'm the one who forced you to make the audience laugh during your big romantic scene, even though I wasn't involved?' asked Rebecca.

'It didn't matter if you were there or not by then. You'd already done the damage.'

'God you're self-centred,' exclaimed Rebecca. 'Can't you ever take any blame for yourself. I was bad and so were you. That's all there is to it.'

'It's that bastard Damon's fault,' hissed Christopher. 'I don't know what came over him. He's never been like that before.'

'He was certainly good,' said Rebecca, unable to keep the admiration out of her voice.

'I'm surprised you're not hanging round him, then,' said Christopher, petulantly.

'He isn't my type,' said Rebecca, 'otherwise I probably would be.'

'Why did you lose it?' Christopher demanded. 'You've made me look such a bloody fool. I've been telling everyone how good you were; I even likened you to the next Vanessa Redgrave. Nobody's going to listen to me after this.'

'You just want to hope somebody employs you after this,' said Rebecca.

'You might be interested to know that the RSC have already asked me back,' said Christopher, his tone suddenly silky.

'Really? As what? Second sword carrier?' Rebecca laughed.

'They're staging a really innovative *Hamlet*. It's going to be completely different from anything anyone's ever done before. It's going to be linked in with what they've discovered about the effects of child abuse and Polonius is going to be played as a kind of therapist.'

'You hate all that pretentious nonsense,' said Rebecca in astonishment. 'That's why you formed this company; to do plays in traditional style.'

'It's a good director,' said Christopher defensively. 'Apparently they're confident it'll be a sell-out, both at Stratford and the Barbican. I can't fail.'

'You said that about *Time and the Conways*,' Rebecca pointed out to him, 'but you seem to have cocked it up pretty thoroughly. Well, do what you like. I always thought this company was really formed for your benefit. Now I know I was right.'

'God, I hadn't realised what a bitch you were,' said Christopher.

'Takes one to know one,' replied Rebecca.

Just then there was a light tap at the door. 'Come in,' called Christopher.

The door opened and Theresa entered. She was smiling, but when she saw Rebecca the smile disappeared and she glanced uneasily at Christopher.

'Don't mind her,' said Christopher. 'You were wonderful tonight, darling, really wonderful.'

'Do you mean that?' asked Theresa.

'Of course he means it,' said Rebecca. 'At least you didn't show him up or even let him trip you up, which was quite an achievement the way he was carrying on tonight.'

Theresa stood uncertainly by the door. 'Perhaps I should come back another time,' she suggested.

'No, I'd like your company now,' said Christopher and, as Rebecca watched, he walked across the room, took Theresa's face between his hands and then started to kiss her – softly at first but with gradually increasing passion.

Rebecca waited. There was something she had to say but she wanted to choose her moment carefully, so she watched as Christopher gradually manoeuvred Theresa against the wall before unbuttoning her blouse and burying his head between her incredible breasts. After about five minutes the pair of them seemed lost in their own world as their excitement mounted. Rebecca waited until Christopher had let his trousers slide round his ankles and was about to thrust himself into the red-haired girl before she spoke.

'There's something you ought to know,' she said, in a clear voice.

Startled by the interruption Christopher turned and looked over his shoulder at Rebecca. 'I'm sure it can wait,' he said hoarsely as Theresa moaned slightly, thrusting her hips towards him.

'As a matter of fact it can't,' said Rebecca, icily. 'I'm leaving you.'

Immediately Christopher released Theresa, pulled up his trousers and turned to face her. 'No one ever leaves me,' he said.

'This seems to be a night for firsts, doesn't it?' laughed Rebecca. 'I'm afraid I am. I'm just going to pack a few things and that's it.'

'Where are you going? Don't tell me you've been offered a job. Not after tonight's fiasco.'

'I'm going away with Nick,' said Rebecca, and at the expression of pained astonishment on his face she smiled.

'Nicholas?' This was no act. Christopher was stunned.

'Yes, we've been having an affair right under your nose most of the tour,' Rebecca continued with relish. 'Tonight he was approached for a lead role in a new TV soap. Obviously it isn't something he can turn down and, as we want to be together, I shall have to leave you. Still, think of it this way, at least no one found out you were being two-timed with a potential TV soap star involved.'

'I can't believe this,' said Christopher. 'What about your own career?'

'My agent thinks it will do me good to get away from you,' said Rebecca.

'But Nick can't act!' exclaimed Christopher.

'Nor could you tonight,' said Rebecca and she glanced at the red-haired girl. 'I hope I haven't ruined the evening for you but he probably won't be able to manage it for about half an hour, and even then you'll have to dress up in the leather gear before he really gets going.'

'I don't mind,' said Theresa.

'Really? I thought you and Mary Fuller were very close,' said Rebecca maliciously.

'Is that true?' asked Christopher.

Theresa looked uncomfortable. 'We have been close,' she admitted, 'but I was lonely. You lost interest in me and I didn't have anyone else.'

Christopher's expression softened. 'Poor little thing,' he said stroking her hair. 'Don't worry, I'll take care of you from now on.'

'He certainly will,' said Rebecca. 'I think you'll be quite safe. There isn't much chance *you'll* ever out-shine him, on stage or off.'

'Just go if you're going,' shouted Christopher.

As Rebecca left, Theresa was peeling off her clothes to change into the black-leather boots and Christopher was busy finding the riding crop. Rebecca hoped they'd be happy together; she was simply grateful to be free of him and wondered how he'd managed to hold her in his spell for so long.

As Rebecca left the hotel to join Nick, who'd been waiting outside, she saw Esther and Damon walking hand in hand down the street and suddenly Esther turned and gave the other girl a wave. Rebecca waved back. It wasn't likely that their paths would cross again and, in any case, she no longer felt any animosity towards Esther.

For her part Esther was walking on air. She still couldn't believe that it had gone so well. 'I think you'd better pinch me,' she said to Damon as they took the lift to his room.

He pinched her very lightly on her buttocks and

then smiled at the expression on her face. 'Didn't you think I'd do it?'

'Yes, but not there,' laughed Esther. 'We really did manage it, didn't we, Damon?'

'And then some,' he said with feeling. 'I just wish Suzie could have been there.'

'She probably wouldn't have appreciated it as much as you did,' Esther pointed out. 'If she's still in love with Christopher she wouldn't have relished seeing him make such a fool of himself.'

'I suppose you're right,' conceded Damon. 'Do you think she'll ever get over him?'

'I should think she will. Especially after the reviews for this. He isn't going to keep hogging the headlines now and she'll have the chance to forget. If she's as good as you say she is then I'm sure she'll soon get back on her feet and parts shouldn't be difficult to come by. Let's be honest, Christopher isn't going to have the influence he used to have.'

The pair talked long into the night discussing the various offers they'd been made and what each of them wanted to do. Esther was dismayed to realise that Damon was talking as though they would now be separating – each following a different career path. Then, when they got into bed, he started to make love to her again and her fears were briefly forgotten as he slowly aroused her already sensitive body to orgasm and continued to make love to her late into the night as she responded with ever-increasing ardour.

They slept briefly but when Esther awoke around dawn she couldn't resist reaching out and running a hand down his stomach and into his crisp pubic hair, lightly fondling his sleeping penis until it started to stir. Then she slid down the bed and took it into her mouth, gently licking and sucking until it grew hard. At that moment Damon awoke with a sigh of contentment.

Esther wanted him to come in her mouth but Damon had other ideas. He pulled her up over his body before rolling over so that she was beneath him. Then he lifted her legs so that they were resting on his shoulders and thrust deeply into her, all the time gazing into her blue eyes.

'Touch yourself while I'm inside you,' he said.

Swiftly Esther obeyed and as her fingers found her favourite rhythm her breathing grew ragged. Suddenly she was soaring again and her body grew damp with perspiration as the darts of arousal strengthened and grew. She could feel the heavy throb of her impending climax. Damon's hips moved even faster and now the pair of them were rapidly approaching orgasm. Suddenly they tumbled into the abyss together, groaning their pleasure before Damon collapsed on top of her, wrapping her in his arms and holding her close against the long, lean length of him.

'What are we going to do?' asked Esther when her breathing was even again.

'Do?' queried Damon.

'About work,' explained Esther.

'I thought we sorted that out last night,' said Damon in apparent surprise. 'You want to go to America, don't you?'

'Yes,' admitted Esther.

'You don't sound too sure,' said Damon.

'It's just that suddenly I don't want to leave you,' Esther confessed awkwardly.

'Why on earth should you leave me?' asked Damon. 'You don't think I'd let you go off there without me at your side, do you? We've both had offers. We'll fly out together. Who's to say *we* can't become Hollywood's golden couple?'

'But that's not you,' exclaimed Esther. 'You don't like the limelight; you're only interested in acting.'

'Acting and you,' Damon corrected her. 'Anyway, I've been offered the starring role in a film of *Richard II*. God knows what the Americans are going to do with that but I've told them I'll only sign on condition I'm consulted over any cuts so it shouldn't be too awful.'

'I wonder if we'll meet Marcus?' Esther asked him.

'It doesn't bother me one way or the other,' said Damon, 'but no doubt it would be the perfect ending for you.'

'Oh, I don't know,' said Esther. 'Marcus seems a long time ago now. It was never like this with Marcus,' she added, and Damon's eyes darkened with rekindling desire. As he started to caress her body again, Esther wondered if it would always be like this. She hoped so. The prospect of an exciting career in America with Damon as her lover seemed too good to be true, and yet it really was going to happen.

Two months later, when all the fuss and commotion about Esther and Damon's success in *Time and the Conways* had finally died away, and contracts had been signed, Esther was packing to leave for America. Suddenly the phone rang.

'Hello?'

'Esther? It's Rosie here.'

'Rosie, hi, great to hear from you. What are you up to at the moment?'

She heard Rosie's familiar giggle. 'Do you mean that literally?'

'No I don't,' laughed Esther. 'What are you doing professionally?'

'It's like I told you before. I'm off abroad with this touring company and Noel and Michael are coming too. Theresa dropped out at the last moment. I think she's probably involved with Christopher although she won't admit it.'

'What about all the others?'

'Well no one's had the same success as you and Damon but everyone's about to work again and that's something in our profession. I expect you heard Chris is going back to the RSC to play Hamlet, and Rebecca and Nick are living together in Kensington because he's filming a new TV soap, while Mary Fuller's been offered loads of work.'

'That's great,' said Esther. 'How about George and Ellie?'

'It's funny you should mention them in the same breath because Noel saw them together only last week. He said George looked really tired, which isn't surprising.'

Esther laughed. 'You mean Ellie's living with George?'

'She may not be living with him but she's certainly sleeping with him and he's got a lot more work than he's had for ages; probably because of his Lear.'

'I thought Ellie had plans for a musical in the West End,' said Esther.

'Oh, she's still got plans for that but the director's abroad and won't be back until Christmas, so I think she's making do with George in the meantime. She's probably using him as practice for living with an older man. I don't think she's working herself, but she's taking singing and dancing lessons so no doubt she'll get that part in the musical.'

'She's determined enough,' conceded Esther.

'But what about you?' asked Rosie. 'When are you off?'

'Tonight,' exclaimed Esther. 'I still can't believe it's all happening and neither can Damon, really.'

'Have you heard anything from Marcus?' asked Rosie.

Esther was silent for a moment. 'No,' she said slowly, 'and I don't suppose I ever will but I honestly don't care. He must have heard what happened in Regent's Park and I should think by now he knows about Damon and me too. That's all I ever wanted – that and success.'

'Well, lucky you,' said Rosie. 'Not that I'd want Damon. He's far too serious for me but I know you fancied him right from the beginning.'

'I did,' admitted Esther.

'Don't forget your old friends when you're famous, will you?' asked Rosie.

'Of course not,' said Esther, but both of them knew that she probably would. That was always the way of things.

On the way to the airport that evening Esther told Damon about the conversation she'd had with Rosie. 'It worked out pretty well for almost everyone, didn't it?' he said casually. 'No real disasters apart from Christopher.' He and Esther glanced at each other with satisfaction.

Eventually, after hanging about at the airport for hours, they were called to board their flight and, as

265

they walked through the terminal, Esther saw a familiar figure coming towards her. It was Marcus, but a very different-looking Marcus. His hair was long and shaggy, his face pale and drawn, and he'd lost his old confident way of walking.

Esther's eyes met his and she knew that she had to speak. 'What on earth are you doing back here?' she asked him, very aware of Damon standing at her shoulder with his hand resting lightly on her elbow.

'Haven't you heard?' asked Marcus.

'Heard what?'

'The film fell through. The dream's over for me, I'm afraid, but I gather it's just beginning for you.' He tried to disguise his bitterness but didn't quite pull it off.

'That's right,' said Esther. 'Where's Claudine?' she added, looking around her.

'Still in America. Her modelling career's going strong. But she'll be joining me later,' Marcus added hastily although without true conviction.

'I must be going,' said Esther after an awkward silence.

'You're looking stunning, you know,' said Marcus in a subdued voice.

'Isn't she just,' said Damon with enthusiasm. 'Nice to see you again, Marcus. It's a funny life, isn't it?'

'You could put it like that,' Marcus said sourly.

'Well, keep in touch,' said Esther and, as she walked on ahead, Damon turned and smiled at Marcus. Marcus stared sullenly back at him. Damon could understand that because he knew that he both looked and felt like a cat who'd eaten all the cream.

He didn't feel sorry for Marcus. Marcus had brought it all on himself. In their profession, even if you had talent a lot of things were down to luck and good judgement. In Damon's opinion Marcus had shown very poor judgement when he dumped Esther for Claudine and had gone to Hollywood to make a blockbuster movie for which his talents were ill-suited.

Damon had no intention of making the same mistake and nor, he knew, had Esther. They'd both learnt a lot during this dramatic summer and he saw no reason why their affair shouldn't continue for a long time. Even now, as he watched her walking towards the plane, he felt a rush of desire and couldn't wait for the moment when they could make love again. He was going to do all he could to make sure that the passion and lust in their relationship never lessened. He felt certain that Esther had the same hopes for them both.

Finally, as they were flying over the Atlantic, they toasted each other with champagne. 'To our affair,' said Damon, his eyes almost devouring Esther. 'Long may it continue.'

'I want you now,' Esther whispered to him as she sipped from her glass. 'I don't think I can wait.'

'That's not a problem,' said Damon casually. 'Haven't you ever heard of the Mile High Club?'

BLACK LACE NEW BOOKS

Published in August

DRAMATIC AFFAIRS
Fredrica Alleyn
£5.99

Esther Reid is relaunching her career as a stage actress after being publicly dumped by her famous actor boyfriend. As the acting troupe she is with begins a national tour, she realises that she's harbouring powerful passions for more than one man in the company. Her admirers have hidden agendas, however, and she will have to keep her wits about her if she is to steal the show and satisfy her desires.

ISBN 0 352 33289 1

PANDORA'S BOX 3
ed. Kerri Sharp
£5.99

Anthologies of erotic writing are very popular. To coincide with the fifth anniversary of Black Lace, we're bringing out the third collection of extracts from the best of this revolutionary imprint. The diversity of the material, including four previously unpublished short stories, is a celebration of the female erotic imagination. This is unashamed sensual indulgence for women.

ISBN 0 352 33274 3

To be published in September

DARKER THAN LOVE
Kristina Lloyd
£5.99

It's 1875 and the morals of Queen Victoria have no hold over London's debauched elite. Young and naïve Clarissa is eager to meet Lord Marldon, the man to whom she is betrothed. She knows he is handsome, dark and sophisticated. He is, in fact, depraved and louche with a taste for sexual excess.

ISBN 0 352 33279 4

RISKY BUSINESS
Lisette Allen
£5.99

Liam is a hard-working journalist fighting a battle against injustice. Rebecca is a spoilt rich girl used to having her own way. Their lives collide when they are thrown into a dangerous intimacy with each other. His rugged charm is about to turn her world upside down.

ISBN 0 352 33280 8

DARK OBSESSION
Fredrica Alleyn
£7.99

Ambitious young interior designer Annabel Moss is delighted when a new assignment takes her to the country estate of Lord and Lady Corbett-Wynne. The grandeur of the house and the impeccable family credentials are a façade for shockingly salacious practices. Lord James, Lady Marina, their family and their subservient staff maintain a veneer of respectability over some highly esoteric sexual practices and Annabel is drawn into a world of decadence where anything is allowed as long as a respectable appearance prevails.

ISBN 0 352 33281 6

To be published in October

SEARCHING FOR VENUS
Ella Broussard
£5.99

Art history student Louise decides to travel to rural France to track down a lost painting – the sensuous *Venus of Collioure* – whose disappearance is one of the mysteries of the art world. She is about to embark on another quest: one which will bring her sexual fulfilment with a number of dashing Frenchmen!

ISBN 0 352 33284 0

UNDERCOVER SECRETS
Zoe le Verdier
£5.99

Anna Caplin is a TV reporter. When her boss offers her the chance to infiltrate a secret medical institute, she grabs the opportunity – not realising the institute specialises in human sexual response. It isn't long before Anna finds herself involved in some highly unorthodox situations with Doctor Galloway – the institute's director.

ISBN 0 352 33285 9

If you would like a complete list of plot summaries of Black Lace titles, please fill out the questionnaire overleaf or send a stamped addressed envelope to:

Black Lace, Thames Wharf Studios, Rainville Road, London W6 9HT

BLACK LACE BOOKLIST

All books are priced £4.99 unless another price is given.

Black Lace books with a contemporary setting

ODALISQUE	Fleur Reynolds ISBN 0 352 32887 8	☐
VIRTUOSO	Katrina Vincenzi ISBN 0 352 32907 6	☐
THE SILKEN CAGE	Sophie Danson ISBN 0 352 32928 9	☐
RIVER OF SECRETS	Saskia Hope & Georgia Angelis ISBN 0 352 32925 4	☐
SUMMER OF ENLIGHTENMENT	Cheryl Mildenhall ISBN 0 352 32937 8	☐
MOON OF DESIRE	Sophie Danson ISBN 0 352 32911 4	☐
A BOUQUET OF BLACK ORCHIDS	Roxanne Carr ISBN 0 352 32939 4	☐
THE TUTOR	Portia Da Costa ISBN 0 352 32946 7	☐
THE HOUSE IN NEW ORLEANS	Fleur Reynolds ISBN 0 352 32951 3	☐
WICKED WORK	Pamela Kyle ISBN 0 352 32958 0	☐
DREAM LOVER	Katrina Vincenzi ISBN 0 352 32956 4	☐
UNFINISHED BUSINESS	Sarah Hope-Walker ISBN 0 352 32983 1	☐
THE DEVIL INSIDE	Portia Da Costa ISBN 0 352 32993 9	☐
HEALING PASSION	Sylvie Ouellette ISBN 0 352 32998 X	☐
THE STALLION	Georgina Brown ISBN 0 352 33005 8	☐

Black Lace books with an historical setting

THE CAPTIVE FLESH	Cleo Cordell ISBN 0 352 32872 X	☐
THE SENSES BEJEWELLED	Cleo Cordell ISBN 0 352 32904 1	☐
HANDMAIDEN OF PALMYRA	Fleur Reynolds ISBN 0 352 32919 X	☐
JULIET RISING	Cleo Cordell ISBN 0 352 32938 6	☐
ELENA'S CONQUEST	Lisette Allen ISBN 0 352 32950 5	☐
PATH OF THE TIGER	Cleo Cordell ISBN 0 352 32959 9	☐
BELLA'S BLADE	Georgia Angelis ISBN 0 352 32965 3	☐
WESTERN STAR	Roxanne Carr ISBN 0 352 32969 6	☐
CRIMSON BUCCANEER	Cleo Cordell ISBN 0 352 32987 4	☐
LA BASQUIASE	Angel Strand ISBN 0 352 32988 2	☐
THE LURE OF SATYRIA	Cheryl Mildenhall ISBN 0 352 32994 7	☐
THE INTIMATE EYE	Georgia Angelis ISBN 0 352 33004 X	☐
THE AMULET	Lisette Allen ISBN 0 352 33019 8	☐
CONQUERED	Fleur Reynolds ISBN 0 352 33025 2	☐
JEWEL OF XANADU	Roxanne Carr ISBN 0 352 33037 6	☐
THE MISTRESS	Vivienne LaFay ISBN 0 352 33057 0	☐
LORD WRAXALL'S FANCY	Anna Lieff Saxby ISBN 0 352 33080 5	☐
FORBIDDEN CRUSADE	Juliet Hastings ISBN 0 352 33079 1	☐
TO TAKE A QUEEN	Jan Smith ISBN 0 352 33098 8	☐
ILE DE PARADIS	Mercedes Kelly ISBN 0 352 33121 6	☐

---------✂------------------

Please send me the books I have ticked above.

Name ....

Address ....

....

....

.... Post Code ....

Send to: **Cash Sales, Black Lace Books, Thames Wharf
Studios, Rainville Road, London W6 9HT.**

US customers: for prices and details of how to order
books for delivery by mail, call 1-800-805-1083.

Please enclose a cheque or postal order, made payable
to **Virgin Publishing Ltd**, to the value of the books you
have ordered plus postage and packing costs as follows:
   UK and BFPO – £1.00 for the first book, 50p for each
subsequent book.
   Overseas (including Republic of Ireland) – £2.00 for
the first book, £1.00 each subsequent book.

If you would prefer to pay by VISA or ACCESS/
MASTERCARD, please write your card number and
expiry date here:

....

Please allow up to 28 days for delivery.

Signature ....

---------✂------------------

BLACK
lace

WE NEED YOUR HELP . . .
to plan the future of women's erotic fiction –

– and no stamp required!

Yours are the only opinions that matter.

Black Lace is the first series of books devoted to erotic fiction by women for women.

We intend to keep providing the best-written, sexiest books you can buy. And we'd appreciate your help and valued opinion of the books so far. Tell us what you want to read.

THE BLACK LACE QUESTIONNAIRE

SECTION ONE: ABOUT YOU

1.1 Sex (*we presume you are female, but so as not to discriminate*)
Are you?
Male ☐
Female ☐

1.2 Age
under 21 ☐ 21–30 ☐
31–40 ☐ 41–50 ☐
51–60 ☐ over 60 ☐

1.3 At what age did you leave full-time education?
still in education ☐ 16 or younger ☐
17–19 ☐ 20 or older ☐

1.4 Occupation _____

1.5 Annual household income _____

1.6 We are perfectly happy for you to remain anonymous;
but if you would like to receive information on other
publications available, please insert your name and
address

_____

_____

_____

_____

SECTION TWO: ABOUT BUYING BLACK LACE BOOKS

2.1 Where did you get this copy of *Dramatic Affairs*?
    Bought at chain book shop   ☐
    Bought at independent book shop   ☐
    Bought at supermarket   ☐
    Bought at book exchange or used book shop   ☐
    I borrowed it/found it   ☐
    My partner bought it   ☐

2.2 How did you find out about Black Lace books?
    I saw them in a shop   ☐
    I saw them advertised in a magazine   ☐
    I read about them in _____
    Other _____

2.3 Please tick the following statements you agree with:
    I would be less embarrassed about buying Black
    Lace books if the cover pictures were less explicit   ☐
    I think that in general the pictures on Black
    Lace books are about right   ☐
    I think Black Lace cover pictures should be as
    explicit as possible   ☐

2.4 Would you read a Black Lace book in a public place – on
a train for instance?
    Yes   ☐   No   ☐

SECTION THREE: ABOUT THIS BLACK LACE BOOK

3.1 Do you think the sex content in this book is:
   Too much ☐   About right ☐
   Not enough ☐

3.2 Do you think the writing style in this book is:
   Too unreal/escapist ☐   About right ☐
   Too down to earth ☐

3.3 Do you think the story in this book is:
   Too complicated ☐   About right ☐
   Too boring/simple ☐

3.4 Do you think the cover of this book is:
   Too explicit ☐   About right ☐
   Not explicit enough ☐

Here's a space for any other comments:

SECTION FOUR: ABOUT OTHER BLACK LACE BOOKS

4.1 How many Black Lace books have you read? ☐

4.2 If more than one, which one did you prefer?

4.3 Why?

SECTION FIVE: ABOUT YOUR IDEAL EROTIC NOVEL

We want to publish the books you want to read – so this is your chance to tell us exactly what your ideal erotic novel would be like.

5.1 Using a scale of 1 to 5 (1 = no interest at all, 5 = your ideal), please rate the following possible settings for an erotic novel:

Medieval/barbarian/sword 'n' sorcery	☐
Renaissance/Elizabethan/Restoration	☐
Victorian/Edwardian	☐
1920s & 1930s – the Jazz Age	☐
Present day	☐
Future/Science Fiction	☐

5.2 Using the same scale of 1 to 5, please rate the following themes you may find in an erotic novel:

Submissive male/dominant female	☐
Submissive female/dominant male	☐
Lesbianism	☐
Bondage/fetishism	☐
Romantic love	☐
Experimental sex e.g. anal/watersports/sex toys	☐
Gay male sex	☐
Group sex	☐

5.3 Using the same scale of 1 to 5, please rate the following styles in which an erotic novel could be written:

Realistic, down to earth, set in real life	☐
Escapist fantasy, but just about believable	☐
Completely unreal, impressionistic, dreamlike	☐

5.4 Would you prefer your ideal erotic novel to be written from the viewpoint of the main male characters or the main female characters?

Male	☐	Female	☐
Both	☐		

5.5 What would your ideal Black Lace heroine be like? Tick as many as you like:

Dominant	☐	Glamorous	☐
Extroverted	☐	Contemporary	☐
Independent	☐	Bisexual	☐
Adventurous	☐	Naive	☐
Intellectual	☐	Introverted	☐
Professional	☐	Kinky	☐
Submissive	☐	Anything else?	☐
Ordinary	☐	_____	

5.6 What would your ideal male lead character be like? Again, tick as many as you like:

Rugged	☐		
Athletic	☐	Caring	☐
Sophisticated	☐	Cruel	☐
Retiring	☐	Debonair	☐
Outdoor-type	☐	Naive	☐
Executive-type	☐	Intellectual	☐
Ordinary	☐	Professional	☐
Kinky	☐	Romantic	☐
Hunky	☐		
Sexually dominant	☐	Anything else?	☐
Sexually submissive	☐	_____	

5.7 Is there one particular setting or subject matter that your ideal erotic novel would contain?

_____

SECTION SIX: LAST WORDS

6.1 What do you like best about Black Lace books?

_____

6.2 What do you most dislike about Black Lace books?

_____

6.3 In what way, if any, would you like to change Black Lace covers?

_____

6.4 Here's a space for any other comments:

_____

_____

_____

_____

Thank you for completing this questionnaire. Now tear it out of the book – carefully! – put it in an envelope and send it to:

Black Lace
FREEPOST
London
W10 5BR

No stamp is required if you are resident in the U.K.